# JOHN MADDOX ROBERTS
## CINGULUM III:
# THE SWORD, THE JEWEL AND THE MIRROR

TOR

A TOM DOHERTY ASSOCIATES BOOK

This is a work of fiction. All the characters and events portrayed in this book are fictional, and any resemblance to real people or incidents is purely coincidental.

THE SWORD, THE JEWEL, AND THE MIRROR

Copyright © 1988 by John Maddox Roberts

First printing: May 1988

A TOR book

Published by Tom Doherty Associates
49 West 24 Street
New York, N.Y. 10010

Cover art by Bob Petillo

ISBN: 0-812-55204-0
CAN. ED.: 0-812-55205-9

Printed in the United States

0  9  8  7  6  5  4  3  2  1

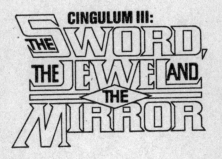

CINGULUM III:
THE SWORD,
THE JEWEL AND
THE MIRROR

# One

HAAKON SAT IN HIS CAPTAIN'S CHAIR WITH HIS BOOTED feet propped on the console before him. He liked sitting here, mainly because he liked the feeling of being the ship's commander and the knowledge that he was absolute monarch of the vessel. That did not always apply in other parts of the ship, which tended to be chaotic. Here he could banish all others and rule in lonely splendor. A speaker squawked beside him.

"Hey, Boss. Jem says for you to get down here so we can get this deal settled."

Haakon ran a palm over his bare scalp. Time to quit fantasizing and get back to work. He rose from the chair in a ripple of springy muscles and headed for the companionway. He was big and rough-hewn, and he looked like a convict, which he had been. His face was more battered than some of the rocks he had been forced to break during his years in the pits. It gave him a certain moral ascendancy in his business dealings.

As his father had once told him: "Hack, if you can't be smart, at least be intimidating."

He had found it to be good advice, which was just as well, because advice was about all he had been able to salvage from his inheritance. His father had been a viscount and so was Haakon, technically. The problem was that the planet where the family estates had been was now in the hands of the Bahadurans, a people notoriously reluctant to give back what they had taken.

That left him with this ship, *Eurynome*, which was without question a spacer's fantasy of a vessel, and his crewmen, who were somewhat less than ideal from a captain's viewpoint. There was also his business, which today was smuggling. The crew was entertaining a syndicate of local businessmen in *Eurynome*'s sumptuous main salon while the latest deal was being closed.

As he entered the salon, a small 'bot floated up to him and extended one of the tequila-and-lime concoctions he favored. The frosted glass was cool in his hand as he crossed to where Soong was displaying his Han calligraphy to a pair of merchants who shared his ethnic and cultural origins. On a sheet of off-white paper, he had brushed a complicated character in red ink. The two merchants examined it closely and expressed both admiration and puzzlement.

"I intend to have it registered among the official Han symbols," said the small, neat man, "as soon as we reach a world where there is a guild house of Master Scribes."

2

"I am at a loss to interpret it," said one of the merchants. "Of course, I recognize the character for 'ship,' but what is this one which is repeated twice?"

"It looks like a combination of the characters for 'human' and 'cat,'" said the other.

"You are most perceptive," Soong assured them. "The character breaks down as 'two Felids in one ship.' Properly, it translates as 'discord.'"

"Ah, I see," said one, looking just as mystified as before. He caught sight of the approaching Haakon. "Come join us, Captain. Mr. Soong has been enthralling us with his mastery of the brush."

"He's a man of many talents," said Haakon with massive understatement. Soong had once been an assassin in the wars between Han and Bahadur. He was making a living as a gambler when he joined *Eurynome*'s crew.

A big, ugly man in flashy clothing walked over to Haakon, a steaming, multilayered drink in one beringed fist. "Fantastic ship you have here, Captain. Does it help you in moving goods that your ship looks like a space-going bordello?" He pushed a hand through his elegant coiffure. Neither clothes nor hairdo softened the toughness of his face. This particular man, Penrose, headed this planet's largest and most prestigious smuggling firm.

"Customs authorities seldom deal thoroughly with a luxury yacht," Haakon acknowledged. "I'm not sure why. There wouldn't be much to find on this trip anyhow." He nodded toward the woman who sat in an alcove near them. Six others—three men, two women, and a herm—sat across from her, all speaking at once in

3

a high-speed, incomprehensible babble. It was the secret language of technothieves, by which they transmitted, stored, and delivered data otherwise accessible only to computers.

Haakon's technothief was Mirabelle. She was small, brown-haired and voluptuous, and just now she was taking on their cargo: a list of transfer coordinates for hundreds of deep-space rendezvous to be carried out over the next standard year by vessels of Penrose's firm and their customers. It was a sight he never quite believed, no matter how many times he'd seen it: Mirabelle could feed all this information back to a computer, or to another technothief, any time she was called to. She could also erase it from her memory instantly, which was what made technothieves the best method of smuggling contraband data.

"She has the schedule of contacts, of course," Penrose said. "I am assured that you shall be able to make all of them on time over the next six months standard." He did not inflect it as a question, so Haakon did not answer it as such. "That leaves only the closing, then," Penrose said, holding out an open palm. The two men touched palms and the deal was made. There could, of course, be no official record, but if Haakon reneged on the agreement, he would never get another contract from the sub-Bahadur underworld. Penrose would suffer likewise if payment were not to be forthcoming at the contact points.

Jemal came in, accompanied by a man with long hair that had once been yellow, but was now heavily shot with gray. "Hack," Jemal said, "meet Hamish Connaught. He's Delian."

"Jem and I are from Delius," Haakon said.

"So he's told me," Connaught said. He was slightly drunk. "Says you were both in the war. Which fleet?"

"Sixth," said Haakon. "Lord Hatch's. You?"

"Forty-seventh, the Prince's Own. Put up a good fight, didn't we?"

"That we did," Haakon answered.

"Well, maybe we're not through yet," Connaught said, the words coming a little thickly. "We can always—"

"It's time we were going," Penrose interrupted. He glanced at a readout floating in front of a wall-screen. "These people have an optimum exit window to catch, and it's coming up within the hour. Captain, it's been a pleasure and I look forward to a mutually profitable association."

Haakon saw the syndicate dignitaries to the airlock and went back into the salon. The 'bots were tidying up as Alexander came in. Alex was a Singeur, with genetic properties of both human and monkey. His feet were like hands and he had a prehensile tail decorated with several jeweled rings. "We heading out, Boss?" From a passing 'bot, he grabbed a stein of beer and sucked up half of it. Alex looked to be about fourteen standard years, but then he had looked that way since joining *Eurynome*, some years earlier.

"In about"—Haakon cocked an eye toward the floating readout—"twenty minutes. What's Her Lady-ship up to?"

Alex shrugged, a gesture performed with his entire body. "Ain't seen her in a couple of days. She keeps to her room. She's had the medbot in there a lot, but she won't let it record or transmit no data. Me'n Soong got a bet going about which it's gonna be, but even Mirabelle can't get the word."

"What about Numa?"

"Keeps to himself mostly. Been hiding down by hydroponics lately. Why do you keep him around?"

"Why do I keep you around?" Haakon asked. "Felids. Jesus! I guess I'd better go see her."

"Must be tough being captain," Alex commiserated.

"You don't know the half of it. Go tell Rand we're about to move out. Go find Jem—"

"I'm right here," said Jemal. He was sitting in one of the little alcoves off the main salon, sipping a drink and staring out the big bubble window. The planet below was spectacular, and the nearby station with its parked ships had a certain elegant beauty. Haakon walked over and sat in one of the plush chairs, which curved itself to fit him and began to hum softly.

"It's a good contract," Haakon said. "Easy, safe, and it pays well. We seem to be working with pretty good people, too."

"Business looks good," Jemal agreed, "but our personnel situation is getting out of hand. The six of us who started this business didn't have any choice. Then Alex showed up. Now we have Numa hanging around for his own Felid reasons. And in a few weeks you know what Rama's going to present us with. Hack, we just can't keep taking these—these" Jemal waved his hands in an uncharacteristic search for the proper word, "these *civilians* onto the ship."

"They know the risks," Haakon said. "At least, Alex and Numa were told. As for Rama . . ." he said, trailing off into expressive silence. "I'd better go see her. I've put it off long enough." He downed the last of his drink and took a last look at the spectacular view out the bubble. It was the kind of sight that a real spacer never tired of, no matter how long he'd been in space. "If I'm not on the bridge within a half hour, send a rescue party."

Rama's suite was the most splendid on the ship. It had been designed as the Prince-Admiral's quarters, back when *Eurynome* had been a royal yacht-cum-light cruiser. Haakon knocked at the exotic-wood door.

"Go away! I hate you!" Rama squalled from inside.

"How did you know it was me?" Haakon asked.

"There is nobody out there I don't hate," Rama said. "Well, come in if you must."

Cautiously, Haakon entered. Rama was a Felid, and Felids were among humanity's deadlier variations. She was vicious at the best of times and lately she had been impossible. Besides that, when she was in a bad mood her smell could raise bubbles on durasteel. Haakon checked his nose filters as he came in.

Rama lay in her immense bed, her silver-and-black-striped hair in disarray, her claws unpainted. She was wearing only the lower half of a filmy pajama suit, which was probably all she had that would fit these days.

"You see?" she hissed. "Does it give you satisfaction to behold the ruin of my beauty?" She gestured at her immensely swollen belly, her distended breasts with their

7

elongated, black nipples. Even the double row of vestigial nipples that dotted her ribs had become enlarged slightly. Her whole white-skinned body was enveloped in a net of blue veins. She glared at him with her slit-pupiled eyes. "Go head, you horrible person, gloat!"

"You don't look half bad, Rama," Haakon said. "Once the baby's born, you'll be right back up to snuff in a few days." He wasn't sure what snuff was, but it seemed to be a good thing to be up to. In fact, even in this condition, Rama was still beautiful enough to take his breath away. Why did the cat-woman have to be such a pain?

"Do you really think so?" Rama asked, a little mollified. "I would hate to think of my magnificence being dimmed permanently. What did you come to tell me?"

"We leave orbit in about twenty minutes. Mirabelle has all the data. Our next scheduled stop is Krishna in about a month, so we can take a side trip to Balder. It's about time we had a little fun." Balder was the spacer's paradise, an unexampled den of iniquity.

"Have fun if you must," said Rama tragically. "I am denied such things now. The demands of the species override that kind of self-indulgence." She wiped away a tear, which Haakon knew was fake since Felids could not weep.

"Look, Rama," he said confidentially, "there are a lot of bets on the ship whether it's going to be a boy or a girl. If you'd just tell me, we could split—"

"Get out of here, bald one!" she shouted, flinging a pillow. "My offspring shall never be the mere object of

8

your greed! Go! And seventy-five/twenty-five my favor is the best deal you'll ever get from me!"

"To hell with that," Haakon said. "Strap your distended bulk in. We're on our way."

He whirled and stalked out. She radiated a wave of scent that he couldn't smell through his filters, but it was strong enough to feel through his skin.

The door shut behind him as he turned right and sprinted up the companionway. The main salon was battened down already. Ordinarily, *Eurynome* made her jumps so smoothly that all these precautions were unnecessary, but spacers were creatures of habit, especially those who had learned their trade in the navies of the recent wars.

When he got to the bridge, he found Jemal already there. Jemal was his second in command and copilot. Rama was his—actually, he wasn't sure just what Rama was. He plopped into his captain's chair. "Let's set course for Balder."

Wordlessly, Jemal pointed to a globe of light that hung above the console. Haakon let loose a stream of *sotto voce* profanity. "Damn!" he finished off. "If it's Timur Khan, I'll—"

"Don't say it. Who else would it be?" Jemal hit the interpreter. The ball expanded into a holographic representation of Timur Khan Bey himself. The image spoke. "You are summoned." Then it winked out.

"A man of few words," Jemal commented.

"Too damn many for me," Haakon said. For months he had been able to hang on to the illusion that he was the captain-adventurer of a free ship. Now he was once again

9

faced with the hard fact that he was a slave; a convict under suspended death sentence, no different from what he had been in the pits. He began to dictate coordinates for Bahadur.

The Lower City of Baikal was the same as always. It was a warren of low establishments catering to the wants and needs of spacers of the "inferior peoples," but not nearly as much fun as Balder. The crew took a shuttle down from parking orbit to the port. Rama stayed with the ship, being in no mood for parties. So did Rand, the engineer. It would be some years before the pleasures of the flesh appealed to him once more.

They couldn't just go to the Black Obelisk without arousing suspicion among people whose good opinion they valued, so an excursion among the fleshpots of Lower Baikal was called for. The array of low dives available was staggering, but they decided to begin with Star Hell. They were well-known there and it was as good a place as any to let the word get around that *Eurynome* was back.

The Pirian bouncer at the door gave them the once-over with its eyeless face, but it was soon replaced by the owner, a small man in a sweep-sleeved evening tunic. "Haakon! Dear boy, where have you been? And you, too, Jemal, your fans have missed you! Soong, Mirabelle, your tables await. I'm so sorry about that little contretemps last time. It was nothing personal, just that BT swine showing up as he did, I'm sure you understand. And where is dear Rama? We'll be disappointed if she doesn't dance and fight. Where is—" The next word caught in his throat as he saw the man following Mirabelle into the foyer.

"Orozco," Alexander said, "meet Numa. Rama's a little indisposed just now. Numa's kind of her mate, you know?"

Numa put a massive, clawed hand on Orozco's embroidered shoulder. "Pleased to meet you. I've been hearing about the place."

"Ah, charmed, I'm sure, dear boy," Orozco said. He took in the sight before him with more than customary appreciation.

Numa was a Felid, and even bigger than Rama, and just as beautiful. His mane was golden and spread from his brow across his shoulders and well down his back. As with Rama, his features were perfectly human except for the slit-pupiled eyes, the bristly whiskers flanking the nose, and the generally catlike cast of countenance.

"And the, ah, nature of dear Rama's indisposition?" asked Orozco.

"She's great with kitten," Mirabelle explained. "Numa's the daddy."

"My congratulations," Orozco said to Numa, who merely grunted. "Ah, what might the little creature be?"

"We still don't know," Haakon said. "But Soong's keeping book."

They went down the multiple levels into the amphithe-ater-style interior of Star Hell. The descending tiers were packed with tables—the top ones for eating, those lower for drinking or just watching the activities in the pit. Everywhere, chemical smokes and gasses laced the air,

11

and the noise was uproarious. On platforms in the pit there were dancers and fighters going through their acts.

Jemal watched bemusedly as a fighter was carried out, bleeding profusely from a powerblade cut on the thigh. "I used to make my living that way," Jemal said to no one in particular.

"How come you're still alive?" Numa asked.

Jemal shrugged. "Some of us are destined for greater things, I suppose." Overhead a police 'bot floated by and Numa snarled and fanned his mane as it floated too close. Jemal put a restraining hand on his arm. "Easy, there. Those 'bots are never in working condition down here. The cops don't care what foreigners do to one another. The 'bots are just to remind us that we're still under police authority." As the thing floated past, they could see a long crack running across its main visual sensor plate.

A band began a pounding rendition of an ancient piece by Bach. The Old-Earth musical instrument revival was in full swing, and the band was equipped with electronic bagpipes, alpenhorn, and digeridoo. They took seats around one of the tables and looked over the crowd. It was a typical assemblage: mostly humans of varying sorts, with a sprinkling of aliens. There was no day or night in this place, because it catered largely to spacers, and the ships came in at all hours, discharging passengers and crew anxious for a little diversion. Rumor had it that Star Hell had not been closed in more than a century.

A towering herm threaded a way through the gaming tables to the one occupied by the *Eurynome* crew. For reasons of their own, the majority of herms preferred to be regarded as female, despite their possession of two sets of fully functional reproductive organs—male and female. The minority preferred to be male. Attempts had been made to devise and institute new genders and pronouns in the common languages, but these expedients had met with little enthusiasm, even among the herms.

"Good to see you, Hack," the herm said, looking pointedly at a vacant seat next to Haakon.

"Sit, Roche," Haakon said. "What's your pleasure?"

Roche talked to the waiterbot and received a glass of something layered in shades of purple and a small inhaler. Roche was one of the minority of "male" herms, massively muscled with small but prominent breasts. The curvature of hips was restrained and the male genitals made a noticeable bulge in the codpiece of his balloon-thighed trousers. He sniffed from the inhaler and sipped off the top layer of his drink.

"How long's it been since you were here, Hack? A year?"

"A little more than that. Why? Did you miss me?" Haakon was curious. Roche was an acquaintance, not the type he would have expected to be the first to seek him out as soon as he made planetfall.

"There are people who've been missing you," Roche said.

Haakon was mystified, which translated as suspicious. "What are you trying to tell me, Roche?"

"We could go someplace private," Roche said.

"What for? You know my taste doesn't run to herms."

Roche glared. Haakon was being deliberately obtuse.

"C'mon, Roche," Jemal said. "This is Star Hell."

Star Hell had three basic appeals: all tastes were catered to, patrons were as safe from the authorities as anyone could be on Bahadur, and there was absolutely no eavesdropping. Anyone bringing a snoop device onto the premises was immediately crucified to one of the walls.

Roche shot a glance at Numa. "He's crew, Roche," Haakon said. "Now give us your message."

"They want you at the Cingulum."

"We were there within the last year to drop people off," Haakon said. "They were no happier than usual to see us then. Why this sudden interest?"

Roche shrugged. He took another sniff and sip. "How should I know? I got word from my contact. You're wanted there."

"When did this word come down?" asked Mirabelle.

"Eighteen days ago, Bahadur. About sixteen-point-five standard."

"Thanks, Roche," Haakon said. "I appreciate getting the word."

"You'll be going, then?" Roche asked.

"I said thanks for delivering the message. We'll take it from here." Damned if he'd let anybody know what his plans were. Especially since he didn't know himself.

"Well, just so you got the word. I said I'd deliver it."

"Thanks," Haakon said. "Can I buy you another?"

"No. I'll be going. See you." The herm rose and made a sketchy bow to the others before leaving.

"I don't trust him," Mirabelle said when the herm was gone.

"Why?" Haakon asked. "Just because he has tits the size of yours and a schlong to his knees."

14

"No," she said imperturbably. "And don't think you can rattle me with vulgarity. I've spent too much time in jail. No, his timing is wrong, and he's too nervous. I vote we ignore this summons."

"I'd go along with you," Haakon said, "but it's kind of irrelevant, don't you think? We've been called by Timur Khan, and our main problem is how to survive whatever he has in store for us. The folks in the Cingulum just have to take second place. Come on, let's tie one on. We go meet with Timur Khan in the morning, and I'd hate to have to face him sober."

"Is he so fearsome?" Numa rumbled.

"We've told you about him," Jemal said. "In any case, you aren't going. Pray he never takes notice of you."

Timur Khan Bey hung his bow on its peg. The bow, along with its bow case and quiver, was the only decoration on the severely plain wall of his office in the Black Obelisk. A tall, intense, slender man of middle years, Timur Khan was the most feared human being of much of human-occupied space. He turned toward his desk.

"Send in the *Eurynome* team."

The door opened and a pair of BT guards led four humans into the office. The four were forced to their knees and made to bow until their foreheads touched the floor. "There aren't as many of you as there used to be," observed Timur Khan.

"Rand stays with the engines, as usual, Noyon," said

Haakon, his voice somewhat muffled from speaking directly into the floor. "Rama is not well."

"Illness and injury are not sufficient excuse to ignore a summons from this office. I choose to overlook the offence this time. I have a mission for you."

"Let's hear it, Noyon," said Haakon, his face pressed to the floor.

"You are aware of the planet named Chamuka?"

If Haakon had had any hair, it would have been standing up. "Yes, Noyon." Chamuka was a notorious hellhole of a planet.

"Some time ago, I sent an elite regiment of my Black Tumans to quell a rebellion there with minimum disruption of the local economy. They have been taking excessive casualties both from the local rebels and from the natural hazards of the place. I want to know how it occurs that a miserable population of subhuman peasants can wreak such destruction among the best troops in the galaxy. Your task will be to infiltrate this movement and report to me. I do not expect you to destroy the rebellion, just observe and report, is that understood?"

"Understood, Noyon," Haakon said, relieved. Infiltrating a rebellion was deadly enough without having to take subversive action against it.

"Then go at once and do my bidding. Fear me and obey."

# TWO

HAAKON SAT AMID THE DIMNESS OF HIS BRIDGE, THINKING over the new assignment. It was far from the worst Timur Khan had handed him. At least, this time, they weren't being asked to bring back any heads. That made him suspicious. There had to be some ulterior factor here. Timur Khan had never used the *Eurynome* team for mere spying. There was, of course, the planet itself.

"May I enter the bridge, Captain?" Soong interrupted his musings.

"Of course. Have a seat. I was about to see what we've got on this planet Chamuka."

"I have just been absorbing some of our data on the subject. Perhaps I can save you some time by abstracting a few of the more cogent points." He took a cup of steaming tea from a 'bot and settled into the copilot's chair.

17

"I'd appreciate it," Haakon said. "All I know about Chamuka is that it's proverbially the last place anyone wants to be."

"And with excellent reason. Much of the animal life is hostile to human presence. Many of the plants are poisonous or dangerous in some other fashion. The climates are mostly ferocious and the terrain ranges from swamp to desert to forbidding mountains with very little inviting land to be had. The inhabitants are warlike and deeply divided into small, independent groups."

"Sounds like a real vacation spot. What makes such a godforsaken place important?"

"Catalytic crystals are produced there. Apparently these crystals are of supreme importance in producing many of the exotic alloys necessary for ships' engines. They are horrendously expensive to make under laboratory conditions, but they occur naturally on Chamuka. It seems they grow there, rather like plants."

Haakon leaned back in his chair and laced his fingers behind his head. "Why are the Bahadurans so tolerant with these people? Ordinarily, they don't hesitate to sterilize a whole planet if it gives them too much trouble."

"It seems that these crystals must have a terribly precise balance of chemicals and atmospheric conditions and such. If the environment is disturbed too much, they might cease to grow."

"That explains a lot. Timur Khan sent in his BT's to surgically excise the source of this rebellion, only they haven't been successful. What do we know about the natives?"

18

"Not much. The original colonists seem to have been Japanese, or at least Japanese-speaking. Incidentally, the name 'Chamuka' is one the Bahadurans gave the place. The local name is a Japanese expression meaning 'Grass Cutter.'"

"Odd name for a planet."

"I checked on it. Grass Cutter was the name of a legendary sword in ancient Japanese history. Only one small continent is settled, little more than a large island. It is divided into districts by numerous, intersecting mountain ranges. All the districts seem to be named after swords as well."

"These people have swords on the brain," Haakon mused.

"I suppose they have taken feudal Japan as their prime myth."

"Prime myth?" Haakon said.

"Yes. Many colonial peoples have them. When men left Earth, they tried to take much of their old culture with them. Often they latched on to some phase of their ancestral history and clung to it. Look at the Bahadurans. They idolize the ancient steppe horsemen: the Hiung-Nu, the Turks, especially the Mongols. To listen to Timur Khan speak, you would think that he and all his people were the direct descendants of Genghis Khan. Yet anyone with eyes can see that the Bahadurans are made up of a great mixture of races. My own people of Han chose to emulate the great age of China, yet I am certain that the great bulk of the early colonists could not have read the ancient Chinese characters until they were revived on Han. I am told that my clan came from northern China, up near the Wall. I probably have more steppe blood in my veins than most Bahadurans."

"So these people on Chamuka may not be Japanese at all?"

Soong shrugged. "Undoubtedly many of the original colonists were, but their attachment to feudal Japan is more likely to be a revival than a continuous tradition."

"We'll know more when we get there. I'm suspicious of Timur Khan's motives, though."

"It is never a good idea to relax your suspicion of that man," Soong concurred. He looked up to see Jemal standing in the doorway.

"Permission to enter," Jemal recited.

"Come on in and join our council. You been studying up on Chamuka?" Haakon waved to a navigator's seat and Jemal took it.

"Yes. Nasty place. What I came to see about is what's our cover? Timur Khan gave us a carte blanche, and I'm damned if I know what to do with it. If we don't know what's going on down there, how can we know what cover to use?"

"Good question. I suggest we keep the ship in high orbit and shuttle down to the main port. Then we just hang around and behave suspiciously."

"Not a bad idea," Jemal said. "If you want to contact rebels, it's best to have a reputation for being anti-social. Finding the right port won't be difficult, either, since there's only one."

"That's not so good," Haakon said. "I hate to go into a place that doesn't have a back door."

20

"Our data," Soong said, "lists only one *official* port."

"Hmm," Haakon mused. "There could be any number of smugglers' ports. Better make that one of our first orders of business. We'll find out what they like to bring in, hint that we're smuggling it, and get some coordinates for a quick getaway port."

"That would be prudent," Soong said.

"First party to go down," Haakon directed, "will be just the three of us. Alex and Numa might attract too much attention. Rama's indisposed, and Rand stays with the engines. If it looks like the kind of place where Mirabelle can pick up information easily, she can come down next. I figure if we act shifty enough, somebody should contact us pretty soon. Once we have contact with the underground market, contact with the rebels should be close behind."

That evening Haakon wandered back to the engine room. It was the one part of his ship he rarely visited. Like everyone else, the big Teslas that powered the ship made him nervous. They were notoriously temperamental, and were given to spontaneous expulsions of nameless, deadly radiation, for reasons nobody had ever been able to figure out.

He found Rand seated at the engineer's small desk next to the humped, hulking shapes of the Tesla engines. Rand was completely sheathed in a therapeutic suit of Galen manufacture. It looked like a suit of battle armor except for some external tubes through which liquids bubbled. Rand had once been standing near a Tesla engine when it blew. Burned down to little more than a skeleton and a brain, he had been regenerating in the suit ever since. At least, that was his story. There was much disagreement within the crew whether there was really a human being in there at all.

Haakon stopped short when he saw what lay on Rand's desk. The engineer had taken one of his gloves off. Holding his wrist with the other hand, he was slowly flexing the fingers and thumb of the bare hand. The fingers were thin and spidery, the bones nearly visible through the thin, pale flesh. Blue veins laced the back of the hand and the nails had grown long, curling inward. The sight made Haakon a little queasy. He had never seen any of Rand's flesh before.

"Come in, Captain," said Rand through his voice grill. "I just took this off for the first time in years. The regenerative process seems to be working." He wiggled the fingers proudly.

"Congratulations. When will you be able to dispense with the suit?"

"Oh, a good many years yet. This hand's still so weak I couldn't pick up a stylus with it. The skin's so delicate you could rub it off with your fingertips. I took off the glove because from now on I'll have to cut my nails regularly. They started to grow back in a few months ago."

"Good to know it's working, anyway. What I came down to tell you is, we're going to be staying in high orbit on this job, and I want the engines to be ready for an instant jump if there should be trouble and we need to make a fast getaway."

"You know there's no such thing as an instant jump, Captain. I'll keep them on standby ready to fire up for the first exit window, but that's the best I can do. Anything more, and we'd be in more danger from the engines than we'd be from whomever's chasing you."

"It's your department," Haakon said. "But we rarely have time to spare when we have to cut and run."

He hurried from the engine area. The place gave him the creeps. He found most of the others in the main lounge. "Guess what I just saw? Rand had one of his gloves off, and there's a real hand in there. Flesh and blood, although not much of either."

Soong turned to Jemal in triumph. "Pay me." Jemal had been of the opinion that Rand was really a machine.

"Wait," Haakon told Soong, "you pay me first. Our bet was which part of him we'd see first. I bet his hands and you—"

They were interrupted by a summons from the planet-to-ship communicator. "Looks like the people downstairs want to talk to us," said Mirabelle.

Haakon summoned one of the floating 'bots and used its remote commo-receiver. "Identify yourself," droned a bored voice. "This is Chamuka transport control. Identify yourself."

"Ship *Eurynome*, free trader, Captain Haakon speaking. Request permission for a shuttle landing."

"What is the nature of your business, Captain?"

"Repair and maintenance of our ship. We need parts and provisions." This was the usual excuse for visiting someplace when they had no cargo to load or discharge.

"How many in the landing party?"

"Three. Myself and crewmen Jeman and Soong. It is possible that others may wish to come down at some later time." He saw Alexander sulking at not being allowed to go down.

"Permission granted for the first party to land. Use Dock Eight. Report immediately to customs and quarantine officers for examination. Do you have personal armor?"

"Yes," Haakon answered the unexpected question.

"Wear it."

"Why armor?" Jemal wondered.

"We'll find out soon." Haakon adjusted the sleeves of his armorcloth singlet over the steel bracelets he always wore. "Trouble is, I can't think of any pleasant reason for wearing armor."

The ground was coming up quickly now. They could see spectacularly rugged mountains, largely covered with luxuriant vegetation. The spaceport was little more than a clearing in the woods at the bottom of a narrow valley. The untidy sprawl of buildings had a prefabricated look, and the vegetation had been cleared back from the port for half a kilometer.

"I see gun emplacements and search towers down there. All of it aimed outward. No anti-ship defenses visible, but that kind of thing is usually buried anyway."

The shuttle docked at Dock Eight and a blast of warm, humid air struck them as the hatch cycled open. The ladder unfolded to the port surface and they descended. The landing pad area was paved with fused glass, made many years ago with atomics. Now the thick glass was cracked extensively, and plant life was pushing its way through. Burned and blackened vegetation showed where the growth had been poisoned, but fresh growth was pushing up everywhere.

There were several shuttles present, and cargo pallets were being guided among them. All the port laborers were oddly dressed in plates of loosely fitted, ceramic armor. They wore wide helmets with spreading neck guards that covered much of their shoulders. A towering wall of black cloud was coming over one of the nearby mountain ridges.

"Odd folk costume they wear around here," Haakon said. There was a functionary coming toward them, fiddling with a recording device at his belt. He wore a suit of the peculiar armor but his was plain brown.

"You are from *Eurynome*?"

"Yes," Haakon said. "Why—"

"Weren't you warned to wear armor?" the man interrupted. He glanced nervously at the approaching cloud.

"We are," protested Jemal.

"I'm afraid you were inadequately warned," the functionary said. "Armorcloth is not sufficient. Come on, we might make it to the customs building on time, but you'd better run."

"Anything you say," Haakon answered. They broke into a trot and headed for the nearby cluster of buildings. "Were we supposed to wear *battle* armor?"

"That would have been better." It was getting very

25

dark. "Too late," the official said. "Better take cover under there." He pointed to a parked pallet. There was a half-meter of space under it. Mystified, they dived beneath the little vehicle. They had no idea what was going on, but they had not lived this long by ignoring warnings. The official crowded in with them. Out on the field, the pallet drivers were seeking shelter or erecting collapsible roofs over their vehicles.

With absolutely no prelude, the air was full of fist-sized hailstones. They crashed to the glass, showering the huddling crewmen with stinging chips of ice, smashing overhead on the pallet with a roar so deafening that it could have been mistaken for shelling. The racket continued for five minutes, then stopped abruptly.

"Welcome to Chamuka," said the official. He began, to push the piled hailstones away so that they could clamber out from under the pallet. Outside, the landing field was completely invisible beneath a slush of smashed hailstones, already steaming and melting in the renewed heat of afternoon.

"Does that happen often?" asked Jemal, aghast.

"A dozen or so times per day. Now you see why you need armor."

"How do they practice agriculture around here?" Haakon asked.

"It's not easy," the official said. He led them into the customs shed, which was at least cool, although austere. Armored suits hung on racks near the doors. The functionary stepped around behind the customs table and assumed his official mein. "Now, you say you're here for parts and provisions. What kind of parts do you need?"

"The engineer gave me a shopping list. Nothing exotic. Is there a salvage yard around here?" Jemal nudged him and he looked up to see a man entering the station. He wore the black uniform of the Black Tumans, with the addition of curtainlike plate armor.

"About two kilometers from here. Pretty limited stock, but you might find what you need. Your ship war surplus?"

"Right," Haakon answered. "It's a light cruiser frame."

"I think they've been wrecking a couple of light cruisers, write-offs from the end of the war. As for provisions, you might find enough food to get you to the next decent port, but you won't want to lay in more than that. The grub here isn't what you're used to, I can guarantee it."

The man in the BT uniform pulled off his helmet and dropped it onto the customs table. It was close-fitting, without the spreading neck-and-shoulder guard of the local helmets. He had close-cropped hair and the narrow features of the Bahadur upper classes. "You're from the ship that just arrived." It wasn't a question.

"That's right," Haakon answered. "*Eurynome*, free trader. I'm Captain Haakon.

"What cargo do you carry?"

"Actually, we aren't unloading anything here. Just stopped to—"

"I said what cargo. Answer only what you are asked." True to type, the man was insufferably arrogant.

Haakon fiddled in his belt pouch and came up with a

thin disc. "Here's our manifest. General cargo, nothing very interesting."

The BT took the disc and inserted it in his belt recorder. It popped out within a second and he tossed it onto the table. "Transact your business and be on your way. Things are unsettled here and we have no time to protect transients. Your presence is now registered with the local police authority. Restrict your activities to the port and the town of Masamune. If you are found outside these areas, or more than fifty meters from the road connecting them, you'll be shot on sight." He collected his helmet, jammed it over his head, and left.

"He's just a bundle of charm, isn't he?" asked Jemal.

"How come the BT's are here?" asked Haakon.

The customs man looked quickly about to see if anyone was standing too near. "There's continuous rebellion going on here. Used to be, they'd send regular Bahadur troops and rotate them out every year. The BT's got here a few months ago. Word is, they're here for five years."

"Why such a long tour?" Jemal asked idly.

"You ask me, they're here for punishment. Somebody must have screwed up bad. More than two-thirds of them'll be dead in five years."

"It is so bad?" Soong asked.

"Worse. The locals are always up in arms about something, and even without them there's plenty of other ways to die here."

"I take it you aren't local," Haakon prodded.

"I hope to all the gods not!" the official said

vehemently. "No, this is a hardship post for System Port Authority. Sixteen inhabited planets in this system, and every one of them a garden spot compared to this one. Two years here with double pay and I get a promotion and the post of my choice at the end of it. Every day I ask myself if it's worth it. I'm short now, though. Fifty-two and a wake-up."

"Perhaps," Soong said, "it would be prudent to learn about the dangers awaiting us. Have you any information modules concerning such things?"

"There's a bus runs every hour into Masamune. It runs a briefing program for newcomers. Keep your armor-cloth buttoned up, the insects here are fierce. And get some hail armor as soon as you get to town, is my advice. And be polite to the natives. They'll kill you for looking cross-eyed at them. There's the bus now. In town you can arrange for transportation to the salvage yard. Hope you make it back alive."

They boarded the bus—an antiquated air-cushion vehicle with an opaqued dome top—and sat. "We were lucky to encounter such a talkative functionary," Soong said.

"He was jittery," Haakon observed. "Typical short-timer. He wants to get away so bad, time seems to be standing still."

During their trip into town, a running hologram entertained them with the many ways one could die on Chamuka. There were the giant flying insects with buzz-saw noses, the plant that shot twenty-centimeter bolts like a crossbow, the flash floods, the poisonous gas vents

29

that might erupt at any time from innocent-looking ground, the extremes of temperature and, of course, the hailstorms. This, they were assured, merely scratched the surface of Chamuka's lethality. Even more entertaining ways to expire were to be found in the hinterlands. There was no mention of the natives, rebellious or otherwise.

The town was a sprawl of incongruously delicate-looking buildings, with slender beams supporting high-pitched roofs of hard ceramic. The muddy streets were broad and the blocks of buildings were widely separated, apparently as a precaution against the spread of fires. Walkways between buildings had overhead protection. Armored people strolled in the streets, unconcerned at the buildup of black clouds in the near distance.

The bus stopped and settled to the ground in an open square, and the passengers departed into the shelter of one of the covered walkways. When the hailstorm hit they had to cover their ears with their hands against the thundering racket.

"Soong, can you read any of the signs?" Haakon asked when the hail let up.

Soong tried to decipher the extravagant calligraphy, which ran vertically down the front of some buildings, but shook his head. "No. They use many of the old Chinese characters, but they use them to mean different things. From the way they are arranged, I suspect that each character represents a syllable in their language."

By asking bystanders, they were able to make their way to a shop selling protective gear. Like most port cities, this one abounded in people able to speak some of the spacer dialects. The shop building consisted of little more than a wooden platform, some support posts of local wood, and a ceramic roof. A few interior spaces were closed off with hanging curtains.

"Most of the men here wear swords, I've noticed," said Jemal, examining a rack of the weapons. He took one down and drew it from its sheath. It roughly resembled the ancient Japanese sword, with a very plain handle and a flat metal plate for a guard, but the blade was short, about sixty centimeters in length, and very broad, widening somewhat toward the tip. It ended in an abrupt hatchet point. It was made of plain steel but a pearly color along the edge meant some sort of special treatment.

"Looks as much like a machete as a sword," Jemal said.

"Be most careful of the edge," said the proprietor, a roly-poly man whose movements were surprisingly swift and deft. "It is as keen as your powerblade, without the messy sparks and annoying noise. These swords are first sharpened as perfectly as it is possible to sharpen steel, then a second edge of perfectly aligned crystals is grown atop the first edge. You can shave with it after spending the day splitting wood with that edge."

"Why are they carried?" Haakon asked. "I haven't seen more than ten worlds where swords were worn with daily attire. Even on those worlds it was mostly for show."

"These are not show weapons," said the proprietor,

31

smiling. He picked one up and went through a dazzling sword drill with it. "It is a descendant of the ancient katana of our people, adapted for conditions on Grass Cutter. With one of these, you can shear through a python vine at a single stroke, before it has a chance to strangle you. Also handy for dueling, a popular pastime here."

"What we stand in most need of is hailstone protection," Haakon said. "Can you outfit us?"

"I have everything you need," he assured them.

"Why are the buildings constructed in this fashion?" Soong asked as he was measured for his armor.

"It is light and airy, which is a blessing in this climate, and there is little to crush you when the earthquakes strike."

"I might have known that you had earthquakes," Haakon said. "Very frequent?"

"Nothing like the hailstorms," the shopkeeper said. "We have severe ones no more than once or perhaps twice per month. The roofs come down in one piece, so if you aren't directly under one of the corners—you notice how the sides arch up?—you have an excellent chance of escaping serious injury. Most partitions are made of cloth or paper and the support poles are hollow." He rapped one to demonstrate.

"What recreational facilities are available here?" Haakon asked.

"Probably nothing as lavish as you are accustomed to. There is an inn at the edge of town, if you plan to stay for the night. The service there is adequate. Most of our few transient spacers and the port personnel and the odd military person frequent the tavern across the square, the one with scarlet lettering on a gold background. Do your boots have armored insoles?" They answered in the affirmative. "Good. There is a little plant here called a pungi. It grows in depressions in the ground, disguised by grass. About fifteen centimeters in length, perhaps five millimeters in diameter, very sharp point. It will go right through your foot."

"No poison?" Haakon asked.

"Oh, no. But it stays in your foot. There is a little insect which lays its eggs in the pungi. At the proper temperature they hatch, and—"

"Don't tell us," Haakon said hastily. "We'll just keep our boots on and try to avoid the wilds." He tried on a rectangular plate that was designed to hang from the shoulder and protect the whole upper arm. A skirt of similar plates protected the body from waist to knees. Shin-plates strapped on over their boots, with projections to cover knee and instep. A boxlike cuirass covered the torso with four hinged plates and buckled at the sides. The upper shoulders were covered by the helmet's spreading brim. There were close-fitting plates for the forearms, but Haakon elected to retain his steel bracelets.

Soong selected a shallow, conical helmet and tried it on. "We still wear a hat like this at home. Made of straw, though."

Haakon tried one with a dome-shaped crown and a wide neck guard. "Why isn't it made like battle armor?" he asked. "Close-fitting, with articulated joints. This system of curtains seems awkward."

"We have found this type to be superior," the shopkeeper assured him. "It is light and does not hamper movement; it allows air to circulate. After you have worn it a while, you will feel relatively comfortable in it. The local contingent of the Black Tuman have insisted upon wearing their conventional battle armor, and their casualties have been high."

"From Chamukan Mama Nature or from the Chamukans?" Jemal asked.

"Oh, from both," said the shopkeeper, beaming.

Dressed in their new finery, they stood on the veranda of the shop. The ceramic armor was finished in a multitude of bright colors to simulate lacquer. They had added swords of the local type. "I never felt so silly in my life," Haakon said.

"It's light, though, and easy to move around in," Jemal said. "Tell me, Soong, did the old Japanese warriors wear armor like this?"

"I believe so. Old paintings I have seen show samurai dressed in roughly similar armor. It may be coincidence that the same design is suited to the exigencies of life here."

"Let's find that tavern," Haakon said. "We haven't been acting suspicious enough so far."

There were few people in the streets. Two men were passing in front of them when they heard a loud buzzing. A big blur was coming down the street at about shoulder level. It was headed straight for one of the two men in front of them. Before they could say a word, one of the men ripped out his sword and cut straight out in a single motion. The blur intersected the blade and flew off in two pieces. The two men laughed and the swordwielder wiped off his blade with a piece of tissue and sheathed the weapon without looking at his scabbard.

Half of the blur had landed at Jemal's feet. It was a fist-sized insect equivalent, divided neatly from a spot between the compound eyes, down the thorax and abdomen, and through its long, pointed tail. The side they could see bore five jointed legs and a pair of large, gauzy wings. "No wonder they use steel," Jemal said. "I don't think a powerblade could charge up that fast. Remind me not to tangle with these people." Coming from a bladesman like Jemal, it was high praise.

They crossed the square, scanning their surroundings warily, and mounted the veranda of the tavern. A number of loungers sat at tables drinking from small cups. Conversation was notably muted, presumably so people would be able to hear the warning buzz of approaching insects. Some of the loungers were clearly local, others wore their armor awkwardly.

Like the shopkeeper, the bartender spoke fluent spacer. "What will you gentlemen have?"

"What's the local specialty?" Haakon asked.

"We have wines, brandy, and beer. Nothing else is drunk here, I fear."

"Let's have a representative sample of everything," Jemal suggested, "then we'll decide what to stay with."

The bartender set up several tiny cups of various liquids and they tried them all. The wines and brandies were far too sweet for their taste, so they settled on beer.

It came in liter bottles with a stylized picture of some horrible beast on the printed label.

"I hope that thing's mythical," Jemal said, brooding over a beer label.

"In this place I wouldn't count on it," Haakon cautioned. He turned to the bartender. "Tell me, friend— I've seen BT's around here. They aren't stationed nearby, are they?"

"They have a fortified encampment about three kilometers north of the spaceport. We seldom see them here in town."

"Good," Haakon said. He signaled for another beer.

The barkeep brought it. "You have no love for the BT's?"

"You ever hear of anybody who had?" Jemal said. The level of conversation at the tables had dropped fractionally. People were trying to eavesdrop.

"One never knows," the bartender temporized. "You are free traders?"

"Freer than most," Haakon assured him. If that didn't attract some outlaw attention, nothing would.

A small man rose from one of the tables and came to the bar. His armor rattled as if he were not used to it. "Just arrived, I take it?" His head was shaved, but he had a tiny chin beard that was bright blue, either dyed or a gene-sport.

"That's right," Haakon said.

"Come sit at our table. We always buy newcomers a drink."

"That's hospitable of you." They took the remains of

36

their beers to the table as another deafening hailstorm began. All conversation stopped of necessity until the storm passed. Haakon took the opportunity to study the table's other inhabitant. He was another short man, stumpy where the bluebeard was slender. Obviously a local, he was dressed in old, worn armor decorated with a string of big beads passing over one shoulder and beneath the opposite arm. His head and face were clean-shaven and heavily scarred.

"I'm Serge LeMat. This is Hori Soun, the abbot of Amida Temple in New Kaga Province." Besides the usual sword, the abbot wore a long dirk and the hand-plates of his armor had spikes over the knuckles. His was clearly not one of the pacifist sects. Haakon made introductions all around. The proposition arrived before the first round of drinks.

"You have a good ship?" croaked the abbot in a voice that fitted his frog face. "Fast? Able to make lengthy voyages?"

"That's right," Haakon said. "Are ships of some interest to you?"

"We'd like to talk a little business," LeMat said. "I'm afraid my colleague here is a little precipitate."

"We're not here for business," Haakon said. "Just routine repair and maintenance, maybe take on a few stores, the usual. This is pretty good beer, for instance; I might order a few hundred liters."

"Of course," LeMat said, "it goes without saying that you aren't here for business. On the other hand, I never saw a free trader who wasn't interested in a little serendipitous action that might fall his way by chance, especially if it looked profitable."

"If it isn't profitable," Haakon pointed out, "it isn't business. However, I have no licenses or permits to trade on this world. You know how stuffy the Bahadurans can be about people treading on their commercial corns. It's not worth it to me to lose my trading license, not to mention my freedom, my ship, and maybe my head, just for a little impromptu cargo run."

"There's really no reason to trouble the authorities about this," LeMat assured him. "Poor dears, they work so hard as it is. Let's just leave them out of this, shall we?" The man was all bland assuredness.

"Smuggling?" Haakon asked. He looked around. "Isn't this place a little public to be discussing such things?"

"Who's talking about smuggling?" LeMat asked, his eyes widening in a parody of innocence. "What we need to transport isn't contraband."

"Then why not just hire space on a commercial freighter?" Jemal asked.

"You know how tedious that would be," LeMat said. "There're forms to go through and questions to answer and we really would rather not involve the authorities."

"Why not?" Haakon asked. "Since, as you say, your cargo isn't contraband."

"Oh, the items themselves are perfectly legal. You could walk through the port with them dangling from your fist and nobody'd say boo to you. It's the matter of their destination that's tricky, you see. The Bahadurans are picky about items leaving the worlds they claim, especially this one. It's not enough to send something off this planet; you also have to state where it's going and it has to go there with no side trips."

Now we reach the crux of the matter, Haakon thought. "All right, where do you want these mysterious items to go?"

LeMat leaned close. "Have you people ever heard of a place called the Cingulum?"

# Three

SENIOR SUBADAR HULAGU SWEATED IN HIS BATTLE ARMOR as the transport bore him and his squad along the road from the BT encampment to Masamune. BT armor was supposed to maintain a steady, optimum body temperature and process any excess perspiration, but nothing seemed to work properly on this hellhole of a world. The transport had lightly armored sides to waist height and an armored roof. Each man held a short beam rifle upright by his side, with its power jack plugged into the forearm of his armor.

"I think I saw an oni back there," the driver said to Hulagu. "It was in the trees, ducked back just as I caught sight of it. Want to go after it, Noyon?"

Hulagu considered. Two of his men had been eaten by oni in the last thirty-day cycle. But the ghastly creatures were hard to kill, and hunting them sometimes multiplied the problem. When the unit had first come here, an oni had been seen lurking outside the camp perimeter. A sentry had cut it in two with a heavy-duty beamer. By the time Hulagu had gone out to investigate, the two halves had crawled off into the bush. Within ten days, they had two full-sized oni to contend with.

"Let it go," Hulagu said. "This near the town it will only eat locals, which it may do with my blessing." He sat back but did not relax his vigilance. Occasionally, a needlenose would come buzzing for the men, but someone would swiftly shoot it before it got near enough to do any harm. All of Hulagu's men were superb shots, although few could cut the insects from the air with swords as the locals could.

They passed a small Buddhist shrine, and again he cursed the Bahadur policy of not interfering with local religion. It made him feel slightly disloyal to resent a government policy, but it had been formulated for worlds where religion was a stabilizing, rather than a rebellion-fomenting element. The one saving grace was that here the various sects fought each other almost as ferociously as they did the Bahadurans.

By the time they reached the town, the stones of the most recent hailstorm had melted and already the air was dusty. It never failed to amaze Hulagu that a place with so much precipitation could be so dusty. Like everything else here, all the elements conspired to annoy human interlopers. The transport pulled into the little town plaza and settled to its landing struts, which adjusted their height to keep the vehicle level.

Hulagu climbed from his seat and blinked away the sweat that seeped from beneath his helmet. "Don't wander too far from the transport," Hulagu warned the squad. "Avoid trouble with the locals, but if you're attacked, kill them. I don't want our infirmary or our stockade cluttered with prisoners."

The men dismounted and stretched. They were not the usual Bahaduran troops, recruited from the lower classes. The Black Tumans were recruited exclusively from the best families, and most of the men were tall, with the narrow features common to the aristocratic caste of Bahadur. They despised the stocky, round-faced natives of Chamuka and the sentiment was richly reciprocated.

Hulagu and his men had no particular reason for visiting Masamune today, but it was wise to remind people of their presence from time to time. The sight of the black armor brought the usual scowls and spittings from the natives, but there was no immediate hostile action. He looked toward the communal tavern, where the troublemakers were usually to be found. The place was nearly empty, but his gaze was drawn back to a shaven-headed man at one of the tables. Bald men were common here, since about half the male population were adherents of one Buddhist sect or another, but this man did not look like a local. Something about him stirred a memory.

"Stay here," he said to his men as he walked toward the tavern.

"Trouble, Captain?" murmured Soong. All conversation had stopped upon the appearance of the BT wagon. Now an officer wearing a Subadar insignia was coming toward them.

"No problem," Haakon said. "We're just law-abiding spacers, after all." He had a feeling that Soong meant more than just ordinary BT trouble. Had they run into this Subadar before?

The officer mounted the veranda and came straight to their table. "You're new here," he said.

"That's right," Haakon affirmed. "We just arrived this morning." He handed over the transient's permit he had been given at the port. The officer scanned it, his eyes slitted and mouth compressed into a thin line.

"You've come to the scummiest dive first thing, I see."

"Second," Haakon said, gesturing to his armor. "We thought it best to lay in some weather protection first. Besides," he said, looking around at the little town, "is there anyplace else around here to sample the delights of urban Chamuka?"

The officer went on as if he had not heard. "And you've taken up with some low companions."

LeMat smiled and shrugged. "Just buying the newcomers a drink, Subadar. I always do."

"Be careful of this one, spacers. Just being in his company puts you under suspicion. That one, too. Don't let his priestly pose fool you. The monasteries here are nests of bandits and rebels."

Soun raised both hands with palms outward at shoulder height. It was not a gesture of supplication, but of ritual. "Even a BT may be saved by calling upon the name of Amida."

"I am almost as suspicious of transients as I am of these two. Watch your step while you are here and don't stay long."

"Much as I hate the thought of leaving a garden spot like this," Haakon said, "I'll take your words to heart. We'll transact our business and be on our way."

"Where do you go from here?" Hulagu demanded.

"We need some replacement parts. We were told at the port that there's a wrecking yard not far from here, back toward the port someplace. When we've had a few more of these," he said and held up an empty bottle, "we'll go find it and see if it has what we need."

"Keep to the areas closely patrolled by the official forces," Hulagu ordered, "and don't go wandering or exploring. You will give me cause to be suspicious. Besides, this is the deadliest planet in all of Bahadur's possessions that is even remotely habitable by humans."

"So I deduced," Jemal said, looking at Hulagu's men grouped around the transport. "I never saw a full senior Subador in charge of a mere squad. Casualties been heavy?"

Hulagu's expression did not change, but his attitude became that of a man about to commit violence. The tension crackled for a few seconds, then abruptly relaxed. He tossed the permit back to Haakon. "Watch yourself," he said.

Hulagu kept himself under extreme control all the way back to his transport. His instinct had been correct. The three newcomers were the ones he had encountered before, far from here. He also suspected them of being the cause for his being transferred to this hideous place. Now what could he do? He remembered them, but he also remembered where he had last seen them, and in whose presence. He climbed into the transport and the others scrambled aboard. "Back to the camp," he said.

"Looks to me like you've run into BT's before," LeMat said.

"Who hasn't?" Haakon asked. "Any free spacer who does business within the Bahadur hegemony has to take a lot of crap from BT soldiers like that one."

"He's no toy soldier," LeMat said, "and neither are the rest of them. They're tough, and they know their work."

"They are much better than the old troops," Soun agreed. "We used to joke about the foolish Bahadur soldiers who died so easily here. We joke no more. They are not as fine as the people of Grass Cutter, but they are fierce and skillful."

"Now that we've attracted attention," Soong suggested, "it might be best if we did not tarry here long."

"I agree," Haakon said. "If you gentlemen want to continue a business discussion, we'd better pick some other place to do it."

"No problem," LeMat said. "Just have a few more cold ones and go about your business. When you get to the wrecking yard, somebody will be there to meet you."

LeMat and Soun left the tavern, and Haakon ordered fresh ones all around before commencing serious discussion. "Was that the Subadar we met a while back, when Timur Khan sent us to Mughal?" he asked, first checking to make sure they were out of hearing distance from the other customers.

"That is the one," Soong confirmed. "I believe his name is Hulagu, one of those names out of Mongol history that the Bahadurans are so fond of. He spotted us from the street. I could see his expression from where I sat. He might easily have made trouble for us."

"I wish he had," Haakon said. "Then, if we got out of here alive, we could go back to Timur Khan and tell him one of his own boys blew our cover."

"He probably blames us for his being here. This is quite a comedown from Timur's own personal guard. We humiliated him in front of his boss and he got sent here as a reprimand."

"I have always thought that you behaved precipitately in that incident," Soong said.

"I wonder what Timur's pets are doing here?" Haakon pondered. "Do you think it's really for punishment?"

"Undoubtedly," Soong said, "it reflects some internecine power struggle within the Serene Powers. That is the kind of situation one is well advised to leave strictly alone."

"Except that it may well be why we're here," Jemal pointed out.

"Why are things always so complicated?" Haakon bemoaned. "Why doesn't he ever give us a simple job?"

"If it were simple," Soong pointed out, "he would not send the best."

They hired a small transport to take them to the wrecking yard and backtracked along the road to the port. Two or three kilometers from the port, they turned off onto a path surfaced only with stabilized dirt. Apparently, the vicissitudes of nature on Chamuka made paved roads more trouble than they were worth. The dense growth grew close to the road, and they kept a wary eye out for flying lethalities. Once in a while they glimpsed odd creatures fading back into the brush and they were not tempted to investigate.

The wrecking yard was an unfenced area dotted with the gutted hulks of several cannibalized ships. Most of them were vessels never designed to land, and they sagged and collapsed in a disconsolate fashion as age and the human urge for bargain prices reduced them to scraps of metal and plastic. Rand had equipped Haakon with a shopping list of the kind of items an ordinary free trader might need to keep his overaged ship spacing.

A man came out of a dome-shaped plastic structure wiping his hands with a scrap of cloth. His helmet had a face plate which was pushed up clear of his face, disclosing a countenance that was not native to Chamuka. "How may I be of service?" he asked.

Haakon handed him the list. "Do you have any of these whitchits?"

The man scanned the list. "Some of this we have. These Tesla transmission nodes, though, they deteriorate pretty fast. There should be some in that hulk over there." He pointed to the sad tail section of an old cruiser.

"You'll have to show me what they are," Haakon said.

The man looked at him suspiciously. "You're a ship's captain, and you don't know anything about Teslas?"

"Are you serious?" Haakon asked. "I have nothing to do with them. I wouldn't have the damn things on my ship except it won't go anywhere without them."

"Can't say I blame you. I spaced for twenty years and had to abandon ship three times because of blown Teslas. The last time the lifeboat just barely made it here, and I haven't gone offworld since. Come on." He led the way toward the hulk and the rest fell in behind.

"Why does your helmet have a face plate?" Jemal asked.

"You work in a junkyard, sometimes you got both hands full when the bugs come at you. Besides, you have to be born on this place before you can cut the bugs out of the air. I like to have a second chance."

"I've noticed that nobody carries guns or beamers around here," Haakon said. "We were warned not to bring any down. The Bahaduran authorities pretty strict on weapons control?"

"Yeah, but I don't think the locals would use them anyway, much as they love to fight. They prefer hand weapons."

"Why don't they at least set up electronic bug screens?" Jemal asked. "Even the Bahadurans wouldn't give them any trouble over that. Do they have some kind of taboo against them?"

"Naw," the man answered. "They just think cutting them down on the wing is more fun."

They poked through the ruined Tesla engines only to find that the transmission nodes were indeed deteriorated past any possible use. They returned to the dome to look for some of the smaller items on the list. They found a small reception committee waiting for them.

Three were burly, shaven-headed men who wore the strings of beads they had seen Soun wearing. Their armor and clothes were colored a subdued saffron. The fourth person was plainly a woman, although a close-fitting metal mask covered her features. She was taller than her male companions and looked willowy even in her bulky armor.

"You are the ones who have agreed to take our treasures offworld, to the Cingulum?" the woman asked.

"We haven't agreed to anything," Haakon said. "And nobody mentioned treasures. We told LeMat and Soun that we'd talk further about a job, and we got some cagey talk about some items innocuous enough to be carried openly through customs. Now we're ready to hear more."

"Very well," the woman said. "We—"

Haakon interrupted. "If you don't mind, I'd prefer it if you'd take off that mask. I like to see who I'm talking to when I'm discussing sensitive business."

The bald men bristled but, after a moment's hesitation, the woman removed her helmet and then the metal mask. She handed them to the nearest of the men and faced Haakon. She was stunningly beautiful, with high cheekbones and a high-bridged, aristocratic nose. Despite her old-ivory coloration and the slight epicanthic fold in the inner corners of her eyes, her features were unlike those of the Chamukan natives they had seen so far. Her shiny black hair was gathered into a waist-length tail and her face was sheened with fine sweat from wearing the mask.

"Is that satisfactory?" she asked.

"Much better. I'm Captain Haakon. These men are my officers, Jemal and Soong."

She scanned them briefly with enormous brown eyes that were intimidatingly cool. "You've lived dangerously," she said, "and you are dangerous men." Startlingly, her teeth were lacquered glossy black.

"We've done what was necessary to stay alive," Haakon said. He was always cautious with people who possessed that easy ability to read character.

"Just as well," she said. "We weren't looking for saintly people. I don't suppose ordinary people would be entrusted with the coordinates to the Cingulum."

"How do you know we have them?" Haakon asked.

"How could you hope to carry out our mission if you didn't have them? Of course," she said and scanned them bleakly, "there is always the possibility that you intended to take our pay without holding up your end of the bargain. That would be unwise."

"No need for threats. We're reputable smugglers. Ask anybody. We'll undertake no job we can't see through."

"Captain," Jemal said, "before things proceed any further, I think it's time for the lecture."

"Lecture?" the woman asked.

"We have to caution you about our relationship with

50

the Cingulum," Haakon said. "You're aware that those coordinates change from time to time?"

"I know. Is it really true that the whole planetary system can be moved at will?"

"Quite true. In telling you that, I'm revealing nothing that Bahadur doesn't already know. The inhabitants of the Cingulum are a truly hardcore pack of resisters. If we ever brought them anybody or anything that was in the slightest way dangerous or compromising to them, we'd be executed immediately. We don't take people there just for the asking. We're regarded with suspicion there at the best of times. They think, quite correctly, that we lack proper revolutionary fervor."

"I think," Soong said, "that these people have heard enough from us for now. It is time that we learn something about them and their mysterious mission."

The woman turned to the wrecking yard man. "Kiley, keep a lookout and make sure to warn us if anyone comes close."

The man nodded and left. The woman sat cross-legged on the floor and the three native men sank beside her in a peculiar crouch, with one knee on the floor and the other foot planted flat, left hands grasping their sheaths. They appeared to be as ready for action as when standing. Haakon and his men sat as well, cross-legged like the woman.

"The people of this planet," the woman began, "are without question the most intransigent foes of Bahadur in existence. I realize that they continue to exist only because of the unique economics of the planet. Courage and character are as nothing in the face of modern weapons."

"As I understand it," Haakon said, "this character doesn't extend to any degree of unity."

"That is true," the woman admitted. "They are deeply divided by regional and religious differences especially. Still, there is a single rallying point: The ancient royal line still lives here."

"That is not in agreement with the data in our banks," Soong protested. "According to our information, some members of a cadet branch of the old Imperial house were among the early settlers. There is no record of any pretenders to a throne of Chamuka."

"Our royal house," growled one of the warrior-monks, "is not a foreigner's illusion of thrones and palaces. Their Majesties have always been our connection with the gods of our ancestors. They are our living gods, and we have protected them from the upstarts of Bahadur by a conspiracy of silence."

Being told other people's secrets always made Haakon nervous. "What has all this to do with the goods you want taken to the Cingulum?"

"The old Emperor," the woman said, "Go-Hosokawa III, is dying. He cannot last out the year. He wishes to send the Three Treasures of the Imperial Regalia to his son, Tametomo. Tametomo is believed to be living somewhere in the Cingulum."

"Believed?" Haakon asked. "You mean, you've lost track of the royal heir?"

"He disappeared during the last great war that

Bahadur fought. One morning he picked up his sword, left the royal residence, and bribed his way onto a smuggler's vessel. He left a note saying, in verse form, that he was going to join a Han fleet and fight against Bahadur. Since he had six older brothers, he said, the family would not miss him. He was sixteen years old."

"I take it the six brothers are no longer among us?" Soong asked.

"Three of them also ran off to war and died. The others died of natural causes here on Grass Cutter. Tametomo is the only one left of that generation. We were able to trace the fleet that he joined. The greater part of it was destroyed in a great battle within the Han system. Tametomo's ship escaped with some others and they linked with the Delian League. There was another battle, another defeat.

"After that, matters were so confused that we have been unable to find records of the ships and their crews. There was desperation. Ships were attached to whatever little fleet was still fighting. Eventually, there was nothing but a few shiploads of fugitives looking for any sort of refuge to avoid the Bahadur pits."

"I went through the same process," Haakon said. "All three of us did. In my case, I ended up in the pits. What makes you think he made it to the Cingulum?"

"His ship made it. At least, it was the ship he was last assigned to. Its manifest still carried a Captain of Marines T. Minamoto. That must be Tametomo. He was very fond of the tales of his namesake, the ancient warrior Minamoto Tametomo. He undoubtedly chose it so he would not have to use his family name."

"How did you get hold of this ship's manifest?" Haakon asked.

"From a contact," the woman said coolly. "You need not trouble yourself about that."

"Why didn't he just come home, or at least send word?" Jemal asked. "The war's over, you know."

"He thinks," said the monk who had spoken earlier, "that it is not honorable to return from defeat. The boy left here with a head stuffed full of old poems and tales of heroes. If he had paid more attention to the holy scriptures, he would not be so full of empty pride, but more mindful of his duty to his family."

"Maybe he just wants to keep on fighting," Haakon pointed out. "The Cingulum is a hotbed of resistance movements. None of it's ever come to anything, but if you want to sit around with your friends and plot a comeback against Bahadur, the Cingulum is the place to be."

"You don't sound very impressed with the Cingulans," the woman said.

Haakon shrugged. "It's not our kind of show. Bahadur won. We just try to get along as best we can. Someday the Cingulum may be an organized republic with a fleet and a real chance against the Powers, but that's a long way off." This was only partially true, but he saw no reason to be excessively candid with these people. He knew that the woman, for one, wasn't being completely open with them.

"He must be convinced," she said, "that this is one place where he can do Bahadur some real damage. He must come home!"

"So that's how it is," Haakon said rhetorically. "And why must he have these Three Treasures? Wouldn't a simple summons from papa do as well?"

"He would not trust the word of a stranger, or even a hologram of his father speaking. Remember how young he was when he left here, how many years and hardships have intervened. He is in his early thirties now; his memories of home will be distorted. He remembers his father as a vigorous man in the prime of life. The Three Treasures are eternal. They cannot be duplicated, and he will know that with them, he holds the future of the royal line, and therefore, of Grass Cutter and all its people. He must come home."

It made sense, Haakon had to admit. He remembered what it was like, being an enthusiastic young man, charging off to war full of ideals. He knew the humiliation of defeat, the disorientation of a cause irretrievably lost, the shame of returning home beaten. Of course, in his case, there had been no choice about the last point. The aristocrat-officer class was forbidden to return to Delius on pain of death.

"All right," he said. "We'll give it a try. I can't guarantee that he's alive, or even that we can find him if he is. The Cingulum is a stranger place than you can imagine. Of what do these treasures consist?"

"They are not bulky," the woman said. "They do not really look like treasures. Their significance is spiritual, almost mystic for the people of Grass Cutter."

"The Sword," said the monk. "The Sword from the tail of the Cloud Cluster Dragon. The Mirror, which brought the Sun back to us, and the Jewel, which——"

"Those are the Three Treasures," the woman interrupted. "Three rather small objects, unknown to the authorities, which you may take up to your ship without arousing official suspicion in the slightest."

"This all sounds extremely simple," Jemal said. "Extremely agreeable and risk-free. Why, I ask myself, why do I keep getting the impression that there's something we haven't heard yet, something that's going to call for a really good price for our services?" He wiggled his eyebrows in a comical gesture of query.

For the first time, the woman smiled very slightly. "As you say, it isn't as simple as all that. You will have to come with us to see the Emperor. He is old, and he trusts only his own instincts. He will have to interview the couriers before he will entrust the Three Treasures to them."

"Ah, the light dawns," Haakon said. "Will this involve a lengthy trip? You understand, we've been warned by the local BT's that they'll kill us if we stray too far off the officially permitted road."

The monk snorted. "You may depend on us to protect you from the Bahadurans!"

"It pleases me no end," Haakon said, "that you have so high an opinion of yourselves. It's a pretty extreme leap in credulity to trust our lives to it, though. How long a journey are we talking about?"

"His Majesty," the woman said, "keeps his residence

at the Great Boddhisatva Temple in this province. Leaving Masamune, and traveling by animal transport, it will take no more than two days to go there."

"That's plenty to get us killed," Haakon pointed out. "We've already attracted some attention from the BT's. If they notice us taking a little jaunt into unauthorized territory, there could be trouble for us."

"You let us worry about the BT's," the monk said. "While you go to see His Majesty, we shall arrange a diversion for the Bahadurans. Nothing shall disturb the serenity of His Majesty's hours."

"We've dealt with these people before," said Haakon doubtfully, "and we know that they don't spook easily. They're tough, smart, professional soldiers. It'll take a little more than some shouting and shooting to take their attention off suspicious characters like us."

"Will an uprising of about fifty thousand guerrilla fighters suffice?" the woman asked. "With a major offensive against some twenty Bahaduran positions, hundreds, perhaps thousands of casualties on both sides, and reprisals afterwards by the BT's consisting of, say, ten thousand noncombatants executed as an example?" She stared at them without flinching. The monks stared likewise.

There was a period of silence. Then Haakon said, "You people are serious."

"We do not speak here," said the monk, "of petty wars fought by little noblemen for contemptible gains of power and influence. We speak here of racial survival, of the preservation of a people and a culture. We are not a great, numerous people like some others." He stared at Soong. "The Han own many worlds; they are a numerous minority on many others. You," he said, looking Haakon in the eye, "represent the old European culture, from which sprang the expansion of men from Earth into the stars. No amount of slaughter, even the Bahaduran sterilization of worlds, would wipe out your heritage.

"We," he said, sweat shining on his brow, "are a small people. Not numerous, not even unified, but a people. As far as we know, the culture of the Home Islands is lost except for Grass Cutter. Our language, our legends, our customs and religions may exist nowhere else except here. We are quite willing to accept casualties in order to preserve these things. To you, we may appear to be a backward people—divided into warring religious and political sects, an agricultural, iron-age race on a primitive planet. To us, we are the conservators of an ancient cultural tradition. Any of us will happily die to preserve it."

There was another short silence, then Haakon said, "All right, I'll go for it. We need a little time, though. I want to bring another of my crew down. When do you want to set off on this expedition?"

"The day after tomorrow will be convenient," the woman said.

"We'll stay in the inn at Masamune we were told about," Haakon said. "Are there any other surprises we should be looking for?"

She smiled once again. "No, all the cards are on the table now."

58

I'll bet, Haakon thought. "We'll need an excuse to prolong our stay. Bring Kiley back in."

One of the monks got up and ran out of the shed. After a few minutes, he returned with the junkyard-keeper in tow.

"Kiley," Haakon said, "how long was it you figured it'd take to get those Tesla nodes pried out?"

"Tesla nodes?" asked Kiley, mystified. "I already explained, they deteriorate so fast."

"Kiley," Jemal said, "we need an excuse to stay here about four or five days."

"Oh, *Tesla* nodes! Well, like I was telling you, they get covered with all this corrosion that takes days to chip away. You gotta do it careful, too. Job like that, it could take five, six days easy."

"That's better," Haakon said. "One thing we can be pretty sure the BT's will know nothing about, it's Teslas. Now I think it's time we had a look at that inn. When you're ready to leave, bring transport for four of us."

"You'll have it." The woman rose and redonned her metal mask and helmet. She left the shed, trailing her escort of warrior-monks. Overhead, another thundering hailstorm commenced.

As they rode back to the town, Haakon said, "How do you read that woman? She's not Chamukan."

"Unless my ethnological analysis is terribly inaccurate," Soong said, "she is a high-born lady of some Bahaduran house. During my years as an assassin, I studied those people in great detail. She shows gene traces of some of the very highest houses. Those families are so inbred that their genetic signatures are quite distinct."

"Now what's a Bahaduran noblewoman doing involved in an anti-Bahadur movement on a place like Chamuka?" Jemal asked.

"Damned if I know," Haakon said. "But we don't trust her."

"When did we ever trust any but our own shipmates?" Soong asked.

# Four

NUMA DIDN'T SMELL HAPPY. TO EVERYBODY'S GREAT relief, Felid males were not nearly the scent factories that the females were, but his changes of mood were nevertheless signaled by different odors.

"I've always hated wearing armor," he rumbled.

His large, clawed fingers adjusted the laces of his suit with incongruous delicacy. It had taken them most of a day to find armor large enough to fit him. They had had to hire a craftsman to fashion some of the plates especially for the Felid.

The locals had never seen a Felid, and many had wandered by to gawk, further irritating his already uncertain temper. He hissed at a bystander as they awaited their transport on the veranda of the inn.

"You look splendid," Soong assured him. "The red armor sets off your gold coloration to perfection. That particular color combination is regarded as most felicitous by Asian cultures."

"Makes you look mean as hell, too," Jemal said.

Numa's rumbling subsided. Felids also had a weakness for flattery.

Haakon scanned the area. The inn was set in a picturesque grove of local foilage and some kind of modified bamboo. The buildings were set on posts that had been soaked in poison, to keep local wildlife from crawling in. There was a rock garden with a pool and an ornamental bridge, giving a deceptive aura of peace in the midst of this deadly environment. The bridge looked fragile, but it was made of the same durable ceramic as their armor. He had carefully examined some of the local trees. Their trunks were hard as stone and the leaflike appendages were tough and leathery. Everything here was adapted to resist the hailstones, winds, and earthquakes.

Their transport arrived to take them to the wrecking yard and they climbed in. "I hope we don't run into the BT's on the road," Jemal said.

"We have our excuse ready," Haakon reminded him.

"I just don't want to attract attention. Hulagu may just be looking for an excuse to kill us."

"He knows he'd have to answer to his boss for that," Haakon objected.

"With a situation as confused and volatile as this," Soong pointed out, "one can get away with many things. Unsettled times are the traditional opportunity for settling old scores."

"You two are just doing wonders for my equanimity,"

Haakon groused. "Why not just shut up and let's deal with our problems as they arise?" He could only take so much pessimism, especially when it was justified.

Their traveling party did not appear until after the transport had returned to town. They rushed for cover as a hailstorm arrived, and when it was safe to leave the shed, they saw what was emerging from the tree line.

"What the hell are those things?" asked Jemal, aghast.

"Those are turkles," Kiley said. The creatures being ridden or led were about four meters long and moved on four short, stumpy legs. Their backs were covered with a jointed carapace and their low-slung heads were capped with a plate of knobby horn.

"I can't decide," Haakon said, "whether they're incredibly ugly or just plain dumb-looking."

Kiley shrugged. "They ain't pretty, but they're about the only animals on this planet that won't deliberately try to kill you. Might accidentally stomp you to death, though."

"I don't think I like this idea," Jemal said. There was an ancient spacer's superstition that said it was bad luck for a spacer to climb aboard any riding animal.

"Best not sleep too close to them, either," Kiley said helpfully. "Sometimes they roll over in their sleep and squash people."

"I can't imagine sleeping in the open in this place," Haakon told him. They went out of the fenced area and joined their escort, which turned out to be the woman and the four monks, with the addition of the abbot, Soun.

"This trip will go a lot easier," Haakon said, "if we have a name to call you by."

"My name is Sarai," she said.

"Now we're making progress," Haakon said. "Are we really supposed to ride these beasts?"

"That is why we brought them," she said. "You mount by stepping on top of its head and climbing up its back to your saddle."

Haakon surveyed the head in question doubtfully. The blunt face was divided by a mouth that ran its entire width. The mouth was slightly open, revealing a veritable pavement of small, flat teeth. The creature stared back with an amazing absence of intelligence. This thing was definitely designed for durability rather than brain power.

Cautiously, he stepped up onto the head. It held steady enough for him to walk up to the short neck and onto the carapace. The saddle was a padded seat with a folding roof stored behind it. When he sat, his legs stretched before him almost to its neck.

"How do I steer it?" he asked.

"You don't," she answered. "One of us will be in the lead at all times. The others will follow. Guidance is rather complicated, so don't even try it. A tug on that strap behind you will unfold your shelter."

"What do we do about the bugs?" Jemal asked. "I'm pretty quick with a blade, but I don't think I'm that quick."

"You needn't worry," she said. "They seldom attack recent arrivals. After you've lived on Chamukan food and water for a year or so, they start to notice you. They seem to home on body chemistry."

Sarai noticed Numa for the first time. "What kind of person are you?"

"The best kind," he answered. "A Felid." Two bounds put him in the saddle, his foot scarcely touching the top of his mount's head. The monks spoke excitedly when they realized that Numa, beneath his armor, was not a standard human.

"They think you look like one of the old guardian spirits," she explained. "They have statues of them in the temples. Don't be offended. They say it's a sign that the gods favor their mission."

"Gods?" Haakon asked, settling himself gingerly onto his saddle pad. "I thought this outfit was Buddhist."

"They are," she said, "but they've also incorporated Shinto into their sect. Buddha is the supreme teacher, but the smaller gods also exist and have their own realms, along with spirits of other sorts. They maintain that it doesn't conflict with the teachings of the Buddha."

"Nor should it," Soun said. "Where in the sutras does it say that—"

"We have a long trip ahead of us, folks," Haakon said. "I suggest we get going."

Soun looked incensed, but Soong said soothingly, "My Lord Abbot, while we are on this journey, would you be so kind as to impart to me some of the teachings of your sect? In all my wanderings I have come to realize that it is impossible to exhaust the possibilities of the words of the Lord Buddha."

Soun regarded him with a certain respect. "You are a pilgrim?"

"I strive to regulate my life properly, and any new facet of the Enlightened One's teaching can only help me to that end."

"We shall talk, then," Soun said. "I shall keep your beast and mine in mind-yoke."

Haakon wasn't sure what that last reference meant, but there was no question that Soong was a first-rate diplomat. When he thought about it, it seemed that Soong and Mirabelle were about the only members of his crew who could be depended on to show a few social graces. An assassin and a thief. He was sure there was a moral to be found in there somewhere, but he wasn't sure what it might be. Eventually, everybody was mounted and more or less ready to go.

"We'll travel in double file," Sarai announced. "That gives each of us only one side to keep full lookout on. First will go two of the monks, then Abbot Soun and Soong, then Captain Haakon and me. Jemal and the Felid, Mr.—"

"Numa. We only use one name."

"Numa, then. Since you're both new arrivals, there's little chance you'll be attacked right away by the native life forms. Last of all, the other two monks. Any questions?"

"One," Haakon said. "We may be safe from the native life forms, but what about the local human population?"

Soun looked at the woman and grunted. It was an I-told-you-so sound.

"You needn't concern yourself about that," Sarai insisted. "There are several squabbling sects here, but they won't endanger you. If there should be a fight, it will be me, Soun, and the other monks who will take the brunt of it."

Haakon looked idly at the backs of his hands. "I've been wounded many times in combat. Sometimes it was by the enemy. Just about as often, though, it was an accidental wound from my own side. Happens all the time in war. I figure a neutral in a crossfire is about twice as likely to get hit as someone on either of the warring sides."

"Our warriors will keep you safe," Soun barked. "If there is fighting, it will be close, with blades and spears. Since the BT's came, none of us goes armed with beam weapons, or with firearms or bows. They are most apprehensive of missile weapons, as well they might be. Our people were the finest marksmen and archers they had ever encountered. One is seldom injured by an ill-aimed sword."

"I believe you," Haakon said. "I just like to know what I'm getting into."

"Are you satisfied?" asked Sarai impatiently. "Shall we go now?"

Haakon regarded her blandly. "Let's go."

The turkles lurched into stately progress. For such enormous animals, they made remarkably little noise. It took Haakon a while to realize what was strangest about them. Then he noticed that he could not hear their breathing. He had never encountered a beast so large that did not breathe like an ancient steam engine.

67

"Animal transport isn't our favorite means of travel," Haakon remarked.

"Would you rather walk?" Sarai demanded.

"Not at all, but wouldn't some kind of powered vehicle be more practical, not to mention faster?"

"Conditions here are hard on mechanical devices. Besides, anything that flies or travels on the ground under power is easily spotted by BT surveillance."

"I suppose we're stuck with these beasts." He sat back and admired the scenery.

For all the ferocity of its climate, Chamuka was an extraordinarily beautiful place. This part of it was, at any rate. The land was mountainous, densely covered with rich, green vegetation. Picturesque, rocky crags jutted from the mountainsides, many of them spouting graceful waterfalls. Something was missing, though.

"No flowers," he noted.

"Nothing so delicate could live here. The plants have developed other means of reproduction. Some keep their reproductive apparatus inside their stems or trunks, and lure insect vectors in through small holes, using smells or colors as bait. Some can even make sounds like insect prey to lure them in. Grass Cutter teaches all her children to be resourceful."

"And deadly."

She smiled. "That, too. Even in the relatively tranquil field of plant reproduction, there can be dangers. You see that stand of trees on that knoll?" She pointed to a close-set group of trees with squat trunks and frond-tipped branches sprouting in a helical pattern. "They are bisexual, and each produces sperm that is stored in small thorns. Gas builds up in tubes behind the thorns. In the proper season, the trees fire their thorns like darts, hard enough to penetrate the bark of neighboring trees of the same species. It is very hard bark, too. Every thorn in that stand will be launched at once, thousands from each tree. If you were wandering through those trees, you would be cut to pieces in the crossfire."

"Nice place you have here," Haakon said. "I'm going to miss it."

From time to time, they passed small shrines in the forest. Some housed carved Buddhas, others held seemingly random objects: a helmet, a bamboo tea ladle, a bolt of brightly dyed cloth. Sarai explained that the objects had some sort of cult significance.

"I would not have taken you for an avid sightseer," Sarai said.

"I'm not, but it helps keep my mind off what's going on here on Chamuka. When does the hell-raising start?"

"The offensive began before we started out. There is major combat in progress right now."

It was hard to believe in such tranquil surroundings. "You take it all calmly."

She shrugged. "Life is terribly hard and brutal on this world. One comes to accept violent death as a given."

"A rather Bahaduran attitude," Haakon said.

She glared venomously. "Bahadur accepts the slaughter of subject peoples and enemies. We do not hold life cheap here; we merely understand its inevitable brevity." She pulled up her shelter as hailstones began to bounce from the armored hides of the turkles.

* * *

Hulagu's duty day began at sunrise. Light coming through the translucent plastiyurt woke him moments before the duty officer's runner rapped on his door. He rose from his hard pallet and splashed cold water on his face. Dressed only in shorts, he walked outside along a covered walkway to the exercise field, where every man of the Tuman who was not on guard duty or in the infirmary was already assembled. There were too few of them, he noted, as he had every morning for a long time. Too many casualties. How would his Tuman survive a full five years of this?

Twenty minutes of stretching exercises were followed by an hour of violent calisthenics. This ritual was followed religiously by every Tuman in the Empire on every morning that he was not in the field. A temporary force shield kept out the hailstones and marauding life forms of Chamuka. Later in the day would be weapons practice, patrolling, and other activities of the year-round training schedule peculiar to the Black Tumans. Timur Khan Bey insisted that his pet troops be given the most rigorous and demanding training imaginable. To this end, common Bahadur troops performed all their maintenance and support functions. The BT's were reserved strictly for combat.

Sweaty but exhilarated, Hulagu returned to his yurt to dress. The demands of his work always gave him a renewed sense of purpose. He hated this place, but those who survived five years on Chamuka proved themselves worthy, indeed. He could look forward to important posts and rapid promotion, if he could just survive.

He arrived at the officers' mess immaculate in his

black uniform. There were few other black uniforms in the mess. Most wore the red of common Bahadur units or the colors of subject races. Hulagu saw one of his Jemadars beckoning him to a table he shared with a red-clad officer. Ordinarily, the BT's did not fraternize with the other arms, but on a post as remote as this, some things could be relaxed.

Hulagu sat on the cushioned floor and took a cup of tea from the low table.

"Good morning, Subadar," intoned the two men.

Hulagu nodded first to the Jemadar and said, "Juchi." To the other he said, "Subadar Mahmud Shevket."

Technically, Shevket outranked Juchi and was equal in rank to Hulagu, and somewhat senior as well. In practice, any BT outranked anyone of any other service, at least in their own estimation. If Shevket resented the slight in protocol, he displayed nothing.

Shevket grinned at Hulagu. "Young Juchi and I have a wager, Subadar."

Hulagu's eyes narrowed slightly at the patronizing reference to his junior officer. Shevket had the round, bullet head of the Turkic peoples. He was of the upper classes of that race, but not of the pure Bahadur blood.

"And the nature of this wager?" Hulagu asked.

"Shevket thinks the natives are ripe for a new rebellion," Juchi said indignantly. "I say they are beaten and cowed. We'll see nothing from here on except banditry and petty guerrilla action."

Shevket flashed his insolent grin again. "There speaks one who has never been to the wars." He continued to grin at Hulagu, who flushed slightly.

Neither had he been to the *real* wars, and veterans like

Shevket never let him forget it. He wondered whether he might someday have to call Shevket out. The Turk was high enough in birth to duel with Hulagu. How might Timur Khan take it, though? Ordinarily, he encouraged his officers to brook no insolence from lesser services, but he might prove merciless to any who took part in something as self-indulgent as a duel in so volatile a place as Chamuka. Best to show a mild face.

"Our next month's pay rides on the outcome," Juchi said.

"Seriously, Subadar," Shevket said and dropped the grin, "I have ordered my men to double the guard and sleep on their arms. I think you should do the same."

"It is never amiss to err on the side of caution," Hulagu said judiciously. "At least, when the only consequence will be a bit of lost sleep. What makes you think an uprising is due?"

"It's the attitude of the people in the villages around here. It has been changing of late."

"How so?" Hulagu asked. A 'bot deposited a platter of rice and sliced lamb atop pieces of flat bread on the table and the men began to help themselves. "Are they sharpening their swords? Do they glare sullenly? Do they mutter curses and prayers? They have been doing those things since I arrived here."

"Oh, no, Subadar, that would not disturb me at all." He bit into a piece of the bread piled with lamb and rice.

"Then what does?" Hulagu demanded impatiently.

"They look happy."

The first explosion shook the mess hall. It came from the northern edge of the camp. There was no confusion and no idle chatter. They all knew how to take emergency stations. Most had presence of mind to scoop up some food, and Shevket even stuffed bread into the leg pockets of his battle gear. They ate on the run as they took up their stations, for once action started, a soldier never knew when he might expect to eat again.

Shevket smiled at Juchi as they crowded through the door. "Laugh when you live to collect it, Turk!" Juchi spat.

The firebase shield was active by the time they exited the mess hall. It would not last under repeated attacks, but it ought to hold until everyone was in position. Hulagu ran for the command post, a humped structure of fused rock that overlooked the whole firebase. A guard passed him through the portal and shut the armored door behind him. He passed the dogged hatches of the hardened gun positions and climbed the stairs to the command room. "Report!" he barked.

"Three-hundred-sixty-degree attack, Subadar," reported a black-clad Jemadar. The man recited in a calm, almost bored voice. Hulagu approved. Let these mongrels see how a BT of the true blood could act under pressure. "No penetrations. They are using some heavy weaponry we have not encountered here before. First estimation, backed by remote sensor intelligence, numbers the forces attacking this firebase in regimental strength, say, four to five thousand men."

Hulagu looked to a red-clad private who sat behind a strange-looking apparatus. "All contact with other firebases ceased seconds before the first denotation, Subadar," the private said.

"Have you tried the alternate frequencies?"

"I am working on them, sir. So far, all are seriously jammed."

Some antiquarian in the Signal Corps had resurrected ancient radio for battlefield communication. It was dreadfully inefficient compared to more modern systems, but what the enemy did not know about, they could not jam. Somehow they had learned of this ploy. They were on their own until the attack stopped.

"We can expect no help from the other Tumans, then," Hulagu said. "We don't need it in any case. Are all defenses in place?"

The battlemaster watched the tiny spherical lights floating above the holographic projection of the firebase. The last winked from red to green. "All ready, Subadar."

"Then lift the shield so we can kill them."

"Yes, sir!" The battlemaster grinned. BT's were assault troops and they hated to fight defensively. He spoke into his intercom: "Shield raised five meters. Kill them!"

Immediately, a ferocious fire sprayed from the redoubts encircling the firebase. Overhead, the shield remained to defend against high-trajectory fire. Beams and bullets laced the surrounding jungle, and sonics brayed from projectors on the outer defense wall. They were not allowed to use chemical weapons, lest the crystal-farming be disrupted.

"Let's have visual," Hulagu ordered. The holo of the firebase winked out and was replaced by concentric circles of imagery, revealing their attackers. There were faint variations in the colors of the circles, indicating distance from the firebase. To eyes untrained to such imaging, it would have been confusing and incomprehensible, but the men in the control room could interpret it easily.

"They're dying by the hundreds," grunted the battlemaster. In all the circles, men in the drab clothing and armor of guerrillas were charging in to be felled by the defense. A few had modern beam rifles, others had obsolete beam or projectile weapons. Many had only swords, spears, and bows.

"Where are they getting the new beam rifles?" mused an officer.

"We shall find out," Hulagu said. "Target plenty of villages for reprisal annihilation when this is over, no one to be spared. We must begin the instant the attack ends, before they can escape to the hills."

"Masamune?" an officer asked.

Hulagu thought. "No. It serves the port, much as I would like to scour the place."

"Let's win here before we start reprisals," muttered a red-clad officer. Hulagu took note of him. Weakness of spirit had to be punished.

"Look at those," said the battlemaster. He pointed to the fifth ring, almost outside the defensive fire of the base. Shaven-headed men in blue clothing and armor were entering the fight. "Those are warrior-monks from the Mount Nara Temple."

"It shall be destroyed," Hulagu said. Of them all, he hated the Buddhist monasteries the most. The monks whipped people up to anti-Bahadur activity with relentless dedication.

"They're getting close to the southwest quadrant. There's more natural cover there." The attackers were recklessly taking terrible casualties to force themselves closer to the outer defenses.

"I said years ago we should have leveled that terrain." It was the same red-clad officer who had spoken before.

"Would you have Bahadurans appear afraid of this scum?" Hulagu asked coldly.

The man glared back just as coldly. "Does this great armored fort look like the work of men confident in their superiority?"

Hulagu stared back but could think of nothing to say. Unfortunately, he agreed with the man. They were interrupted by the communications private.

"Sir, I'm getting something on the Mayday frequency. BT transport coming in with wounded."

"I have it on visual," the holograph officer said. He brought in an enlargement of a lurching transport, smoke trailing from its power plant, black-uniformed figures slumped over its rails, blood trickling in thin streams from its deck.

"They want us to raise the shield to twenty meters to let them in," the private reported. "Attitude controls are out, but he still has acceleration and braking. It's urgent, sir."

"Shoot it down," advised the battlemaster. "It's a ruse!"

"How could they have taken a transport full of BT's?" Hulagu demanded. He hesitated. "Still, there is a risk.

76

Shoot it down." He hoped nobody had noticed his moment of indecision.

The battlemaster gave the order and five beams converged on the frail craft. It disappeared in an immense fireball that temporarily blacked out the sensors. The battlemaster's mouth twitched slightly upward at the corners. "What did I tell you? It was poor strategy. I'll wager that blast took out half their men in that quadrant."

At that instant, the command post shook with an explosion that dwarfed anything that had gone before. Lights blinked and sirens shrieked. "What was that?" shouted Hulagu, notably ruffled for the first time.

"At a guess," said the red-clad officer, "I'd say while we were distracted by that transport, they launched the real attack a hundred-eighty degrees on the other side of the base."

"Bring up the holos," Hulagu ordered. "I want damage assessment!"

Slowly, flickering, the firebase holograph took shape. The whole southwest quadrant was a mass of blinking red lights. All the bunkers and redoubts in that section were out of commission, at least as far as their major weapons systems were concerned. One building glowed red in its entirety. "They got the shield generator," Hulagu said. "What was it? A missile?"

"That would be my guess," the battlemaster said. "It came in low at high speed, and launched from no more than a kilometer away, or our satellite defenses would have had plenty of time to shoot it down. Praise the Everlasting Sky these subhumans don't have nukes."

Hulagu shook his head. "Thay dare not endanger the crystal-farming any more than do we. It's all that keeps them alive. What do you think they'll try next?"

"That thing went straight for the shield generator," the battlemaster said. "Taking out the perimeter defenses was a side effect. Now they'll bring in high-trajectory fire, mass on the southwest quadrant, and mount a wave attack against the southwest."

Within minutes, the interior of the holograph began to blossom with explosions.

"Those are rockets," the battlemaster reported. "Maybe even mortars, God knows these people are primitive enough. And they are breaking off heavy contact everywhere but the southwest."

"Strip the other sides of superfluous personnel," Hulagu ordered. "Mass them with the reserve and get them into the breach the instant the bombardment lets up, BT's in front, with small arms and hand weapons. I'll lead them myself. You can handle the overall perimeter defence from here, Battlemaster. This defense work gets tiresome. A little close action will be a relief." He was not merely putting a good face on things. He was genuinely anxious to get out of the control room and into real action.

Hulagu pulled on his helmet as he went down to the shuttle tunnel. He boarded a ten-man car as it pulled up by the control room station. It was already packed with men headed for the reserve room, but they made space for him. The car glided silently over electromagnetic tracks, and the loudest sound was the nervous chatter of the men. Hulagu was too occupied with his own thoughts to rebuke any of them.

The reserve room was an immense chamber beneath the center of the firebase. Men stood in formation in the areas marked off for their units. Four wide ramps led up to surface doors to allow reserves to reach any given side of the base as quickly as possible. A muffled thumping overhead told Hulagu that the shelling was still in progress. The men fell silent as Hulagu mounted the commander's platform. He punched a control on the low podium and the floor rotated to bring the men face-on to the southern ramp. At the head of one company he saw Shevket, grinning.

"By now you all know that the big explosion took out most of our southwest perimeter defense. In a few minutes, the shelling will stop and they'll come pouring in. We shall see to it that none pass the breach. They are tough, but Bahadurans have never been defeated by subhumans. Shoot them down! Avoid hand-to-hand combat whenever you can. They were born with those blades in their fists, and you were not. Your armor is better designed for battle than theirs. Use it. Take no prisoners, and accept no surrenders. They have killed Bahadurans, so they must all die. Kill them!"

The battlemaster's voice came over his helmet receiver: "The shelling has stopped, Subadar. I am opening the gate."

Hulagu unclipped a stubby beam rifle from the side of the podium, and both podium and platform sank to floor level. He climbed the ramp as the men surged behind him, voicing a variety of battle chants. The gate slid smoothly upward and Hulagu was out as soon as it was high enough to duck through. The BT contingent was close on his heels as he crossed the shell-pocked courtyard. Smoke rose from the ruins of the shield building, and there was smoking litter everywhere. They were two-thirds of the way to the perimeter wall when the shelling resumed.

Explosions bloomed among the running men, dropping them like tenpins. The BT's, in front, took the fewest casualties. Most of them made it into the safety of the perimeter wall. Hulagu looked back at the ground he had just crossed, now dotted with dead and wounded men.

"They're getting clever, Subadar," said Shevket. The man was gripping a heavy-duty beam rifle, and beneath his mustache he still wore his maddening grin. "Drew us into the open and let us have it. Those were primitive fragmentation bombs, though. Our armor stops all shrapnel. Concussion and blows have knocked those men down. Most will live."

"Meanwhile," Hulagu pointed out, "they're out of the fight."

"Yes," Shevket said, nodding. "Now we get to find out if we're as good as we keep saying we are." Once again the shelling stopped. "Here they come."

The first of the Chamukans were already at the wall before the last echoes of the shelling had stopped. They had risked being hit by their own shrapnel to get close to the wall while the Bahadurans kept their heads down. The double wall formed a raised trench with firing loops and there was no overhead cover. Fifty meters to either side of Hulagu, hulking redoubts squatted impotently, their heavy weapons silent until power could be restored to them.

Hulagu began firing through his loop in short, economical bursts, dropping natives as he tracked from left to right, then back again. Stone fused and spattered near his face as shots from beam rifles found his loop. He winced slightly as tiny drops of molten rock got through the breath opening of his helmet and stung his face. These savages might be good with their blades, he thought, but they couldn't shoot like his BT's. All along the wall, his BT's and auxiliaries were dropping them as calmly as men at target practice. Here and there, a guerrilla broke through and scrambled over the wall, growling and laying about with his blade, only to be cut down by gunfire almost instantly.

A loud hum and crackle announced that the redoubts were functional again. Broad beams lashed into the attackers, vaporizing men and churning rock to lava. The beams were invisible, but colored light was added to them to make them visible to observers. A backlash of heat tightened the exposed skin of Hulagu's face.

"Good work, Battlemaster. They fall back quickly now." He stood and fired into the retreating backs. Now that the redoubts were functional, few would escape.

Shevket came over to him, checking a power pack at his belt. "Why did they do it?" the Turk asked. "They have lost most of their force, and they've hurt us very little. We can't have more than a hundred casualties, and they've lost thousands."

"We haven't heard from the other bases yet," Hulagu

pointed out. "They might have been hurt worse. And perhaps these expected a greater advantage from their big missile weapon. No matter. They have lost, and they have only begun to suffer. Soon they'll have reason to envy their dead."

Shevket nodded silently. "We'll make them suffer, all right. But these people just don't seem to learn."

# Five

HAAKON DODGED A BUG. ON A CONSCIOUS LEVEL, HE knew the thing wasn't after him, probably wasn't even aware of him. It was just human nature to dodge something big and many-legged and buzzing loudly. "What kind of bug was that?" he asked in annoyance.

"That was a darter," Sarai explained. "Flanking its snout are two long tubes from which it can blow tiny darts for several meters. Poisonous, of course."

"I knew it," Jemal groused. "If I just lived long enough, I'd find a planet where the bugs carry guns." The stood beside their beasts beneath a dense canopy of trees while the monks erected a shelter of bamboo and some kind of hide that was nearly transparent. "Is that real bamboo?" Jemal asked.

"Just about the only Old Earth plant that's tough enough to withstand conditions on this planet without major genetic modification." Her eyes kept a wary lookout for flying dangers. Dusk was falling fast. The turkles were to be loosed for the night. According to Soun, they would wander back by dawn.

"What about food plants?" Soong asked.

"Most are grown under shelters," Sarai said. "Especially delicate ones like rice. A few food-bearing trees have been adapted to conditions here. Very little of the native life is edible. Geneticists developed armored pigs, sheep, and cattle. Poultry are raised under shelter as well."

"Armored pigs," Haakon mused. "The mind boggles."

"Stranger things have been done to adapt to this world. Still, it's a good world. It tests people. The worst it has to offer is sudden, violent death. That's to be found elsewhere, too. Slow and unpleasant ways to die don't abound here as they do on other worlds. Grass Cutter nurtures rigidly moral societies, even though they are a bit contentious."

"I'll admit it has its points," Haakon acknowledged. "Still, I like to relax occasionally. That doesn't seem possible here."

She smiled thinly. "Here we practice meditation instead. With proper training, it's possible to go into a deep meditative trance without relaxing your vigilance."

"I'll stick with extended binges in low dives," Haakon said.

The monks finished their building project. It was a low, domed structure perhaps seven meters in diameter.

The only entrance was a triangular flap with some kind of mechanical closure. Inside, there was barely enough room for the travelers and their gear. Light came through the walls freely, and they could just make out the shapes of the trees outside.

"Cozy, isn't it?" Jemal remarked.

"Beats sleeping outdoors," Haakon said. "At least this way you stand a chance of waking up."

"You need not concern yourself with standing guard," Soun told them. "We shall take night watch in shifts."

Haakon didn't like the sound of that. "Are the bugs that dangerous?"

"We believe in staying alert," Soun said.

"I'm sleeping next to the entrance," Numa rumbled. "I don't want to be slowed down if I should decide to leave in a hurry."

"Probably the best idea in any case," Jemal commented. "The ventilation's better there."

The monks rigged an awning before the entrance and kindled a fire to boil rice and vegetables and heat water for tea. The spacers had brought their own self-heating field rations. They had also brought a few bottles of the local beer. After the monks had eaten, they sat cross-legged in a straight line before Soun, eyes closed and chanting softly. Sarai sat a little apart from them, her own eyes closed, engaged in some form of meditation that did not require chants.

Haakon half whispered to Soong, "Learn anything from the abbot?"

"Fascinating details of their religious practice, but he

clammed up tight when I brought up the subject of the rival monasteries and sects."

"So these people take their religion seriously," Jemal said, shrugging. "Lots of people do. What does that tell us?"

"I think there is more to it than that," Soong insisted. "I've encountered religious strife in many places. Adherents of one sect are never loath to denounce the others at great length. They are seldom silent about their rivalry. I think we are seeing the true workings of Chamukan politics here."

"You think the monasteries control things here?" Haakon asked.

"I think each of them would like to," Soong explained. "From what little I have been able to gather, these monasteries are immense landholding establishments, and I believe they also practice the growing of the catalytic crystals."

"I thought this Emperor was the big boss here," Numa said.

"From what I know of Japanese history," Soong said, "the old Emperors seldom had real power. They were ceremonial leaders, more like high priests than earthly rulers. Often they lived in virtual poverty, their time taken up by endless rituals. Many groups contended for real power: warlords, feudal chiefs, Buddhist monasteries, the occasional conniving adventurer. Often they fought over physical possession of the Emperor. The group that had the Emperor under its 'protection' would claim to be the legitimate government."

"And this Great Boddhisatva Temple we're going to is the one that owns and operates His Majesty right now," Haakon said. "We could be walking into an extremely volatile situation."

"It goes without saying," Soong confirmed. "I think we may also assume that the other parties do not know about the plot to smuggle the imperial regalia off world and bring back the heir apparent."

"What about the massive diversion the monk and the woman spoke of?" Numa asked. "Surely the single monastery can't field as many warriors as they said."

"An alliance of several local forces could do it," Soong said. "Despite the deadlines of this place, it is densely populated, and every adult male fancies himself a great fighter."

Conversation and chanting ceased as they heard a humming in the distance. It was the distinctive sound of an atmosphere transport.

"BT's?" inquired Haakon of no one in particular.

"Bahadurans, at any rate," Sarai said. "Just keep still. The tree canopy shields us from observation."

"They aren't heading this way," Haakon said. "They're a good two kilometers to our southeast and headed due west." There, that'll teach the little twit.

"Show-off," Jemal muttered.

Much to Haakon's surprise, the night passed uneventfully, their sleep disturbed only by the deafening thunder of hailstones pounding on their tent at irregular intervals. The trees gave them protection from observation, but the frondlike branches did not even slow down the hailstones. The monks, who would jerk to immediate action at the breaking of a twig, did not alter the rhythm of their snoring during the hailstorms.

True to promise, the turkles wandered back at first light, and the bleary-eyed spacers climbed aboard. Outdoor living was anathema to any spacer, and the conditions of a planet like Chamuka made it that much worse. Haakon was hardened by his years in the pits, but *Eurynome* had spoiled him. He thought he caught a glint of satisfaction in Sarai's eye as he slumped disconsolately into his seat. Sadistic bitch, he thought.

The day was a repeat of the first, with Sarai and Soun keeping up a running commentary on the many dangers they were passing through. There was an innocent-looking rock that opened up jagged-toothed jaws to snap at them. Sarai explained that it was some sort of camouflaged reptile.

"We never kill them," she explained, "because they eat the acid spitters, which are far more dangerous. The pseudorocks will eat you if you get close enough. Be careful to prod stones with a stick before sitting on them."

"Is there anything here that isn't deadly?" Haakon asked.

"This is trifling," Soun said over his shoulder. "Wait until you see the flamethrowing viper or the giant gulper."

The point was not lost upon them: They had no chance in this deadly landscape without their guides. Haakon presumed that to be the reason for this bone-chilling commentary. As tour guides, these people made him long for the pleasures of deep space.

It was early evening when they arrived within sight of the Great Boddhisatva Temple. It was a rambling pile of interconnected structures cloaking most of the crest of a high hill. A swift-flowing river wound around the base of the hill and the last rays of the sun glanced from the slanting, ceramic roofs of red and gold. The beauty of the scene affected even the tired and disgruntled spacers.

"An exquisite scene," Soong said appreciatively.

"I wouldn't've traveled this far just to see it," Jemal said.

"That is because you lack the aesthetic temperament," Soong told him.

Soun raised himself in his saddle and blew into the top of a spiky, coiled shell. What emerged from its flared opening was a pure, low-pitched note of no great volume.

"Can that sound carry all the way up the hill?" Haakon asked doubtfully.

"Much farther," Sarai said. As if to confirm this, an identical note came from the temple, nearly as loud as Soun's had been. "The shell belongs to a sort of tree snail indigenous to this continent. Its internal chambering is quite unique. Under the right conditions, the sound can be heard for more than three kilometers."

"How does the snail kill you?" Jemal asked.

"It is quite harmless," she assured him.

"You can't mean it!"

They crossed the little river on a high-arched bridge made of an extremely hard wood that was pegged and keyed into place in an amazingly intricate fashion. "Why is it built this way?" Haakon asked.

"This is a 'haystack in the typhoon' bridge. When a single pin is driven out on the temple side, the whole bridge comes apart and falls into the river. A security precaution."

"Why don't they—" Haakon ducked as a buzz-saw-nosed bug screeched over him. A faint click announced its demise on the blade of a monk. "Why don't they just use explosives?"

"You, too," she said, "lack aesthetic appreciation."

"Gods!" Haakon said. "Your Prince Tametomo must feel right at home in the Cingulum. They're all crazy as loons there, too."

From the temple side of the bridge, a narrow track wound up the slope to a main entrance gate, which was flanked by two demonic figures carved in stone. These Soun identified as guardian deities, the wind god and the thunder god, traditional protectors of gateways.

"How many little gods is a monotheistic religion allowed to have?" Haakon asked.

"Your theology is primitive," Soun grunted. The man seemed to grunt everything he said.

The temple complex was large but not terribly impressive. Its few decorative elements were of necessity sublimated to the demands of local architecture—either to withstand the shocks of earthquakes or fall neatly apart with minimal risk to life and limb. Most buildings were of the latter type, but the central structure was a towering pile of cyclopean blocks that looked strong enough to survive collision with a small asteroid.

Heavily armed monks were everywhere. Prayer beads

rattled against ceramic armor and men sitting on the ground chanting were outnumbered by those practicing with sword and bow. "They look tough enough," Haakon said, "but bows are poor weapons when the enemy has beamers."

"We don't keep all our weapons up here where the Bahadurans can see them," Soun said. A young monk ran up to the abbot and reported something in a swift chatter that sounded unlike the ordinary, conversational speech rhythm of the natives. Soun turned to Sarai. "Mount Nara Temple has been destroyed. The monks who survived have gone to join the guerrillas."

She looked down for a few seconds before she spoke. "It was expected. They knew it would happen when they volunteered to take part in the attack."

"They have been our enemies for centuries," Soun said, "but we shall avenge them as if they were our brothers. Villages are being destroyed as well. They spare no one."

"Is this the diversion you spoke of?" Haakon asked.

"It is. Before this is over, it could cost us a million dead."

"You knew that going in," Haakon told him. "By now you know how Bahadurans behave. I've known them to sterilize entire planets. It better be worth it to you."

"It is," Soun insisted. "Suffering is nothing new to us. And we are well-versed in how to take vengeance properly."

They climbed a gradual slope, heading toward the

giant stone temple. "Damn!" Jemal said to Haakon. "If this is what the Buddhist monks are like, I hope we don't run into any really bloody minded warmongers."

They dismounted at a small gate in a stone wall surrounding the great temple. The turkles walked off unescorted, apparently knowing where they were expected to go. Inside the temple, it was all thick-walled dimness, more like a fortress than a place of worship. They traversed a maze of passageways and from time to time one or more of Soun's escort of monks would peel away. They ascended the building until they came to a broad terrace that was open to the sky. By now only the *Eurynome* crew, Soun, and Sarai remained.

"You will meet with His Majesty this evening," Soun announced, "after the sundown bell is rung." He pointed to a long, almost tubular bell which hung from a giant frame upon a battlement at the edge of the terrace. Its external clapper was a log slung horizontally beside it. "Until then, rest in the quarters you have been assigned. Sarai will show you where. Now I must report to His Majesty." He bowed perfunctorily and strode off in a bandy-legged gait.

"Come with me," Sarai said. They followed her along the terrace until they came to a low structure of lightweight materials built out from the main stone tower. It was roofed with ceramic, and Sarai slid a panel aside to show them in. "You'll be happy to know that the insects never ascend this high, and the temple is secure against all other hostile life forms."

"Wonderful. Now all we have to worry about is the

trip back, with BT's crawling all over the landscape."
Haakon looked at Sarai pointedly. "I'm still trying to
figure out your stake in all this."

"If we all knew everything we wanted to," she said,
"life would have fewer mysteries and be infinitely more
dangerous."

"We could live with the danger," Jemal said.

Numa pulled his helmet off and the golden mane
spread over his shoulders. "I'm getting out of this crab
suit. And I'm not nearly as curious as I am hungry. When
do we eat?"

"Our friend has the true Felid's sense of priorities,"
Soong said.

"I'll have food sent up," Sarai promised.

"No rice and seaweed," Numa warned. "I'm a
carnivore, and I've been living on travel rations too
long."

"I'm sure the kitchen staff can come up with something agreeable. Now, if you'll all excuse me, I'll leave
you for a while."

When she had slid the partition shut, they unrolled
their sleeping-bag mattresses, which hissed as they
inflated. Bedding had already been provided; thin pallets
with wooden headrests, but none of them shared the
Chamukan taste for hard living. A monk appeared and
led them to a bath house where they soaked away the
soreness of the long journey.

"I suppose the turkles are better than walking," Jemal
said as he slid deeper into the steaming water, "but not
by much."

"It's hard to believe that such beasts really evolved," Haakon said. "But then, that goes for most of the animal life in this place. It's almost like it was designed to be hostile."

"We have encountered such worlds before," Soong pointed out.

"Right," Haakon said. "In the Cingulum. This is different."

"Our galaxy bears a near infinity of worlds," Soong said. "One such as this could exist purely as a matter of chance."

"Somehow," Jemal added gloomily, "the laws of chance get suspended when we're around."

"I wish you people would stop talking like that," Numa rumbled. "You're spoiling my bath. This isn't such a bad place if you're fast and mean like me."

"It's not just the hostility of the place," Jemal protested. "There are thousands of planets worse than this. Any place with a poisonous atmosphere and pervasive volcanic activity and a surface temperature of six hundred Celsius and ten times Earth gravity is plenty bad. What's odd is that this place is as beautiful as Earth must've been before men evolved and it has a tolerable climate and soil that's suitable for Earth flora. It's almost like a garden world."

"Except that nearly all the native animal and plant life seems to exist for the purpose of killing people," Haakon said, "and the sky drops unbelievable hailstorms and the ground shakes with some regularity."

"So what?" Numa said. "We'll be gone from here soon. What I want to know is what happened to dinner."

When, reluctantly, they hauled themselves from the bath and made their way back to their quarters, they found their meal laid out for them. As usual with the local fare, they found it depressingly bland, except for the raw, bloody hunks of meat that had been provided for Numa.

Numa finished and belched mightily. "First square meal I've had since we landed here. I wonder what it was."

"Turkle steak, maybe," Jemal hazarded.

Haakon ventured no opinion, but visions of armored pigs danced in his head. He was more preoccupied with the prospect of meeting the Emperor that evening. He'd occasionally dealt with sovereigns before, but never with a bona fide Emperor. But then, this Emperor would have to be a pretty minor sort of autocrat. In any case, he wasn't here to deal with the man; the deal had been made. They were here to pick up the goods. Still, it made him uneasy.

The gong sounded shortly after they had finished their meal.

"It occurs to me," Soong said, "that none of us is dressed for a royal audience."

"That's tough," Jemal said succinctly. "If this were a diplomatic function, I'd worry about it. As it is, they'll just have to put up with us the way we are. We're not here to win friends anyway."

Sarai appeared at their doorway. "His Majesty will see you now."

They followed her out onto the terrace, then up several

flights of external stairs, gradually ascending to the tapering peak of the tower. On the topmost level, they found a small, pagoda-roofed building surrounded by an open balcony. On the balcony sat at least one hundred monks, their swords unsheathed across their knees. At the parapets stood sentries with modern beam rifles. The abbot, Soun, stood by the doorway to the small building.

They went inside. The interior was cool and il-luminated by a large number of candles. At the far end of the single room was a long screen decorated with an elaborate battle scene. There was no other interior decoration. Seated before the screen was an elderly man in a plain black robe. In his hands he held a long string of prayer beads over which he muttered. Soun and Sarai walked quietly to the old man and stopped a few paces before him. They knelt, placed their palms against the polished wood floor, and bowed until their foreheads just touched the wood.

The *Eurynome* crew followed. "All right," Haakon muttered, "we've done this before. On your faces." Numa rumbled discontentedly.

The old man's eyes flickered open and focused sharply upon them. "Not necessary. I am not your sovereign. Please be seated, gentlemen. We have affairs to discuss, and very little time for the formalities, I fear."

The four sat cross-legged, flanked by the woman and the abbot. A monk came in with a tray of fragrant tea, then withdrew silently. Haakon studied the Emperor. The face was drawn and lined, the skin paper-thin over prominent bones. His close-cropped hair was white. His hands did not tremble as they raised the teacup, and his eyes were clear. He looked old, but he did not appear to be dying. That meant little in itself. Good medical attention could maintain an appearance of health almost to the moment of death.

Go-Hosokawa III set his cup carefully upon the tray. "So you are the people who are to seek out my son Tametomo."

"We'll give it our best try, Your Majesty," Haakon said, "but what we have to go on is very little. The evidence that your son is still alive is very slim. On top of that, the Cingulum is a haven for refugees. You don't just go in there and ask for someone by name. We can probably locate him in time, *if* he's still alive and in the Cingulum. We can promise no more than that."

"If you had promised more than that," the Emperor said, "I would have been highly suspicious. I like the look of you, and I like the way you speak. I think we have chosen the right people."

Jemal cleared his throat discreetly. "There is the matter of payment, Your Majesty. The risks we run will be considerable, quite aside from smuggling your contraband offworld."

Go-Hosokawa reached inside his sash and withdrew a small gem, dangling on a short chain. He handed it to Haakon, who studied it closely. It looked rather like a diamond, faceted in an archaic pattern. The candlelight shattered from the facets brilliantly. Diamonds were fairly common and not among the more precious gems during the last few centuries, although still much favored for personal jewelry. "A diamond?" Haakon said. "Very pretty, but I don't—"

"Not a diamond," the Emperor corrected, "a catalytic crystal. Such stones are our poor world's only reason for existence. It took a master jeweler two years of terribly dangerous labor to cut a crystal into such an unnatural shape. To make the subterfuge more believable, we chose one of the very rare colorless crystals. I think you will find this ample compensation. In a place like the Cingulum, cut off from most sources of supply, even a small crystal such as this should fetch an adequate price."

"Most adequate," Haakon said. "It will ensure our welcome there, at any rate." He handed the gem to Jemal, who took the chain by its wire catch and hooked it into his earlobe. It dangled there, an adornment no port officer would glance at twice.

"Now," the Emperor said, "the treasures you must deliver to my son." Beside him were three veils. He lifted one and picked up the object it had covered. "The Mirror. I wish I could tell you of the web of myth and legend surrounding these objects, but we lack the time. Rest assured that they are the most precious relics of our culture, dating to the time of the gods." He handed the thing to Haakon, and as the Mirror was passed across, Soun bowed deeply to it. Haakon turned it over in his hands and found it to be merely a disk of bronze, polished on one side and decorated on the other with raised carvings in an abstract design.

The Emperor took another. "The Jewel."

This Haakon also examined. It was a smooth, semi-precious stone of indeterminate color, smaller than the palm of his hand. Its shape was that of a curved teardrop, and it reminded him of something, but he couldn't quite remember what it might be.

"The Sword, which once resided in the tail of a dragon."

This time, the Emperor's hands trembled slightly as the treasure was handed across. Soun's forehead struck the floor with an audible thunk, and he sucked in his breath with a sharp hiss.

Haakon had been expecting a heroic weapon of formidable proportions, bizarre design, and jeweled decoration. Instead, he held an unimpressive little weapon with a blade no more than forty centimeters long, with designs crudely carved on the flat sides. The grip was of bronze worked into some stylized form that he could not recognize. For all the reverence they were being shown, these three objects had to form the dingiest, shabbiest collection of treasure he had ever run across.

"You were right," Haakon admitted. "We should have no trouble at all getting these through customs."

"Although it pains us," Go-Hosokawa said, "you must not treat the treasures with reverence. It would only rouse suspicion. Behave as if they were trifles you picked up here as keepsakes."

Haakon stuck the Jewel into a vest pocket and handed the Mirror to Soong, who thrust it inside his shirt. Jemal wrapped the Sword in a veil and stuck it through his belt. Soun averted his eyes while this was being done.

"Is there anything else we should know?" Haakon asked.

"Yes," the Emperor said. "There has been a change of circumstances here. We must ask you to take Lady Sarai with you to the Cingulum."

"Out of the question!" Haakon barked. "The treasures we can get offworld without suspicion because they're so innocuous. She's contraband of no uncertain nature."

"You need not worry about getting her offworld," Soun assured them. "We have a smuggler ship for that. You can rendezvous within the system before making your jump."

"If you have such a ship," Jemal demanded, "why do you need us to smuggle your treasures offworld? Why can't she just bring them to us?"

"It's the safest way," Soun said. "Chances are too high that her ship will be shot down before escaping. The safety of our Three Treasures comes before all else."

"We still can't take her to the Cingulum," Haakon protested. "Look at her! Anybody with half a brain and one working eye can see she's a highborn Bahaduran! They'd shoot her on sight in the Cingulum just before they shot us for trying to bring her in."

"How do you know there aren't already Bahadurans in the Cingulum?" Sarai demanded.

"What?" Haakon asked brightly.

"You heard me. By your own admission, you are not high in the councils of the Cingulum. You perform occasional errands for them, but you are barely tolerated and are always under suspicion. How can you be sure that there are not numerous Bahadurans within the Cingulum?"

"Logic says no," Haakon insisted.

"History says yes," she countered.

"She is quite right," Soong commented. "Politically influential refugees from an enemy state can usually find a welcome. A cadre of Bahadurans on the Cingulam side would prove most useful if the Cingulum hopes ever to defeat the Powers. They would provide a corps of potential territorial governors after the Bahadurans have been subdued on their own worlds. Pretenders to the throne are even more desirable."

"Right," Jemal concurred. "There was a Spartan king in exile who lived for years at the Persian court. There were the Stuart pretenders at the French court, and Lenin in Germany."

"Never heard of them," Haakon said. Why did Jemal always trot out his historical trivia at moments like this? "All right, I'll take her, out of the goodness of my heart. I'll give you transfer coordinates and a timetable, and if you're ten minutes late for rendezvous, we'll be gone, even if we've picked you up on our screens. That's because I'm going to schedule the rendezvous as close as possible to an exit window and there'll be no time to spare. If you're late, I'll assume there's been trouble, and you have BT's aboard. That kind of problem I don't need."

"I understand, Captain," she said with maddening equanimity. "You needn't impress me with how ruthless you are. I agree to your terms."

"Just so we understand each other," Haakon said. He knew he had just been outmaneuvered, but he wasn't sure just how. Somehow, control of this situation had slipped away from him.

"I would not seem inhospitable," the Emperor said, "but the time has come to hurry. I had intended to offer you temple accommodations for the night, but that will not be possible. You must set out at once." He looked at them with a mixture of confidence and fear. "Go with my blessing. You hold the future of my line and this world."

# **Six**

THEY FOUND THEIR MOUNTS ALREADY SADDLED AND packed in the courtyard. There was a good deal of activity going on all over the temple complex, considering the lateness of the hour. The bustle didn't seem primarily defensive, but Haakon knew the air of a place about to be attacked when he saw it.

Soun came striding up, now rearmored like the rest of them. "We must be away quickly!" he shouted.

"You're expecting an attack?" Haakon asked as he ascended to his saddle.

"Yes. The Black Tumans will be here before first light. We received word only an hour ago. Great Boddhisatva Temple had no men in the attack on the Bahadurans, but it is within the radius of reprisal decreed. I am told that the commander of the BT's extended the death radius beyond the customary limit

103

just to include a few of the more prominent monasteries."

"What will you do?" Haakon asked as they headed out the gate.

"This ancient temple will be destroyed," the abbot said. "We shall rebuild it in time. We removed its treasures long ago. The monks shall take to the mountains and join the guerrillas. His Majesty will be taken to a safe place of refuge."

"You know," Haakon said reluctantly, "maybe you should put the Emperor on that smuggler ship. He'd be welcome in the Cingulum. And he'd be safe."

"Never!" the abbot said vehemently. "Without His Majesty, our link with the gods and the ancestors would be broken. Grass Cutter would wither and its people die. He will be safe here. Every living man and woman on this planet will die in his defense."

"Have it your way," Haakon said, unwilling to argue with someone for whom war, politics, and religion were one and the same.

The little caravan wound through the forests in near silence through the night. Once, near dawn, they felt a faint shaking in the ground, followed moments later by a sound like distant thunder.

"Great Boddhisatva Temple is no more," Soun said gloomily. "We shall build another to the glory of Lord Buddha." The monks began one of their lengthy chants.

Sarai rode in the lead. The dawn was just breaking when she signaled for a rest. They were in a bight of a stream and the beasts lined up at the water to drink. The riders climbed from their saddles, stretching stiff muscles as they walked about the glade.

"Keep close," Sarai warned them. "There are more dangers here than you can imagine."

"Are you referring to the charming flora and fauna hereabout?" Jemal asked.

"Yes," she said, puzzled. "What else?"

"Oh, I just thought you might mean the men surrounding us." His powerblade was in his hand and he thumbed its switch.

"Men?" Her jaw dropped and her eyes widened, but she recovered almost instantly. "Soun!" she shouted, but the attack was already underway.

Even with the element of surprise, the monks were so swift that all had weapons out and in motion before the first of the attackers reached them. Two monks of the escort collapsed with arrows through their faces, but the rest charged to close quarters. The attackers wore black clothing and armor and some wielded curved blades on short poles. They seemed to outnumber the defenders about two to one.

"This looks bad," Jemal said. A black-clad man attacked him with a pole arm, slashing at his legs. Jemal jumped over the weapon and swept his powerblade across the attacker's abdomen. The blade cut an effortless, smoking path across the armor and the man collapsed silently.

There was some shouting and pointing among the attackers, then about half of them converged on the offworlders, who stood with their backs to the turkles.

The beasts were still placidly sucking up water, without a care in the world.

"Looks like they're after us" Haakon said. "Numa, show 'em your stuff."

The Felid hit the pack of advancing attackers with the force of a minor nuke. His paws flashed out too fast to see and two breastplates went flying. Before the entrails of the first two hit the ground, Numa was on two more. The Chamukans, through genetics and long training, were as fast as humans could be. But Felids were faster and stronger than ordinary humans by an order of magnitude. While Numa raised havoc in the midst of the attackers, Haakon and Jemal worked the outskirts, using their powerblades on men distracted by the outrageous Felid.

Soong saw a pair of their assailants driving Sarai back into the woods, the woman hard-pressed to defend herself against their attacks. The Han ran lightly, his hands empty as he caught up with one. His hand moved almost lazily as it stroked the neck beneath the helmet rim and the man fell dead without a sound.

The second man had Sarai down on the ground. She was frantically parrying his sword with her own blade and with her arm plates, but she was clearly at the end of her strength.

"Excuse me," Soong said politely.

The swordsman whirled, then saw only an unarmed man before him and chuckled. The sword made a glittering blur as he sent it into a decapitating slash. Soong stepped within the arc and pushed lightly on the man's trailing shoulder. They spun together in a strange parody of a dance, as if they had rehearsed this move many times before. In the midst of the turn, Soong's hand flashed toward the man's face and the black-clad attacker fell away, quite dead.

Soong took out a tissue and wiped blood and other fluids from his right forefinger. He had thrust the finger through the man's eye and into his brain, breaking through the thin shell of bone behind the eyeball. "That was distasteful," he said, "but he was too expert to waste time with. Are you all right, my lady?"

Sarai was on all fours beside the stream, splashing water on her face with a cupped hand. A cut across her brow was bleeding profusely. "It's superficial," she said shakily. "But the blood keeps blinding me."

Soong knelt beside her. "Let me help." He saw something glittering in the stream bed beneath her and he picked it up. It was a round, cupped piece of soft plastic. Most strange. "Here, sit up for a moment."

He took a spray-tube from his first-aid kit and sprayed the cut. The bleeding stopped within seconds. Soong wiped the excess blood away and pinched the edges of the wound together. He sprayed from another tube and the protective coating hardened, forming a bandage.

"Thank you," she said, her daze dissipating. "What's happening up there?"

"All is quiet now. I believe all is well. I also believe this belongs to you." He held out the brown contact lens.

Her eyes widened when she realized what it was. One of her eyes was still its customary brown, the other bright silver. Her hand crept toward the dagger in her belt.

"Please don't try it, my lady, or should I say

Highness? You may have been taught by experts, but I was for years an assassin of Han, and you could not hope to prevail. Here, resume your disguise. Have no fear, we've agreed to take you to the Cingulum, and we honor our commitments. I wish, though, that you had been more candid with us."

"I had my reasons," she said. She placed the brown lens back over her silver iris. "You'll inform your captain of this, I presume?"

"Of course. As I have said, it has no bearing upon our agreement. It does alter, or should I say clarify, our previous assumptions."

They returned to a scene of utter carnage. Three of the monk escorts were down, presumably dead. All of the attackers appeared to be dead as well, many of them in pieces. Soong rejoined his shipmates, who appeared none the worse for the experience.

"I guess I'd better go wash up," Numa said, looking at his hands. They were bloodied to the elbows. He was liberally bespattered all over.

As Numa wandered off toward the stream, Soun came to them. He bowed stiffly to Sarai. "You were wounded, my lady?"

"Slightly. Mr. Soong rendered me aid. Did you kill all of them?"

"All are dead, but that was largely due to the cat-person. I have seen nothing like it. The rest of you did well, too."

"Always glad to be of help," Haakon said. "Who were they and what was this all about?"

108

Soun spat. "Outlaw monks of the Pure Land sect, enemies of all mankind."

"They were coming for us," Jemal said. "They knew we were carrying your treasures."

"That is not possible!" Soun said. "They hate all foreigners. They are too weak to take on heavily armed Bahaduran convoys. Perhaps four outlanders with but a small escort was too tempting to resist."

"Maybe," Haakon said.

"We must finish caring for our wounded and be on our way," Soun said. "My lady, will you help us with the doctoring?"

Sarai went with him. Many of the monks were wounded, but they made no complaint.

"Captain, we misread Lady Sarai. She is not of the Bahaduran nobility."

Haakon looked at Soong disbelievingly. "She's not Bahaduran? Surgical disguise? Is she some kind of spook?"

"I did not say that. Her only disguise is a pair of colored lenses. Lady Sarai has silver eyes."

"What the hell does that mean?" Jemal demanded.

"She is Bahaduran, but not nobility. She is royalty. It is a rare genetic trait that appears with some frequency in the royal house. There have been several in recent generations, all women. I would hazard that Sarai is a sister or daughter of the Khakhan himself."

Haakon snorted disgustedly. "Why is it always like this? Why do the women in my life always turn out to be so difficult? Rama, Mirabelle, Maya, all the others. Now

109

this one. Why don't I ever encounter the nice, stable ones with nothing to hide?"

"Perhaps," Soong said, "Abbot Soun could provide you with spiritual solace. You seem to have a considerble karmic burden to work off."

Jemal nodded. "Maybe the monk's life would agree with you. No women to complicate your life, plenty of meditation spiced with occasional violence could be just what you need."

"See if I ever look to you two for sympathy again. Let's mount up. Things could start getting serious now. We've got a report to turn in to Timur Khan, you know. What happens if we tell him that a princess of royal blood is behind the problems on Chamuka? We could catch it from both sides."

"But we don't know that," Soong said. "Only that she is here, which proves nothing."

"Another point to consider," Jemal said. "Timur Khan may already know she's here."

"She may even be working in league with him," Soong pointed out.

"The monk's life looks better all the time," Haakon said, settling back into his saddle. "I should have taken it up long ago."

Hulagu spotted the spacers as soon as he entered the port customs office. There was a Felid with them now, not the one that had assisted at his humiliation, but the same breed. They seemed to be in the final stage of customs check before embarkation.

"Just a moment." Hulagu pulled off his helmet as he

walked up to the customs desk. He dropped the helmet on the desk and pointed at the plastic crate at their feet. "What is that?"

"Just used ship parts, Subadar," the official said.

"So your scavenger hunting was successful?" he asked Haakon.

"Reasonably. The man at the junkyard was having a hell of a time reaching those Tesla nodes, so we passed them up. The local fireworks got too rich for us."

"Besides," Jemal added, "the earthquake last night dropped the inn around our heads. Time to get out while we're still alive."

"Are you leaving with anything else you didn't come here with?"

"Just a few souvenirs," Haakon said. He waved a hand at the three objects on the table.

Hulagu picked up the little sword. "What is this? It doesn't look like local manufacture."

"I picked it up for my collection," Jemal said. "I like archaic edged weapons. As you'll recall, I'm pretty good with them."

Hulagu's ears reddened. "I remember."

"Our shuttle awaits, Subadar," Soong said in his most noncommittal voice. "We must check in with our superior."

Hulagu could have killed them all in sheer frustration, but the thought of who that superior was made him swallow his bile. He tossed the sword back on the table. "Go, then. Doubtless we'll meet again." He whirled on his heel and stalked out of the building, jamming the helmet back onto his head.

"I'm sorry to say we probably will." Haakon was sweating with relief.

Reboarding his ship was like the first time he had walked out of prison. Haakon stripped off the armor and tossed it into corners of the airlock for the 'bots to pick up. He barked into a comm-plate: "Rand! Fire up the engines, we're getting out of here!" Where were his welcoming committee? He strode up to the main salon and found Mirabelle playing chess with Alexander. She glanced up at him with annoyance.

"What took you so long? We've been bored stiff."

"So what? We've been enduring earthquake and civil war while you lazed around up here, sopping up the refreshments and improving your game."

While she was distracted, Alexander tried surreptitiously to move a bishop with his tail. Without looking, she grabbed the tail and twisted it. "Did you find out what Timur Khan wanted?" She moved her queen. "Check."

"I'm not sure. We were ass deep in a war so complicated I never did figure who was fighting whom, but I got us a smuggling contract and a passenger."

"Where we going, and who's the passenger?" Alexander demanded. "I hope it's someplace fun and somebody interesting." Abruptly, he grabbed a knight and snapped it down between her queen and his king. "Hah! Bet you didn't see that!"

"Damn! Where'd that come from?" She was in trouble now.

"As to the passenger, she's a princess."

"A princess!" Alex's tail shot straight up. "I'm real

good with them royal and noble types, you know. Must have aristocrats in the ancestral woodpile somewheres. Is she pretty? What kind of princess, local?"

"Very pretty," Haakon said. "She's Bahaduran." Alex's tail drooped.

"That's a tasteless joke," Mirabelle said. She looked at him sharply. "You're not joking."

"Not for a second. And the destination is the Cingulum."

"What happened to you down there, Boss? They scramble your brains for you or something?" Alexander was looking more scared by the minute. "We were on a mission for Timur Khan himself. Now you pick up a Bahadur princess *and* head for the Cingulum? You know what they'll do when we show up, don't you? They'll cut off our—"

"This is the most harebrained—"

"Shut up, both of you." They shut up. Being captain was a pain, but sometimes it had its points. "The deal's been made and I have my reasons for doing it. How's Rama?"

"Unbearable," Mirabelle said. She returned her attention to extricating her queen.

"Alex, go check on her. See if she's too dangerous to approach and report back."

The monkey-boy scampered off and Haakon studied the board for a moment. "How can you play chess with a vacuum-head like him?"

"We're evenly matched. I have impeccable mathematical logic and he has insane intuition. Are we really

113

going to the Cingulum? And is she really a Bahaduran princess?"

"Right on both counts. At least, Soong swears she's of the royal house, and I trust his judgment."

She sipped from a balloon-shaped glass of rare wine. "We're going to need luck to survive this one."

"When have we ever lacked for luck?" he asked cheerfully. "Hell, if we'd depended on planning, good sense, and brain power, we'd've been killed years ago."

Alexander's voice came over the comm: "She's safe, Boss, sort of."

"I'd like to be there when you tell her what you've been up to," Mirabelle said.

"Come along. I could use moral support."

"I'll pass. When did I ever have morals anyway?"

Haakon checked his nose filters and entered Rama's chamber. She glared at him with a barely repressed snarl. "Where have you been?"

"Planetside, remember?"

"Oh, yes. Something about a mission, wasn't it?" Her hair was tumbled into a mass so tangled that the stripes were hard to discern just a few centimeters from her scalp. "Well, did you succeed? Are we safe for a while longer?"

"I'm not certain."

She snorted. "When are you ever certain? When do you ever accomplish something satisfactorily, you bald person? Well, you might as well tell me the worst. I can bear it." She glanced at him narrowly. "You might not survive it, though."

With an eye cocked to his escape route, Haakon told

her what had occurred on the planet. He wasn't sure why. After all, he was captain, not Rama. It was just safer to let her in on his decisions. Having delivered his report, he prepared to endure her tirade. As it turned out, she was uncharacteristically restrained.

"You've bungled it in typical fashion. Agreeing to go to the Cingulum, indeed! And this princess of Bahadur with the silver eyes, I suppose she is attractive?"

"Fairly. Nothing to compare to you, of course."

"I should think not. You've always let your thinking be clouded by your primitive, animal lusts. You have to start thinking beyond your testosterone, Haakon; it is unhealthful and could cause me to kill you. I suppose this princess-person will think that she deserves to be given my royal suite. She is wrong."

"She'll be given passenger accommodations," Haakon assured her.

Rama ran a hand through her tangled hair. "A princess! My hair is a mess and I've nothing to wear. Why didn't you give me more time?" Frantically, she began summoning her 'bots.

"Actually, she doesn't seem to be a princess in good standing. She probably won't stand on ceremony."

"What do you know about it? Get out of here while I make myself stunning." He got out, relieved that it had gone so easily. He decided to go up to the bridge and play captain for a while.

Jemal and Soong were already there. "No sign of pursuit or other second thoughts from the BT's," Soong reported.

"Good," Haakon said. His screens told him the

engines were ready for departure. He entered the coordinates for their rendezvous with Sarai and the ship began to leave orbit. He wouldn't be able to relax until they were well beyond pursuit range of the planet. "I don't know when I've been so glad to leave a planet." He ordered a drink from the nearest hovering 'bot.

"Since the last time we were on the run. A couple of months ago, I think it was." Jemal sipped at a glass tube of something. "How long till rendezvous?"

Haakon swept his fingers over a console plate and the numbers came floating up. "A little over six hours."

"I liked the old screens better," Jemal said. "Floating digits give me a headache after a while. Let's make the transfer quick. I want to be out of this system as soon as possible."

"I don't feel like hanging around myself," Haakon agreed.

"In the meantime," Soong interjected, "we had better be thinking very hard about what we are going to say when we reach the Cingulum. They almost opened fire on us last time."

"Are you two forgetting?" Haakon asked. "They want to see us, remember? What's-his-name back in Lower Baikal said so."

"Roche," Jemal reminded him. "A man I trust slightly more than Timur Khan."

"We seem to be in the unbreakable grip of karma," Soong said. "However reluctantly, every direction leads our steps toward the Cingulum."

* * *

*Eurynome* had all her armament trained on the smuggler ship as contact was made. The welcoming party at the airlock was heavily armed, and unseen weapons had been activated as well, in accordance with the ancient tradition that it was always best to err on the side of caution. The lock cycled open and a small, lonely figure emerged.

"Am I all that dangerous?" Sarai asked. She set a small space bag on the deck.

"You might have been," Haakon said. He held the beamer hanging by his side, but he did not put it away.

"Everything all right?" Haakon recognized the voice over the comm as that of LeMat, the bluebearded smuggler.

"Just fine," Haakon said. "Now beat it. We're taking a Tesla jump in five minutes and you don't want to be around when that happens."

"Breaking contact," LeMat said hastily. "Good luck, Sarai."

"Come with me," Haakon said. "We'll get you settled later. Right now you'd better get strapped in. The salon is as good a place as any."

She stayed studiously unimpressed as they walked from the lock to the salon, but they could see that it was hard work. "Nice ship," she said finally.

"Just think of it as home for a while, Highness," Jemal said. He holstered his beamer as they went into the salon. Sarai settled into a lounge, which shaped itself to her and began to hum soothingly. "My name is Sarai. Since I'm officially dead, my titles have been revoked. That reminds me." She lowered her head and pulled out the lenses. "I don't need these anymore. That's a relief." She gave them, for the first time, the full benefit of her silver-eyed gaze. It was disturbing.

"How close are you, or, rather, were you, to the throne?" Haakon asked bluntly.

"Don't you offer your passengers a drink?"

"What'll you have?" She jumped slightly as Alexander appeared at her elbow.

"Kumiss," she said.

He turned to the 'bot hovering next to him. "You heard her, cough it up, whatever it is." A glass appeared from the 'bot's innards and Alexander presented it to her grandly. "Here ya go. Never let it be said we don't treat our guests good."

"Ah, thank you." She took the glass, which held a pale, sparkling liquid. Kumiss had come a long way since it had been fermented milk of mares. This was more like champagne. A slight trembling went through the ship, causing her to spill a few drops. "What was that?"

"Tesla jump," Haakon said.

"So smooth. This is no ordinary free trader's ship."

"We steal only the best," Haakon assured her. "Now you were about to explain your connection to the Khakhan."

"Haakon, how could you have started this without me?" Mirabelle came in, dressed and groomed for high-fashion society. It was one of her favorite guises and she seldom got a chance to use it. Patiently, Haakon made introductions.

"Now you've met everybody except Rand and Rama.

118

You'll see Rand when you get curious about the engines, and you shouldn't meet Rama until you're really up to it. Now about your recent lineage—"

"I was Third Lady, after my sister Bourtai."

"Then you are the Khakhan's own daughter," Soong said. "I thought as much. It explains little, but I am always pleased to know my deductions justified."

"How did you come to be, ah, officially dead?" Haakon asked.

"You're aware of the fratricide rule? How the male who inherits the Khanate must have all his brothers killed?"

"I've heard of it," Haakon said. "If you don't mind my saying so, it couldn't happen to a nicer bunch of people."

"Well, it isn't required among the female side of the family, but it's extremely popular anyway. My sister Bourtai has been the best practitioner in this generation. She did away with me when I was only ten years old. She was fifteen then. I suppose she wanted to practice on an easy target before she went after my older sisters."

"It is always best," Soong agreed, "to begin with simple tasks before attempting the truly challenging."

"I fear I wasn't much of a challenge. She hired an old family retainer to kill me. He couldn't do it. It had not occurred to her that others were not as ruthless as she. He took me to Chamuka, the remotest part of the empire, and sent word that I was dead and disposed of."

"Didn't she get suspicious when he didn't come back?" Jemal asked.

119

"She had given him a slow-acting poison. He was dead within days of our arrival on Chamuka."

"Couldn't you have complained to Daddy?" Haakon asked.

"That my sister had tried to kill me and I had not killed her instead? He would have killed me himself."

"Nice family," Haakon said. "But, if you think they're bad, remind me to tell you about Timur Khan Bey sometime. So now we have you on Chamuka, ten years old and alone. What next?"

"The monks found me and took me to Amida Temple. I became a temple servant for a while, but the abbot had reported my case to the Emperor. Between them, they guided my training and education. I was trained in war, and administration, and diplomacy."

"So now they want you to establish links with the Cingulum?" Haakon asked.

"And to assist in the search for Prince Tametomo."

"Let us take care of that end of it," Haakon said. "It's what we've contracted to do. You'll have your hands full dealing with the Cingulans. That could be a one-way trip. Is this your first time offworld since you were dropped on Chamuka?"

"No, I've made smuggling runs with LeMat and others. They wanted me accustomed to space travel before I was sent on serious missions."

In a blast of flowery scent, Rama strode in. It was the first time she had been out of her suite in weeks. Her striped hair was immaculate and she wore a billowing, tentlike robe of scarlet silk that completely hid her gravid form. "You must be the princess-person I've been hearing so much about! Welcome to my ship, dear one. Has the bald one been annoying you with his impertinent questions?"

Mirabelle wrinkled her nose and turned away. She hated to be upstaged.

"You must be Rama," Sarai said. "I've met your, ah, husband? Mate?"

Rama looked puzzled. "Mate? Oh, you mean the other Felid, Numa, I think his name is. Something like that. No, he's just the father of my child, a mere matter of instinct and hormones. My, but aren't you beautiful!" She patted Sarai's cheek and Haakon noted, with approval, that Sarai didn't flinch at the half-extruded claws, which Rama had enameled gold. "Such exquisite silver eyes! Come, dear, let me show you to your quarters. The royal quarters would be yours, but I got there first." She glared down at Alexander. "You, monkey-person, take her luggage." She turned back to Sarai, lifted her from her lounge, and put an arm through hers. "Do you find yourself disliking our captain as much as I do? Surely you must. That gives us something in common." Her monologue continued as they exited the salon, with Alexander carrying the space bag behind them.

Mirabelle chuckled. "I'll bet her diplomatic training hasn't prepared her to cope with Rama. Do you think she's telling the truth?"

Haakon shrugged. "Damned if I know. We're just taking her on as a passenger, in any case. When we get to the Cingulum, Lopal Singh will have the truth out of her.

It could be true. The Bahaduran royal line is bizarre enough."

"On the other hand," Mirabelle said, "her little-girl-all-alone-in-a-hostile-universe story is so heartrending it just sounds suspicious as hell."

"Maybe," Haakon said. "Let Lopal Singh worry about it."

"I find myself wondering about our irreplaceable Three Treasures," Soong said.

"What about them?" Haakon asked.

"Japanese history is an obscure study, but I found some information in our banks. The Jewel, the Sword, and the Mirror are indeed the great Three Treasures of those islands. However, they were lost in a sea battle in the twelfth century. At least two of them were supposed to have been retrieved from the sea bottom, but one may be a reproduction dating from that time, and possibly all three. There may have been other replacements at other times in history. Japan had a very colorful past, involving much destruction."

"Irrelevant," Haakon said. "If the treasures are fake, that's between the Chamukans and their gods and ancestors. If we find Prince Tametomo, he'll recognize them as the ones that used to hang on his daddy's bedroom wall or wherever, and that's what counts.

"Now, in my authority as captain, I order you all to stop worrying. We have a lot of trouble behind us, and a lot more coming up all too soon, so let's relax." He turned to a 'bot. "Give me another drink."

# Seven

"WAKE UP, CAPTAIN DARLING!" CHANG FORCED HIS EYES open and saw through gummed-together eyelashes that it was O'Leary shaking his shoulder.

"What is it?" Chang forced out.

"There's a ship approaching, beloved," O'Leary said. "We all thought you should be first to greet them, you being our leader and all."

"Quite right, O'Leary," Chang said patiently. "By the way, don't you have a clean uniform?"

The big, ugly New Hibernian looked down at his stained coveralls. "Sure and I don't, darling man. 'Twas all I had when I left Coventry."

"Well, put it in the airlock and give it a few minutes of vacuum treatment. That should at least kill the micro-organisms."

"Be easy in your mind, your lordship. It shall be

done." O'Leary left and Chang got up and pulled on his uniform and plunged his face into a basin of cold water. Surely, in a reasonable universe, *nobody* really talked like that.

Scanlon looked up cheerily as Chang came onto the bridge. "Hey, Captain, guess who's here?" He gestured at the holographic image in the tank. Chang groaned when he saw what was floating there.

"Not them again! Why? Why do they always show up when I'm on duty? Why do they only arrive in *Sakura*'s picket sector?"

"Terrible sins you committed in a former life?" hazarded Leila, the shuttle pilot.

"Mondragon's Principle of Revised Synchronicity?" suggested Stransky. Stransky was a grad student at the University of the Cingulum, specializing in Enhanced Reality Post-Tesla Neometaphysics. He was, Chang reflected, turning into a real pain in the ass.

"Talk to me, *Eurynome*," Chang ordered.

Haakon's hairless countenance replaced the image of the ship. "That you, Chang? Hey, isn't it a coincidence how we always encounter *Sakura* every time we come to the Cingulum?"

"Tell me about it," Chang muttered. It could have been worse. It might have been the cat-woman.

Haakon turned to somebody out of image range. "Soong, what're the odds against us encountering the same picket ship every time?"

"I would have to know the Cingulum's entire security setup," said Soong's disembodied voice. "We could ask, but they probably wouldn't tell us."

"Have we all clowned enough?" Chang asked. "Why do I get the feeling that you're stalling, Haakon?"

"Stalling?" Haakon asked innocently. "Why should I do that? After all, I heard that the authorities here wanted to see us. We got a summons weeks ago in Lower Baikal."

"The question had occurred to me," Chang said. "What is it, Haakon? Are you carrying contraband again?"

"Something like that," Haakon admitted. "Actually, I have a passenger."

"You've had passengers before. You know the drill. What's so different about this one?" Chang was starting to have a very bad feeling about all this.

"Well, never quite like this one." He turned and beckoned to someone behind him. A woman came into image range and stooped to put her head on a level with Haakon in his captain's chair. "Chang, this is Sarai. Sarai, say hello to Captain Chang." The woman waved politely.

"What makes this lady dangerous?" Chang asked.

"It's not that she's dangerous exactly, but, see the pretty silver eyes? What that means is, she's the Khakhan's number-two daughter."

Chang hit the panic button on the arm of his chair. "Battle stations, everyone! Commo, send full fleet alert. Condition infra-red! Haakon, don't you move. Any action and I'll blow you into your component molecules and use them for fuel in my mass converter."

Scanlon turned to him. "What are you talking about, Skipper? You know *Eurynome* outguns us by about three

125

orders of magnitude. Hell, this tub could be vaporized by a kid with—"

"Shut up!" Chang hissed. "All of you just be quiet and let me handle this. Haakon, are you listening?"

"Attentively."

"Just sit back and keep your hands away from your controls. And no voice orders, mind. From here on in, Lopal Singh handles this. I want no part of it."

"Fine," Haakon said. "Sorry about the inconvenience. I'll buy you a drink when you get off duty. Is the Bloody Bucket still in business?"

"Yeah, but in a new location in the new Meridian atrium. That's opened up since you were last here. Is she really a Bahaduran princess?"

"Absolutely. You didn't think I'd be showing up with just any scruffy refugees, did you?"

"I'll be damned," said Chang, impressed.

"Is he typical of the Cingulans?" Sarai asked. Clearly she was having second thoughts about coming here.

"They're not all as loopy as Chang and his crew," Jemal assured her, "but a certain degree of eccentricity is pretty much the norm." They sat in the salon, awaiting their boarding party.

"And then there's Chang's boss, Lopal Singh. He's head of security for the Cingulum and he's a different proposition entirely." Mirabelle had assumed her mantle of preternatural serenity, which meant that she was prepared for anything. Haakon was still on the bridge, keeping Chang entertained. Soong practiced calligraphy while Alexander sat on a priceless carpet, nervously shooting marbles with hands and feet. Rand, whom Sarai had never seen, was with his engines and Rama had decided that labor was imminent and had taken to her bed, where Numa guarded her.

A bong on the comm announced the arrival of the reception committee, and Jemal left the salon to greet them. He returned a few minutes later with a towering man in a khaki uniform topped with a violet turban. Several less impressive people trailed behind them. The huge man walked up to Sarai and she stood to meet him. She had to look sharply upward to meet his gaze. He was the largest human she had ever seen.

Lopal Singh studied the silver-eyed woman for several seconds without speaking, then he said: "It's true."

Haakon came down from the bridge. "Ah, Lopal Singh, I see you've met our passenger. Sarai, this is—"

The Sikh ignored him. "Your Highness, you must come with me. For reasons of security, you will speak to no one but security personnel until you have been cleared." He turned to Haakon. "Likewise, you are not to speak to anyone about your passenger until I give you permission."

"Actually," Haakon said, "I did kind of let it slip to Chang."

"I know," Lopal Singh said. "Your calculated negligence is nothing new for me. Lucky for you that we have a mission for you to carry out. Otherwise I would have you all in Coventry for this."

"That remains to be seen," Jemal said. "Coventry is preferable to many of your missions."

"But you would lose your ship," Lopal Singh said. "Need I remind you that about half of our captains have requested to be assigned *Eurynome* should we confiscate her?"

That shut them up. They would do anything not to lose *Eurynome*. Almost anything.

The Bloody Bucket, while not quite as flamboyant an establishment as Star Hell in Lower Baikal, was still a rather rough place. The roughness had limits because the Cingulum was well policed, not so much by the authorities as by its citizens. In the Bloody Bucket, it meant that arguments could be settled violently, but only with weapons that would not endanger bystanders.

The bar was tunneled into the rock of the Meridian atrium, its main room perched on a ledge overlooking a vast landing field. The field was surrounded by tiers of ledges backed by doorways and windows and fronted by roadways. Vertical elevators and slide stairs connected the various levels. Meridian was one of the hundreds of worldlets making up the Cingulum. It was an undistinguished hunk of airless rock a few kilometers in diameter. A ragged hole in the surface of Meridian led into the atrium, which was considerably larger than the external worldlet. It was one of the little paradoxes that made the Cingulum such a unique and interesting place.

Haakon sat at a table with Alexander, Chang, and Scanlon. He looked out over the atrium, where a newly arrived refugee ship was disgorging its passengers. "How long did you say this place has been in operation?" he asked.

"About nine months," Scanlon said. "They were still

working on it when you were here last. Beats the old setup, doesn't it?"

"What's that?" Alexander pointed to a huge, furry mass that quivered on the floor near one of the walls. It seemed to be about a quarter-acre in extent and perhaps four meters high, its shape extremely irregular.

"They've called it the Mole," Chang explained. "It tunneled up through the floor a few months back. It's been growing ever since. Some think it's intelligent, others aren't sure it's really alive. I guess something'll have to be done about it sooner or later, if it keeps growing."

A waitress came ot the table. "Can I get you another round?" All the waitresses at the Bloody Bucket were identical and they were all named Margaret. They were actually skinbots designed to look exactly like human women and they shared a common robotic intelligence.

"Bring us another round," Haakon said. "Margaret, what's the political news?" Other Margarets worked in other bars and catering establishments all over the Cingulum. They were an invaluable source of political gossip since nobody had ever built a discretion circuit into them.

"The big debate now is how to get diplomatic recognition for the Cingulum without letting anybody know where it is," Margaret said. "Legal definition is another problem. Most hold for 'Refugee Republic' but DaSilva wants it declared a 'Metaphysical Entity.' Old Baibars say the Cingulum should be declared a legal state of mind."

"Thanks. It's no help, but it means things haven't

changed any. Chang, we've been here four or five days and still no word about this mission they have for us. Do you know anything about it?"

"Not a thing. But you know this place. All kinds of anomalous things are happening continually. They might want you to investigate something. It's what you get for being so expendable."

"Don't use that word," Alexander said. Margaret set a huge stein of beer in front of him, and he sucked up half of it. "One day Lopal Singh's gonna get his wish and we won't come back from one." He pinched Margaret's plastic bottom, and she rewarded him with a backhanded swat that knocked him sprawling on the artificial-sawdust-covered floor.

A knot of merchant smugglers came in and crowded around the Bloody Bucket's latest attraction: a genuine, antique juke box which produced music from spinning petrochemical discs. After much argument, they fed in some metal slugs and heard a scratchy rendition of some primitive song in a language nobody could understand. "What is it, Margaret?" one asked.

"A rendition of a song about hound dogs in a poor Korean translation," said Margaret. The lights of the juke box flashed gaudily.

Haakon sat back and sipped at his tequila-and-lime. Mirabelle was off somewhere raiding the computers for information about the elusive Prince Tametomo. Jemal and Soong were on similar fact-finding expeditions. Lopal Singh had reluctantly given them free run of the place until they should be summoned before the Council.

Sarai's appearance had come as such a bombshell that

everything else had been dropped until her interrogation was completed. She was either the biggest danger ever to hit the Cingulum, or else the most splendid opportunity to come their way since they had learned how to use the place.

Not that they truly knew how to use it. The Cingulum had been built by a race whose physics were indistinguishable from magic or veritable godcraft. The most cautious researchers thought that it would take several thousand years to understand the basic physics governing the Cingulum. Despite its unbending stance of anti-Bahadur resistance, Haakon found almost anyplace in normal space more comfortable than the Cingulum, which was a continual affront to good sense.

He was worried about Rama. He wasn't sure whether she was really near term or just playing for sympathy. Or she might just be malingering, not wanting to have any part of whatever the Cingulum Council had cooked up for them. He wouldn't put anything past her. She was the most vicious, selfish, contrary, sadistic, insufferable half-human he had ever encountered. He still worried about her, though. He ordered another drink to reduce his worry quotient.

Margaret came to the table again. "The Office for Strategic Planning wants to see Captain Haakon and his crew right away."

"Where's that?" Haakon asked.

She pointed across the cavernous expanse. "Fifth level, next to Garbage Control. Just down the blue hallway. There's a row of beer and wine vending machines outside the door. You can't miss it."

"Time to find out what this is all about," Haakon said. "Come on, Alex." Alexander sucked up the last of his beer and followed Haakon out the door. Behind them, the juke box began caterwauling in Turkish about somebody called Sergeant Pepper.

They didn't find the blue corridor right away. There were a number of corridors on the fifth level, and some of them offered distractions. One featured an elaborate herm brothel, outside which a shill tried to allure them with the delights to be had within. Haakon declined, but he had to drag Alexander away by one of his large ears. Across from the brothel was the bright-red door of the cathedral of All Saints of the Cosmos. From inside, they could hear a choir singing "Melita," in the version adapted for spacers.

They found a bar and put away another drink while they got directions from another Margaret. Eventually, they found the blue corridor. It contained the usual crowds of motley-garbed people doing whatever it was people did in Meridian. The first door they came to bore a sign restricting access to authorized personnel only. Characteristically, Alexander had to look inside. He opened it slightly and peeked inside. Beyond the door was nothing but a vista of endless space dotted with bright-green stars. There was no outrush of air through the door. Alexander closed it. Nothing unusual for this place.

They passed a pet shop where a truly disgusting creature scratched at a force screen trying to get their attention. Just beyond the pet shop they spotted the vending machines and a door with a sign reading: OFFICE

FOR STRATEGIC PLANNING. TOP SECRET. KNOCK BEFORE ENTERING. Alexander drew another beer from a machine while Haakon, figuring he might need his wits about him, took a sober-up pill. They knocked and went in.

Sann Tredegar looked up as they entered. He wore broad light filters to protect his huge, sensitive eyes. His race had been adapted to a planet with a dim sun. "You arrive unconscionably late, even for you, Captain Haakon. And not even sober, I see."

"Give me a few minutes," Haakon said. "When did you get an Office for Strategic Planning?"

One of the tiny Janids answered. "The urge to bureaucratize is part of Original Sin, and no messiah has come to deliver us from it." He was perfectly human, and just under a meter in height. There were at least sixty persons seated around the room, all of basic human stock but many of them with altered genes. Lopal Singh was there, as were the rest of his crew, including Rama, who looked huge but otherwise ambulatory. So much for her imminent motherhood.

Haakon found a vacant chair and sat, massaging the bridge of his much-broken nose. "What do you want?"

"A new reality has appeared," Tredegar explained. "About six months ago, a small hole opened up at the extreme end of the atrium and was reported by a maintenance worker. It disappeared after six days, just solid rock where the hole had been. Another six days passed and it reappeared, this time considerably larger. It's been going on in that pattern ever since: There for six days, then gone for six days, and bigger at each reappearance. It's making us nervous because pretty soon the hole is going to be bigger than Meridian. We've gotten used to paradoxes around here, but we might not survive this one."

"What's on the other side of the hole?" Haakon asked.

"We don't know. All we can see is blackness. It's unresponsive to testing. Instruments send back no signals—"

"Let me guess the next part," Haakon interrupted. "You've sent in manned expeditions and they haven't returned. How many?"

"Three," Tredegar said. "The first in vacuum suits as soon as the hole was big enough. One in a scout ship with three volunteers a month later, then a twelve-man team in a converted sloop-of-war."

"Needless to say," Haakon said, "none of them came back."

"If they had," Tredegar pointed out, "we'd have no use for you. The next appearance of the hole is in exactly"—he glanced at his wrist-screen—"six hours, forty-seven minutes. We want you to go in."

"Why us?" Haakon asked wearily.

"Because you have a record of succeeding in expeditions of this sort," Tredegar said.

"And we wouldn't be missed," Haakon pointed out.

"To be honest about it," Lopal Singh rumbled, "there are many of us who feel most uncomfortable knowing that you people are out there, under Timur Khan's thumb and knowing as much about the Cingulum as you do."

"No deal," Haakon said. "You people must be insane if you think we'd touch a thing like this."

"You're probably right," said one of the Janids.

"Most of us are crazy here. If we weren't crazy when we arrived, living here is enough to make us that way."

Tredegar ignored the interruption. "You haven't asked about your payment."

"Not interested," Haakon snapped. Then he asked, "What were you thinking of offering?"

"If you return after a successful mission, which means not just coming back alive, but returning with an answer to the problem we face, we will put all our medical researchers on a crash program to remove the death devices from your heads while doing you minimal harm."

Haakon sat silent for a few moments. "You bastards. I need to take a vote with my crew." Something occurred to him. "That bastard Chang! He knew about this all the time."

"Of course he knew about it," Admiral Roque said. "He's had his dibs in on your ship for months. So have I, for that matter."

"Well, none of you will get it!" Haakon said. "How big is that hole going to be this time, big enough for *Eurynome* to pass through?"

"Yes," Tredegar said reluctantly.

"Then, if we go at all, we go in our ship. If we don't come back, neither does she." He got up and went into an adjoining room, followed by his crew.

"Alex, shut the door," Haakon ordered. He looked from one to another of his crew. "Ordinarily, I wouldn't even consider another mission of this sort, but this time it could mean our freedom at last, so let's discuss it. Jem?"

"It'd be showing some unmerited faith in the medical

135

staff here. If they're as nutty as the rest, I wouldn't trust them with a cut finger." He thought for a moment. "What the hell, it's a chance. I say go."

"Mirabelle?" Haakon asked.

"I was getting bored anyway. Let's try it."

"Soong?"

"I don't like the odds," the Han said, "but I've had good luck with long shots. I say go."

"Rand?"

The engineer gave a metallic shrug. "You couldn't run the engines without me. Sure, I'll go."

"Rama, I don't think you should go in your condition. Stay here until we get back. If we get back."

"I stay with *Eurynome*!" She hissed. "If you are foolish enough to take this mission, then you take me, too. Besides, any risk is worth it if it will gain me my freedom."

"You ain't asked me, Boss," Alexander said.

"You're not going," Haakon insisted. "You have no stake in this. Timur Khan never planted a bomb in your head. You'd just be endangering yourself for nothing."

"I go with my shipmates," Alexander said, for once solemn.

Haakon sighed. "I won't try to stop you. You'd just figure out some way to stow away. It's your choice. Numa, you don't have to go, either."

"I stay with Rama," he said. "At least until she kicks me out. I don't like the idea, but I have to stay with her while her capacity is impaired. It's in my genes."

"That makes it unanimous." They walked back out

into the meeting room. "It's a deal," Haakon announced.

"It seems you'll have one other passenger," Tredegar said.

"We don't take hitchikers," Haakon said. "Who's dumb enough to want to go along?"

Sarai stood up. In the shadows toward the rear of the room, he hadn't noticed her. "I am."

"You seem to have passed the inquisition with flying colors," Haakon said.

"We are quite satisfied that Her Highness is exactly what she claims," Tredegar said. "And she will be a most valuable addition to our growing community of displaced rulers in exile. I strongly urged her not to do this, but she is quite adamant, and I cannot stop her if she wishes to go. However, it is your ship and your mission, so you may forbid it. I urge you to do so."

"For once I agree with you," Haakon said. "It's out of the question, Sarai. We probably won't be coming back."

"Captain," Soong said quietly, "perhaps you ought to ask her why she wants to go with us."

"Who asked you?" Haakon said testily.

"Ask her," Mirabelle said.

"I let you vote on this mission, so suddenly we've become a democracy? All right, just this once. Tell me, Sarai, why do you want to commit suicide with us?"

"Because the third expedition into this mysterious hole was led by Prince Tametomo! I must go in to find him and deliver the Three Treasures."

Haakon looked at Mirabelle. "It's true, Captain," she

said. "I found out this morning." She looked at Tredegar. "Sorry, sir, but your computers are dreadfully insecure."

"Should that surprise me?" he asked disgustedly. "Yes, Prince Tametomo, whom we knew as ex-captain Minamoto, led the third expedition. We had no idea that he was the Crown Prince of Chamuka, but then, neither had he. Believed himself still an unneeded younger son, I suppose. In any case, he had a distinguished combat record when he arrived, and he became an excellent officer in our defense forces. Like most such, with years of warfare against the Powers behind him, he was bored. When the mission came along, he volunteered for it. The other eleven in his crew were just like him."

"We'll need resumes on all of them," Haakon said. "And full specs on both craft that went in."

"You'll have them. Such slight data as we've managed to collect will be transmitted to your computer, although I don't doubt that Mirabelle has most of it already."

"I don't like this," Haakon said. "We should have more time to study the situation. However, we've agreed to give it a try. You'd better clear the atrium. *Eurynome*'s a little fractious in a gravity environment." An official began dictating orders into a belt-comm unit.

"Let's get out of here," Haakon said to his crew. "We have work to do."

"What about me?" Sarai asked. "Am I going?"

"Sure," Haakon said. "If you're intent on suicide, who am I to stop you?"

"We wish you well on your mission," Tredegar said.

"Go to hell," Haakon replied as he led his little troop out the door.

"I must go prepare," Rama said as they reached the corridor outside. "Come, Numa." The two Felids strode off portentiously. Haakon watched them narrowly. The theatrical tone usually meant Rama was up to something.

"Rand, you go along with them," he said. "Keep the engines cool. She might be planning to take off with the ship." The engineer clicked off.

"You don't trust her?" Sarai asked.

"I trust her at my back in a dangerous situation, but that's about it. Felids are pretty, but their alley-cat genes predominate when it comes to loyalty. You'd be well advised to keep that in mind."

"We have a little over six hours," Jemal reminded them. "What's our next move?"

"Find a good bar," Haakon pronounced.

The Bloody Bucket was a changed place when Haakon returned. Jemal, Alex, and Sarai were still with him. Mirabelle and Soong had decided to return to the ship. The desultory business of earlier in the day had given way to a raucous, noisy throng of smugglers, ex-pirates, and more or less respectable refugees. A roar of approval greeted Haakon and his companions as they entered.

"Didn't take long for word to get around," Haakon muttered. He scanned the front room. "Where's Chang?" he demanded.

"He left soon after you did," said Margaret.

"Good for him that he did," Haakon said. They intimidated a few drunks into surrendering a table next to the front window. Down on the landing field, they could see that the clearing procedure was well underway. Within an hour or so, there would be nothing on the field except, perhaps, the Mole.

Sarai pointed to a spot high on the opposite tier where a gigantic set of holographic numerals had appeared in the empty air. "What is that display? Something to do with landing control?" The numerals were lurid scarlet and they continually flickered and changed. Abruptly, a message flashed over the numbers: GOOD LUCK, EURYNOME!

"No," Jemal said, "that's the sign for Alistair Pettigrew and Sons Bookie Joint. They're starting to take bets on whether we'll come back or not."

"At least they're wishing you well," she said feebly.

"They might as well," Haakon said. "They're giving odds of twenty-to-one against." A thought struck him. "Jem, do you have that crystal on you?" Jemal touched his ear, where the stone still dangled. "Then take it over to Honest Achmed's and see how much you can get for it. Put it all on us to come back alive. We can't lose that way."

Jemal got up and took a brandy from the tray that Margaret had just brought. He knocked it back and waved farewell. "I'll see you back at the ship. Be sober."

"Excuse me, sir," said a tentative voice. They looked up to see a young man standing by the table. He wore parti-colored hose and a metallic doublet with a high collar sprouting a broad ruff. "Aren't you the captain of the *Eurynome*?"

140

"That's right," Haakon said.

"Honored to meet you, sir. I'm Tobias Bottsfinger, a student at the University here, specializing in Higher Metaphysics. We're doing a study on defining luck as a quantifiable entity." Proudly, the student withdrew a spiky box from within his doublet. It trailed several thin wires. "This is my own invention, the luck meter. Since you people seem to be the luckiest beings in the universe, judging by past performance, you would be the perfect subjects to test it on. Would you carry this along on your upcoming mission?" He smiled ingratiatingly.

"Lucky, are we?" Haakon asked, dangerously mild.

"Well, sir, according to all reports, your success rate in incredibly dangerous and complicated missions hasn't been due to innately superior qualities."

Haakon grabbed a bunch of the doublet in his fist and drew Bottsfinger's face down level with his own until their noses were almost touching. "Boy, I want you to go out and get yourself disinherited, then lose a war in which most of your friends are killed and spend a few years breaking rocks in a Bahadur slave pit. Spend what's left of your life on the run under a suspended death sentence. Then come back and tell me how lucky you feel." He shoved the boy away from the table, sending him back-pedaling the full length of the barroom, doing the last few meters on his rump, scattering sawdust and drinkers until he fetched up against the bar rail.

Haakon turned back to the others. "God, it feels good to push somebody else around for a change."

The student picked himself up and brushed off the

sawdust. "So you've had it a little rough," he shouted indignantly. "The yang has to balance the yin, you know!" He stalked out of the Bloody Bucket. The words reminded Haakon of something, but for the life of him he couldn't remember what.

# Eight

THE TIERS WERE PACKED WITH SPECTATORS. NEARLY THE whole population of Meridian had turned out to see the legendary ship leave on its unique journey, and to seek favorable odds from the bookies. Wild cheering erupted as the beautiful vessel made its majestic way through the entrance. It lurched slightly as it entered Meridian's as-yet-unexplained gravity field and the ship's repellers went into overdrive to keep it a safe one hundred meters above the landing field.

Haakon studied his screens as the ship creaked alarmingly. "The old girl really doesn't like gravity," he explained to Sarai. "She can fly in an atmosphere if you ask her politely, but floating along on repellers strains her seams. What are the figures, Jem?"

Jemal checked his central screen. "Latest odds are

eighteen-to-one against. That's strange. Our bet shouldn't have dropped the odds that far."

"The last-minute bettors almost always take long shots," Soong explained. "The books close as soon as we enter the hole."

Sarai was looking a little pale. "Are you really concerned with these odds at a time like this?" She occupied one of the temporary chairs on the bridge. Everyone except Rand was on the bridge for their departure.

"What's more important?" Alexander asked.

A one-third scale holographic image of Tredegar appeared above a console. "*Eurynome*, in the past, we have staked much upon your success. This time you could have a strong influence upon our economy as well. As soon as our last meeting was over, most of the council went out and bet heavily upon your success."

"That explains the odds drop," Haakon said.

"We are more aware than most," Tredegar went on, "of the consequences of your failure, since the hole could destroy us all. Good luck to you all. Our lives, our security, our future, and five thousand of my hard-earned credits depend upon your success."

"Kind of makes you feel all choked up, doesn't it?" Jemal asked.

The image of Tredegar was replaced by one of Lopal Singh. "Don't bring back anything dangerous," he said, and winked out.

"Someday I will eat his face," Rama said.

"When should the hole show up?" Haakon asked.

"Should be right about now," Jemal supplied. "Of

course, we can always hope it won't make an appearance this time."

"No such luck," Haakon said. "There it is."

The far wall of the atrium had been a featureless rock face, the unaltered material of Meridian. A small, perfectly circular hole had appeared in the center of the wall and it was expanding.

"I'm beginning to have second thoughts," Jemal said. "What are our chances of backing out now?"

"None," Haakon said. "The whole Cingulum fleet is out there someplace. It's not much of a fleet, but more than adequate to take care of us." The hole had expanded to take up more than half the wall, then it stopped.

"It's big enough for us to go through," Haakon said. "No sense stalling. I'm taking us in." He signaled his orders and *Eurynome* began to move forward, dead slow. Knuckles whitened on chair arms as they neared the hole. A fine sweat shone on Sarai's forehead, and a disagreeable scent came from the Felids. Alexander was huddled in his chair with his tail wrapped tightly around him.

"Here goes," Haakon said.

*Eurynome*'s nose pierced the black disk. The front of the ship disappeared from view and the blackness slid along the sleek hull until it reached the bridge. They saw it as a bright, shimmering veil as it swept over them. They closed their eyes, gritted teeth, muttered curses, and then it was past them.

"We're alive," Jemal noted with some astonishment.

"So far, so good," Haakon sakd. "Are we all the way through? Rand, report."

"All's well in the engine room," Rand said. "Something like a wall of light came through a few seconds ago. It was visible as far along the spectrum as I can see."

"We're in space," Jemal said, noting the star fields in the screens. "Let's get the computer to work and see if it corresponds to any known part of space."

"What's behind us?" Haakon asked. What the screen showed behind them was a huge circle of red light. It flashed on and off every few seconds. The circle was hundreds of meters in diameter but very thin. "Now what the hell is that?"

"I'm getting an analysis," Soong said. He read the symbols as they came up. "It seems that the circle is a glass tube about three centimeters in width. It is hollow and contains an inert gas, apparently neon. An electrical current causes the gas to be florescent. Interruption of the current causes the flashing we see."

"Glass?" Haakon's nonexistent eyebrows went up.

"Exactly," Soong confirmed. "Made from sand."

"Where is the current coming from?" Rama asked.

"Unknown. The tube is continuous."

"Nothing should surprise us by this time," Haakon said.

"What do we do now?" Sarai asked.

"Nothing without further data," Haakon said. "From the look of things, we're in a solar system, but we won't go exploring until we know more about our situation."

Rama got out of her chair. "I'm going back to my suite. Let me know if anything interesting happens." She left, followed by Numa.

"While we're waiting on our information, let's send out a probe and see if it'll return to Meridian through that circle."

The small, unmanned probe left its bay in *Eurynome*'s hull and passed through the circle. It remained visible and Haakon brought it back to the ship. "Nothing," he said. "I really didn't expect any easy answers."

"I'm getting hungry," Alexander said.

"Go eat," Haakon told him. He turned to Sarai. "It doesn't take long for this crowd to revert to routine."

"The glass tube is an enigma," Sarai said, "but this appears to be ordinary space." She had regained her equanimity.

"Don't count on it," Haakon said. "Did you get briefed on our previous experiences in inner-Cingulum space?"

"Yes. I am not sure that I believe it."

"You'll get your chance to see for yourself. The Cingulum was made by beings who might as well be gods. They can do anything they want with space and matter and physics. And they're bored. Human beings are the most fun they've had in millions of years. Be prepared to be played with, but don't think it's just a game. You can die very thoroughly here, or be transformed into something they find amusing."

"The neon light just went out," Jemal said.

"I suppose that's our signal to move," Haakon said. "Any data coming in from the astronomical scan?"

"Just arriving," Soong said. He puzzled over the symbols for a few moments. "The primary star is a Sol-type, but nothing else makes much sense."

"I could've predicted that," Jemal said.

"There is only one planet in the system, orbit distance about equal to Earth from Sol. Gravity about like Earth, but it lacks the mass for such gravity. There are other anomalies."

"Since nothing else in the system looks promising," Haakon said, "let's go have a look at it. I don't know if that six-day interval has any meaning here, but it might. Let's not waste time." He gave the ship's computer instructions to deliver them to an orbit around the planet and the conventional drive engines kicked in. The distance was not great enough to use the Tesla drive.

Haakon climbed out of his chair. "It looks like we have more than a day to kill before we arrive. I think I'll join Alex."

"I'll come with you," Sarai said.

They found Alexander demolishing a huge salad and a tray of dim sum. Now that the transition was over, he seemed relieved of all apprehension. His attention span was never extensive at the best of times. "Couldn't get along without my company, huh?" he said between mouthfuls of food.

Haakon didn't bother to answer as he sat. The 'bot took their orders.

"You didn't tell me you people were agents for Timur Khan," Sarai said accusingly.

"It's not the kind of information we give out to just anybody," Haakon said. "On a place as hostile as Chamuka, it could have been downright indiscreet. Besides, you didn't tell us you were the Khakhan's daughter. Have I complained? Since when were we so intimate as to reveal the innermost secrets of our hearts?"

"You were there as spies!" she spat.

"Of course we were spying," Haakon said. "Timur Khan would've killed us if we'd refused. Do you think we want to die?"

"Some people just ain't reasonable, Boss," Alexander said. "See, lady, these people got little bombs planted in their heads. They make Timur Khan unhappy and blooie! Brains all over the bulkheads. That's why they was spying on you, not anything personal."

"I was told about that," she said. "It's amazingly unreassuring. I had thought you were at least honest smugglers. Now I am not sure you are the kind of people I want to be with on a mission such as this." The 'bot began setting plates on the table before her.

"Nobody twisted your arm," Haakon said. "Anytime you want, you're free to walk back. Now eat up. You may not like the company, but you won't complain about the chow. This ship has a synthesizer that must be a government secret."

"Yeah," Alexander said, "you ought to try the cheeseburgers with truffles. Mirabelle found them in the historical recipes banks."

"I am not interested in the food, or the accommodations, and least of all in this space-faring jewel box."

"Careful, lady," Alexander cautioned, "that's our ship you're talking about."

"All this conversation is bad for my digestion," Haakon said. "If you don't mind, I'll dine in lonely splendor in my quarters." He rose and the 'bot hurried to follow him with the plates.

"I didn't mean to be so abrasive," Sarai said when he was gone. "Something in his attitude makes me want to needle him. I fear that your captain now has a poor opinion of me."

"Naw, he likes you fine," Alexander said, peeling a banana.

"Why do you say that?"

"Well, most people bitching at him like you been doing, they'd be lucky if all he did was break their arm."

"To see this," Jemal said, "mere screens are not adequate. We'll have to go down to the viewing salon to get the full effect."

A few minutes earlier, he had announced that they had reached optimum orbit. They gathered on the bridge to find all the screens blank. Jemal loved theatrical effects. Obviously, the planet had turned out to be something so weird that he wanted to make the viewing an artistic production. They filed down the short ramp into the crystal-sheathed viewing salon. The effect turned out to be worth the extra effort.

"It's *flat*!" Sarai gasped.

"Strictly speaking, it's roughly disk-shaped," Soong said. "However, I agree that the surface looks alarmingly flat."

They seemed to be orbiting just above the edge of the disk, looking down upon a vista of green mountains and valleys cut deeply by silver rivers. The rivers made their ways to the edge of the disk where they tumbled off in gigantic waterfalls, falling for several kilometers, pluming out into spray, then into mist, then into fog. The falls had cut deep notches into the stone edges of the disk. The fog rose as an obscuring haze and made it difficult to make out details near the fall areas.

"Most of the rivers we see," Jemal said, "are the size of the Nile or the Amazon on Earth. There are a lot of them, but no oceans or seas. Probably all to the good when you consider the way this world is built."

"How does the gravity work in such an environment?" Sarai asked.

"Arbitrarily, but consistently," Jemal said. "Atmosphere and gravity are contained in a cylindrical environment, with the planet in the middle. Instead of falling toward the center of the mass, as with sensible gravity, everything falls to the bottom of the cylinder."

"A very clever terrarium effect as well," Soong said. "With no seas to provide atmospheric moisture through evaporation, their place is taken by the rivers. As they fall they turn to vapor and rise to the upper part of the cylinder where they form clouds and fall back as rain."

"Couldn't have done it better myself," Haakon commented. "Any idea what keeps the planet from dropping to the bottom of the cylinder?"

"At that point," Soong said, "our computer quietly lapses into psychosis."

"I may do the same," Sarai said. "I apologize for my former doubts. This is beyond belief."

"Believe it anyway," Haakon cautioned. "The worst mistake you can make here is to think it's all some kind of illusion. It's real, every bit of it."

151

"This is ridiculous," Rama said. "As if morning sickness weren't bad enough. How much do they expect me to put up with?"

"Worse than this, I suspect," Jemal said. "After all, nothing's happened yet."

"It shouldn't take long," Haakon said gloomily. "Soong, give us some statistics on this thing. How big a world are we dealing with?"

"It is approximately six thousand kilometers in diameter and five hundred kilometers thick. In lieu of a sea level, we must establish a median surface level, above which the highest elevations rise some twenty kilometers. By no means the highest mountains on record, but still quite respectable."

"I see snow on the highest peaks," Jemal said. "Is that for a genuine meteorological reason or pure aesthetics?"

Soong shrugged. "We have too little data to speculate at this point."

"Does this place have day and night?" Haakon asked. "If so, the whole damned cylinder must rotate end for end."

"That seems to be how it works," Jemal said. "Actually, it was a kind of relief to discover that. Baroque as it is, I was prepared to find out that the damned sun orbits the planet."

"Let's continue a horizontal orbit along the rim here. Maybe we'll find something interesting. Send out the standard contact signal. If they're alive and listening, Tametomo's expedition may hear us." He looked at Sarai. "Don't get your hopes too high. We can't be sure that they came through in the same place we did. They could be in a different universe entirely."

"Different *universe*?" she asked.

"We used to think that the original Cingulans built their own universe. Current theory holds that they have lots of them," Jemal explained.

She looked at the impossible, disk-shaped world. "A few minutes ago, I would have said you must be insane. I'm prepared to believe anything now."

The vista of the planet continued to slide past beneath them. Terrain varied wildly. Gigantic rivers flowed through valleys of dense, tropical verdure before tumbling off the edge of the planet. On the other side of a mountain range, small streams meandered through vast, dry deserts. In some areas, active volcanoes threw up plumes of ashy smoke. What kind of subterranean activity could cause volcanoes remained a mystery.

"Guess what's dead in the center of this planet?" Jemal asked, as more readings came through the computer.

"I'm afraid to try," Haakon said.

"An ice cap. Glaciers radiate out from it for hundreds of kilometers. At the center it's about twenty kilometers thick."

"I don't like ice and snow," Alexander said. "Let's not go there."

"So far," Rama said, "I've seen nothing here to attract me at all. Is there any civilization? That might provide some diversion."

"Nothing definite," Soong said. "If there is, it must be pre-industrial. Unfortunately, the volcanic activity masks any evidence of burning hydrocarbons. For what it's worth, chemical analysis precludes industrialization much beyond the late nineteenth or early twentieth-century stage. Not that our readings are terribly significant here."

They were about to scatter to various places about the ship when the proximity scanner sounded a warning. Soong checked the reading. "Ship approaching."

"It must be Tametomo," Sarai said. "Or possibly the earlier scout ship."

"Don't count on it," Haakon cautioned.

"Who else could it be?" she demanded.

"Almost anything, dear one," Rama said. "The very thought curls my whiskers."

"Do we have visual yet?" Haakon asked.

"Soon," Soong said. "It's about the same size as *Eurynome*. Material composition—" he said and went over the symbols twice, then muttered, "No, these must be mistaken."

"What type of engines does it have?" Haakon demanded.

"I think," Soong answered, "that we would be ill-advised to make speculations at this point."

"That hard to believe, huh?" Haakon said. "I hope we get visual soon. This must be quite a sight."

"Here it is," Jemal said. The holographic image that took form in the viewing salon's tank was not easy to recognize as any kind of ship they had ever seen. It was irregular in shape, with a rough, lumpy surface, and was dingy brown in color.

"I'm not even going to say what that looks like," Jemal said.

"I'll say it," Alexander chimed in.

"Hold your tongue," Haakon ordered.

"What are those poles sticking out all over it?" Mirabelle asked. Soong zoomed in for a closeup of one of the stubby poles that protruded from the ship in irregular rows. The one he chose showed a rough surface of a grayish-brown color. Its flat end displayed a pattern of irregular, concentric circles.

"Unless I'm sorely mistaken," Jemal said, "that's a log."

"Look at this," Soong said. He got another closeup, this time of one of the ship's square portholes. It was covered with a crude shutter, apparently constructed of roughly sawn wooden planks.

"Wood on a spaceship?" Haakon asked of nobody. "I feel old and tired."

"About a hundred years ago," Jemal said, "didn't the gene-torturers on Mendel try to grow a spaceship from some kind of tree?"

"They were trying to do everything with DNA and protoplasm back then," Haakon said. "Like most of them, the spaceship project never worked out. Anyway, that thing wasn't grown, it was built, using wood as construction material, something to the best of my knowledge never attempted on even the most impoverished worlds."

"Hey, you!" squawked a voice over the ship's comm. "Stop right where you are and identify yourself!"

Haakon opened the transmission link. "I was about to ask you to do the same."

"Is that so?" the voice said. "Well, suppose I was to open fire on you?"

"Then I'd be forced to return fire," Haakon said. "From the looks of that space-going turd you're in, I outgun you."

"Then let's talk. We'll come alongside, you let us have a look at your ship, you look at ours, we sit down, have a few beers, talk things over. No sense shooting each other while we're still perfect strangers."

Haakon looked at the others. "Hell, I guess it's as good a way to get information as any." He opened the link again. "Sure, come alongside. The airlock's the big hatch outlined in red."

"What's an airlock? That like a door? Never mind, we'll figure it out. See you in a few minutes."

"What have we gotten into now?" Mirabelle asked. "What language were they using?"

"An archaic and debased form of Spanish," Soong said. "We'd better put in ear sets to translate when they arrive."

"I am not going to talk to them!" Rama said. "And you had better not allow them in my suite. That sounded like a highly uncultivated person. You deal with them, bald one. Tell them I will kill them if they get too close." She swept out, followed by Numa and an acrid scent.

"Probably just as well she doesn't take part in the diplomatic negotiations," Haakon said. "Impending motherhood hasn't improved her disposition any." He thought a moment. "Hasn't made it all that much worse, really."

A slight bump went through the ship as the other craft made contact. Lights flashed and beepers sounded as *Eurynome* went through her coupling cycle.

"That ship didn't have anything that looked like true airlock facilities," Jemal said nervously.

"No, but our controls say it's safe to cycle open," Soong said. "Let's just be ready to hit the emergency break contact and seal control."

"I already have it set on automatic," Haakon said. He was armed, as were they all except for Alexander. No rule of diplomacy said that one had to be foolish.

The inner lock door opened to reveal a knot of men. They wore big hats and were oddly dressed, most of them in boots with spurs, short jackets, and trousers, all indescribably wrinkled. One had a colorfully striped blanket thrown over a shoulder. Crossed on their chests were broad leather belts studded with little brass tubes, and they all wore waist belts with strange-looking pistols in holsters and sheathed knives. A barrel-shaped man with short, bowed legs shambled forward. Like the others, he was staring around wide-eyed with the unmistakable air of a man looking around for something valuable to lift.

"Hey, this is some place you got here. Which one's the boss?"

"I am," Haakon said. "Captain Haakon, at your service. Who might you be?"

"General Francisco Villa, at yours. I'm commander of

the Northern Division. You're not Carranzistas, are you? Long as you're not Carranzistas or Redflaggers, we can talk."

"We're neither of those things," Haakon assured him, "at least, to the best of my knowledge we aren't."

"If you were, you'd know it," Villa said. He glared at Soong. "Is he a Chinaman? I don't like Chinamen, either."

"I am Han, sir" Soong said.

"He ain't no Chinaman, Chief," said one of the men. "No pigtail, see?"

"They got some nice-looking women, though," said another, eyeing Mirabelle and Sarai.

Villa swept off his hat and swatted the man across the face. "Where are your manners? We are guests here!"

The man looked back resentfully but a huge man beside Villa whipped out a pistol and leveled it in his face. The pistol made a series of mechanical clicks as it was drawn. The man calmed down, the pistol was replaced, and they went on as if nothing had happened.

"Come on over to my ship," Villa said. "We can relax and talk there. Maybe later you can show me this whorehouse."

"All right," Haakon said. "I'll take my second-in-command. The rest stay here." He introduced Jemal.

Villa indicated the big man who had pulled the gun. "This is my number-two man, Rodolfo Fierro."

Fierro was beefy and handsome, with oiled hair and mustache. He wore a gray suit and a white shirt with a dirty collar and a string necktie. His hat was smaller than the others. He swept off the hat, bowed, and smiled politely as he shook hands, but Haakon knew a real killer when he saw one. A gold tooth glinted at the corner of Fierro's smile.

They walked through the airlock, which, unnervingly, simply opened onto a doorway in Villa's ship. A broad band of empty space showed between the ships.

"What's holding the air in?" Jemal muttered.

Haakon just shrugged his shoulders. He saw that some stanchions near the airlock now had lines around them. Apparently, Villa's men had roped the ships together.

"You need some decent couplings, man," Fierro said. "I can show you how to put them in. I used to work on the railroad."

They stepped across onto Villa's ship. It was dim inside, and the first thing to strike their senses was the smell. There was a chemical scent, and a smell of sweetish tobacco smoke, and something else that was highly organic. Dim, smoking lamps on the walls accounted for the chemical smell, and some of Villa's men had cigars or hand-rolled cigarettes in their mouths. As for the other smell—

"It can't be!" Jemal said.

"But it is," Haakon assured him. He pointed to the floor, where he could just make out a pile of unmistakable horse droppings. "We had stables back on my father's estate. I'd know that smell anywhere, even without the horseshit."

"Welcome to the *Adelita*," Villa said proudly. "Finest ship in the whole Aztlan fleet!"

Haakon ran a thumbnail across a wall and a dry, brown powder sifted down. "What's this ship made of?"

Villa gave him the kind of look reserved for the hopelessly simpleminded. "Adobe, what else?"

"Our ship isn't made of adobe," Haakon reminded him.

Villa shrugged. "What do gringos know about building ships?"

They went into a room with a low ceiling supported by wooden poles, the ends of which apparently were the mysterious logs protruding through the outer surface of the ship. The room was furnished with a number of rickety tables and chairs. One wall bore a paper poster of a man in a tight-fitting, colorful suit doing battle with a hideous, multihorned beast, armed only with a red cape and a thin sword. They sat, and a man in an apron began setting bottles on the tables.

Jemal tried a beer. "Not bad," he commented.

Haakon sniffed at a larger bottle. "Tequila," he said, surprised.

"The best," said Fierro. He pushed a plate in front of Haakon. On the plate were wedges of lime and glass saltshakers.

Haakon wasn't sure what he was expected to do with them but Fierro demonstrated. He sprinkled salt on the back of his hand, took a drink of the tequila, licked off the salt, and bit into the lime. Haakon gave it a try. It was raw stuff, but not bad at all. He noticed that Villa was not partaking of the beverages. His men made up for him handsomely.

"Now, you want to tell me why you're hanging around my territory?" Villa asked.

"We're looking for some friends," Haakon said. "A couple in space suits, some in a little ship, a few more in a ship about half the size of ours. They've been sent this way over the last few months. We were sent to look for them. Have you seen any strangers answering such a description?"

Villa pushed back his wide hat. "I tell you, gringo, times being what they are, we get strange people straying into Aztlan all the time. We stop them every day: smugglers, *filibusteros*, Mormons, observers for the goddamn Kaiser, all kinds of *cabrones*." It seemed that some of these words had no convenient translation.

"The ones we're looking for," Jemal said, "would have been really confused."

"Foreigners always act a little crazy," Fierro said. "Sometimes it's just no use talking to them, and we got to shoot them."

"You'll find us perfectly reasonable," Haakon said. "We just want to get in contact with our friends. If you don't have any information for us, we'll just be on our way."

Villa tilted his chair back and propped his boots on the table, carefully so that his spurs would not snag the edge. "Let's not be hasty, gringo. We're just barely getting acquainted, and we ain't yet seen the inside of your ship, or what you're carrying. You're over Aztlan space, so we got a right to collect toll. You plan to do any trading, we can collect duty."

"We're just passing through," Haakon said. "No need to get into tedious business arrangements. You might say we've made a career of avoiding customs regulations."

"Hey, Rodolfo," said a gap-toothed man in a gold-braided hat, "tell 'em how you save ammunition when you get rid of prisoners."

"It's real simple," Fierro explained. "When we get a lot of Carranzistas and we're low on ammo, I tie 'em up in groups of three, front to back. One bullet goes through all three. I tried four, but a forty-five won't always go through four."

Haakon drew his beamer and swept it in a tight circle. A half-meter chunk of adobe fell from a wall and thunked to the floor, smoking and glowing around the edges. There were a lot of clicks as the mechanical pistols were drawn, but most of the men were preoccupied with studying the hot adobe.

"I never tried to see how many people I could shoot through," Haakon said, "but it'll keep on going farther than you can line them up."

"That's a fancy pistol," said Villa, who had not drawn his own. "You got some of those for sale?"

"No, we're not gunrunning this time," Haakon said, "just looking for our friends."

"Well," Villa said, "maybe you got fancy pistols, but I'll bet my ship's better armed than yours. We got French seventy-fives, installed by Felipe Angeles himself. Show 'em, boys."

Two of the men went to a humped shape in a corner of the room. Hauling off a tarpaulin, they exposed a steel-wheeled artillery piece with a short barrel and a big, square shield between breech and barrel. They threw open the shutters of the window in front of the piece and, lifting the rail, ran the barrel out through the window. One opened the breech while the other lifted a long brass shell from a box and shoved it into the breech. The breech block was rotated shut and the men stepped back, one of them holding a long lanyard.

"Now," Villa continued, "was I to tell Pablo to yank on that lanyard, it'd blow a big hole in your pretty ship."

"I wouldn't count on it," Haakon said. "Us gringos have made some advances in weaponry since your French seventy-fives were hot stuff. Our light guns would turn this ship back into river mud. For something like this, we wouldn't even bother to charge up our heavy stuff."

"Chief," Fierro said. "I think we got here a *yanqui* standoff."

"If that means a no-win situation," Haakon said, "you're wrong. We're holding all the winning cards." He let Villa glower for a few seconds. "But there's really no reason why we should be chest-thumping like this. After all, there's no grounds for hostility between us. Maybe now you'd like to see our ship."

Villa grinned. "Sure, why not? We don't need to act like roosters on a dung heap. I haven't killed any gringos in weeks, so it ain't like I make a habit of it. Let's go."

They got up and trooped back out of the adobe ship and into *Eurynome*'s airlock. "What's this ship made of anyway?" Fierro asked. "Carranza has a ship made out

163

of marble, and they say Montezuma the fifteenth has one made out of gold."

"Metals partially," Haakon asked. "Other materials as well. Most of it's made of synthetics and exotics you've never heard of. A lot of what you'll see is window-dressing, though, things added for luxury and comfort. This was built as a warship and that's still what she is." He thought it would do no harm to remind them of the ship's primary function.

Villa's men gaped as they walked into the main salon. "Hey, Chief," a man said, "we ain't seen nothing like this since we took the mayor's palace in Saltillo."

A 'bot came floating in and their eyes widened. Fierro drew his pistol and fired. There was a tremendous bang and a slug caromed off the 'bot and thunked through a tapestry and into an exotic-wood panel behind it. The 'bot merely rocked gently and continued to approach them. A thin, bluish smoke filled the room before the vents sucked it away.

"It just wants to take your drink orders," Haakon said. He shook his head, trying to clear his ringing ears. For such a primitive weapon, the pistol generated a hell of a noise.

Villa glared disgustedly at Fierro, who hung his head sheepishly. "Rodolfo, how many times I got to tell you? Don't shoot the servants." He turned to the 'bot. "You got any root beer?"

"Hell, we got all kinds of beer," said Alexander, bustling into the salon. He looked at the pattern of lights flashing on the 'bot's panel. "It's checking the historical recipe banks. We'll have some of this root beer stuff pretty soon."

"This one's got a tail, Chief," said one of Villa's men. "Must be from Yucatan."

"I can see that," Villa said.

"Order up, gentlemen," Jemal said, "the bar is open." To their amazement, most of Villa's men asked for champagne, brandy, or wine.

"We can get pulque or tequila or beer any day," Fierro explained. "But you loot enough rich men's houses, you get a taste for the finer things. Now the chief, he don't drink no alcohol, nor smoke tobacco or marijuana, but he got a sweet tooth." He glanced up as Mirabelle entered the salon, dismissed her as a threat, and returned his interest to the glass of champagne the 'bot had handed him.

Villa was more appreciative. "Ah, the beautiful lady we saw all too briefly before." He managed an almost-courtly bow and kissed her hand, bumping her nose slightly with the brim of his hat.

"How do you do, General Villa," she said, "and how goes the revolution?" Haakon nodded his head appreciatively. Mirabelle had been doing some homework.

"It changes from day to day, young lady. I hear that General Zapata is doing well in the south. Huerta is rumored to be dead, which is a pity since I wanted to kill him myself. We keep old Carranza busy, and Emperor Montezuma, as always remains aloof and pretends that he rules a peaceful realm."

"But then," she said, "unsettled times are times of opportunity for enterprising people."

"You are a lady after my own heart. I trust that neither of these gentlemen is your husband?"

"That's the chief's other big weakness," Fierro said, *sotto voce*. "Women." For once, he sounded disapproving of his chief.

"No, I'm unattached," Mirabelle said, smiling.

Villa's grin broadened. "My heart takes wing like a dove. You must show me your beautiful ship. I am sure the captain needs to attend to his many duties."

Haakon smiled inwardly as they left. Mirabelle was competent to handle threats far more formidable than General Villa. "Tell me, Colonel Fierro, how might we be of service to your general? We're not on a business trip just now, but we might be later. I've yet to encounter a revolution that wasn't short on basic supplies." He knew that they would get no more information concerning their primary mission until Villa returned, but any information about their current situation would be valuable.

"We can always use good rifles and machine guns," Fierro said. "The Federal troops use Mausers they get from the Kaiser, but we like the gringo guns, especially the Winchesters. Some go for the Model '94 in 30–30, but I prefer the Model '95 in 30–40 Krag." Clearly, they had hit a subject dear to Fierro's heart. "Now the Mausers are good rifles, you understand. They're fine for infantry, but the Northern Division is mostly cavalry, and the lever actions are flat and easy to pack in a saddle scabbard. A bolt action is fat and rubs galls on a horse's flanks after a while."

Haakon couldn't understand a third of this, but they could sort through it later. "I'll check the market as soon as I get a chance," he said.

"We need rolling stock, too," Fierro said. "Locomotives, flat cars, cattle cars, everything. We're short on track and repair tools, too. You got to keep repair crews on the tracks all the time, and most of ours are sitting around drunk all the time because they don't got no spare track or tools to work with."

"We need dynamite, too," said a man wearing silver spurs with huge rowels. "And don't forget medicine," he added.

It figured, Haakon thought. These revolutionaries were short of everything except liquor. And adobe. He wondered where Sarai was. Probably having a breakdown somewhre. No amount of experience in real space travel prepared anyone for inner-Cingulum space.

"Excuse me, Colonel Fierro," Haakon said. "I have to talk with the officer on the bridge." He turned to the 'bot, took another drink from its tray, and keyed the comm to the bridge. "Soong, is everything all right up there?"

"All quiet, Captain," Soong said. "Mirabelle and General Villa came through a moment ago. He seems favorably impressed. I found out why we didn't get any picture when they first contacted us; they are using a primitive form of radio, capable only of sound transmission."

"Wait'll you hear what else is primitive about their ship," Haakon said. "No more ships or contacts?"

"None, Captain. I'll keep you informed."

Haakon returned his attention to Fierro. "Now, in exchange for these goods, what do you people customarily trade?"

"What do you need?" Fierro asked. "We can round up all the cattle you can use. Sometimes we got Federal gold to trade. The chief absolutely refuses to sell concessions on Aztlan oil or mineral rights."

"Oh, we wouldn't think of asking for them," Jemal assured him.

Alexander was having a great time keeping the soldiers entertained. They looked scary, but they were lots of fun. Best of all, they all knew how to play poker, and he had already won a pistol and a silver-braided hat. He demonstrated to much admiration how he could deal with his feet. He didn't show them how he could deal from any part of the deck, because he knew how that kind of revelation could lead to misunderstanding. Everybody was getting happily drunk.

"Hey, Alejandro," said the one called Pablo, "is the rest of the ship as fancy as this? I'd like to see it." The rest of them thought this a fine idea.

"Captain," Alexander said, "is it okay if I take these guys around the ship?"

"Go ahead," Haakon answered. "Just keep them clear of Rama's quarters, and don't let anybody shoot Rand. I'm not sure how strong that suit of his is." After the mishap with the 'bot, Haakon had discreetly set the internal security system to drop any of these men unconscious if he tried anything dangerous, but there

was no such system in the engine section. The Tesla
engines were just too touchy.

The men trooped after Alexander, ogling the sumptuous furnishings as they went. "Hey, that looks just like
my grandfather," a man said, pointing at a painting
hanging in a hallway. It was all in shades of blue and
depicted an old man playing a guitar.

"I never liked that one," Alexander said. "It's too
dark and looks sad." He got them back to the engine
room without incident. They were fascinated by Rand's
therapeutic suit and awed by his tale of how he came by
it. Nobody was reluctant to leave the chamber with the
Tesla engines.

They were headed back up toward the main salon,
passing by the crew quarters area, when they encountered Rama. "Uh-oh," Alexander said. What the hell is
she doing out of her quarters? he thought. Then he saw
the bouquet of catnip in her hand and realized she had
been clipping it in the hydroponics room. Why couldn't
she send a 'bot to do that?

"Where has this pretty lady been hiding?" asked the
man named Sancho. "Come, little one, have a drink with
us." Apparently, the endearment was a standard one, or
else he was too drunk to notice that she was a head taller
than he was. He held out a bottle to her and went for a
sloppy embrace. Alexander cowered and covered his
head with his arms.

Rama bared her teeth and fanned her hair, exuding a
bitter scent. The instant Sancho was in range, she
squalled and the hand not holding the bouquet flashed in

a backhander too swift to see. The blow caught him beneath the jaw and lifted him from the deck, slamming him against the wall to drop in an inert heap on the carpet. There was a deep rumbling sound, and they turned to see Numa standing in the doorway to Rama's quarters. The bone-chilling rumbling was coming from somewhere in his larynx.

"Everybody just keep calm," Alexander said, barely whispering. "Don't nobody go for guns. You got no idea how fast these two can kill you. Rama, why don't you just go into your room and snort your catnip, okay?" With an annoyed toss of her head, she shoved past Numa and went inside. With a snarl, he shut the door.

Alexander let out his breath in a long, shaky wheeze. The others were bent over Sancho. "Is his neck broke?" Alexander asked, near tears. "The captain's gonna kill me for this."

"Naw, he's just drunk and rattled," Pablo said. To Alexander's amazement, they all started laughing up- roariously. They seemed to think the incident was incredibly funny.

"Sancho," Pablo said, "didn't you notice her belly? Don't you know enough to leave cat-ladies alone when they're pregnant?"

"Sancho don't never learn," said another.

"You mean," Alexander said, "you got people like her where you come from?"

"Not exactly," Pablo said. "But down in Yucatan, in the Maya country, there's jaguar-people."

"I hear Montezuma's got a whole bodyguard of 'em,"

said a man called Mateo. "Big, spotted bastards, is what I heard."

"I never seen any with stripes," Pablo said, "but your cat-lady must be a relative. That man of hers looks like he's half puma."

They carried Sancho back to the main salon where Haakon, Jemal, and Mirabelle were still talking with Villa and Fierro. Villa glanced at the half-conscious Sancho and frowned. "He better just be drunk. I won't have my men abusing these people's hospitality." Sheepishly, Pablo described the incident. "Scandalous," Villa muttered. "Captain, please accept my apologies. You may shoot him if you wish. I don't hold with my men troubling married women."

"Think nothing of it," Haakon said. "I'm just glad Rama didn't use her claws and only hit him with her left. Her right is really deadly."

Pablo explained to Alexander, "The chief is very strict when it comes to women. When he sees one he fancies, he always marries her. If she already has a husband, he shoots him first, because adultery is a sin."

"I think, Captain," Villa was saying, "with this ship, you could help us a lot in getting the revolution going again. It's been kind of slow lately. It always is when that bastard Zapata goes back home to Morelos to sulk. Something like this would not only win battles for us in the north, it would get him back out of his canebrakes and onto the battlefield again."

"I'd just love to help, General," Haakon said, "but we really must locate our lost brethren. If you could help us do that, I might give your suggestion deeper consideration." He watched as Villa turned it over in his obviously very capable mind. The man was crude and overbearing, but nobody rode herd on a bunch like this without plenty of native ability.

"Let me return to my base and send some messages," Villa said. "Will you stay here for twenty-four hours? I may have some information for you by then."

"My word of honor, General," Haakon said.

Villa and his men clumped and rattled out to their ship and Haakon watched through one of the salon's ports as the adobe ship cast off and drifted away. As the impossible craft turned away, he saw a cluster of gaping, almost formless clay pipes sticking out of its rear. The pipes belched flame and clouds of dirty-white smoke and the ship tore away at incredible speed.

"What powers it?" asked Jemal, wonder in his voice.

Soong's voice, coming from the bridge, answered him. "It is powered by crude gunpowder."

# Nine

"WHAT DO WE KNOW SO FAR?" JEMAL ASKED. THEY SAT in the salon, comparing notes. Villa's ship had been gone for an hour and there had been no further contacts from the planet.

"All I was able to find out about a historical General Francisco Villa," Mirabelle said, "was a brief reference to one of that name involved in a series of civil wars in Mexico in the second decade of the twentieth century. It was a pretty obscure time and place, and all I could find was that he was part bandit and part revolutionary, also a popular hero who engendered a sizable body of folk-lore."

"And the other people he mentioned?" Haakon asked. Mirabelle had raided the ship's computer searching for correspondences with such skimpy information as they had.

"Nothing of a Felipe Angeles. Emiliano Zapata existed, doing much the same thing in the south of Mexico as Villa in the north. Carranza and Huerta were Federal generals who briefly became presidents of Mexico, as did both Villa and Zapata. That's all I could find on them. There was nothing about Redflaggers. There was a personage called the Kaiser at that time. He was the Emperor of Germany, and there's a great deal about him, but I could find nothing involving him with Mexico. I've set the computer on auto-search for further correspondences."

"What about Montezuma?" Jemal asked.

"That's a puzzler," she said. "It was a name common among the Aztec rulers of Mexico, but that rule and the name died in the sixteenth century, long before Villa's time. It comes in a number of spellings and pronunciations: Montezuma, Moctezuma, Mehocetuzhoma, and several others. The version Villa uses was the one used most outside of Mexico."

"Excuse me," Sarai said, "but why should these people have names from Earth's history at all?" She had viewed the visit from her quarters, trying to get over the culture shock of her life. She felt a little better now.

"You've got to understand," Haakon said, "these places in the Cingulum didn't just happen, they were *built*. For some time now, the Cingulans have been collecting humans who have wandered in and stripped their memories. They are fascinated by our history, and especially by our myths and legends. They don't just get conscious and subconscious memories, they can peel the ancestral memories right off your genes. Then they have fun with them. What we have here is a world that's impossible in our own universe, complete with its own history going back millions of years, for all we know."

"Time doesn't have the same meaning here," Jemal said. "That planet and whoever is on it may have been around for as long as Earth. Or it might have been put together just for our arrival. They can do damn near anything. But they don't seem to just copy from our history or myth. They take things they find intriguing and play with them. God knows what we'll find down there on the planet if we descend, but it'll be real and dangerous."

"Maybe we won't have to go in," Mirabelle said. "With luck, we might be able to take care of our business from here in orbit."

"Dream on," Jemal said.

"Ever the pessimist," she said.

"Alex," Haakon said, "let's see your loot." Alexander picked up a pile of miscellaneous items: coins, knives, a belt and holstered pistol, a pair of spurs with one broken rowel. Haakon sorted through the coins first. One was a big gold piece with a stylized portrait of a personage in an elaborate feather headdress. "I suppose this is Montezuma," he said. Other coins were of silver and copper and bore portraits and symbols. Lettering indicated a number of nations and languages. "Mirabelle, feed these into the computer and see what we get." She took the coins and began to process them with a handset.

Haakon then turned his attention to the pistol. The design looked crude, but its lines were graceful. Although it was heavy compared to his beamer, it balanced superbly. He raised it and aimed at a bust across the salon. The sights were crude; no more than a blade on the end of the barrel and a groove along the top of the frame, but it fell directly on target. The pistol was designed to be pointed rather than aimed. An inscription informed him that the arm had been manufactured by the Colt's Firearms Co., followed by a string of patent dates beginning in 1871. He tossed the hat Alexander had won across the salon, took aim at it, and pulled the trigger. Nothing happened. The trigger wouldn't budge. "How does it work?"

Jemal took the weapon and examined it. As the crew's official antiquarian, he was expected to know things like this. "Let's see, it's a revolver. That means the charges are in this cylinder in the frame." He took a cartridge from a loop in the belt and showed it to Haakon. "This is the ammunition. That conical hunk of lead on one end is the projectile and the brass tube holds the propellant." He turned it so that Haakon could see the flat base of the cartridge. In the center of the base was a tiny copper button. "That button is the primer. When a firing pin strikes the primer, the propellant burns and kicks the slug down the tube."

"What does it use for propellant?" Haakon asked.

"Originally, crude gunpowder. By the twentieth century, most firearms used nitrocellulose but here, who knows? That shot Villa's man fired didn't make much smoke, so it was probably nitrocellulose." He swung out a small gate on the side of the frame, exposing the base of a cartridge. With a little experimentation, he found out that, by pulling the hammer back until it clicked twice, the cylinder would turn freely. "That must be how it loads," he concluded, "and that rod under the barrel punches out the empty shells." He handed it back to Haakon. "On this model, you have to pull back that striker before it'll fire." He handed it back. "Here, now you're an expert like me."

Haakon once again took aim at the hat and thumbed back the hammer, producing the weapon's peculiar series of mechanical clicks. He pulled the trigger and there was an ear-numbing blast as the pistol twisted violently back in his grasp. The hat flew upward as the slug plowed a furrow along the hardwood floor, struck a wall, and ricocheted about the room, hissing and whistling, narrowly missing Mirabelle before it thunked into a bronze sculpture and dropped, flattened, to the floor.

"Will you cut that out, Boss!" Alexander yelled.

"Yes," said Mirabelle, unperturbed, "please commit your acts of vandalism where they won't endanger people."

"The 'bots can fix the damage," he said. "Probably could have fixed you, too." Nevertheless, he was chastened. The thing was far deadlier than its primitive appearance indicated.

"You ruined my hat, too," Alexander complained. The headpiece now sported two ragged holes.

"It lends it a certain character," Haakon said. He spun the pistol around his forefinger by the trigger guard. Its perfect balance allowed it to twirl freely. "You know, I'll bet I could get really good with one of these." The barrel and cylinder were blued by some chemical process and the frame was mottled attractively in subtle colors. The grip was of a yellow-white substance, the ivory or bone of some animal. He was immensely pleased with the look and feel of the handgun. By God, he thought, the Cingulans were really *good* at handling the ancestral memories.

"If you two are through playing with your toy," Mirabelle said, "would you care to see what I've learned from these coins?"

"Sure," Haakon said, holstering the weapon reluctantly. He really wanted to play with it some more, but business was business.

"This one," she said, holding up the big gold coin, "is, as you guessed, a coin of Montezuma, worth fifty pesos. This," she said, flipping him a silver coin, "is one dollar from the Confederate States of America, with a portrait of President Huey Long. We have a half dollar from the Republic of Texas, no head of state indicated, with a star on one side and a beast identified by our banks as an armadillo on the other."

"Very interesting," Haakon said. "But is there anything of importance to us?"

"I think so." Mirabelle tossed a flat, squarish coin to Sarai. "This is a coin from the Empire of Nippon. There is no portrait, but the inscription says that it was issued in the second year of the reign of Emperor Yoshihito, under the Shogun Minamoto Tametomo."

Sarai stared at the coin in disbelief. "It can't be him! He has only been here a few months!"

"You haven't been listening," Jemal said. "I told you that time has a different meaning here. Besides, not everybody makes it through unaltered. We've met people within the Cingulum who were acting out personae completely different from those they came in with. We could find your Tametomo, and he might have no memory of his extra-Cingulum life, even if he isn't the shogun on the coin."

"You've got to face the possibility," Haakon told her. "And our primary mission isn't finding him, it's finding a way to save Meridian from being holed to death."

"Isn't he the most likely answer?" she demanded. "After all, that was his mission as well, and he has had more time to find out, even if time is a bit different here."

"The possibility isn't enough to count on," Haakon said. "All we know for sure is his ship disappeared and didn't come back. We have to assume they're dead and proceed on our own. If our search leads us to him and the others, so much the better."

"Where did you have in mind to start, if not with finding Prince Tametomo?" she asked.

"We'll wait until we hear from Villa first. He's supposed to be making inquiries about the missing expeditions in any case, so we might be able to find out about your prince from him. I expect to find a little more about the local situation down there from him."

"Surely you don't trust him?" she asked.

"Are you kidding? I just want information from him. We're not establishing a deep, mutual confidence. I wouldn't turn my back on him, and I'm not so sure about you, either."

"Your faith is touching," she said heatedly. "How-

179

ever, I suggest we call a truce and cooperate. After all, you did agree to help me find Tametomo and deliver the Three Treasures. You made that commitment before you took on the mission for the Cingulum."

"We agreed to get you to the Cingulum, which we did. At the time, as you'll recall, we said that he might be dead or he might not be at the Cingulum at all. Well, we got you here. You insisted on coming along on this mission, to which I graciously consented. Besides, we have to find a way out of here and back to real space. If we don't, there's no way Tametomo and your Three Treasures can get back to Chamuka anyway. So let's keep a rational set of priorities in mind."

Further argument was cut off by the arrival of Villa's ship. Once again, Villa came stomping across the lock entrance, dusty and spur-jingling. Fierro followed as always, but apparently Villa now felt secure enough to leave the rest of his men behind. "Good day, gringo," he said jovially. "I think we got some good news for you."

"That's good to hear," Haakon said. "I hope you'll accept, as a token of our esteem, this little gift." He waved a hand toward a stack of packing boxes near the lock hatch. "Ten crates of prime root beer, brewed up by our very own synthesizer."

Villa beamed. "Many thanks, gringo. Now, you wanted to know about your friends. What we've been able to find out is, there was a small ship landed near the capital a few months ago. There were three gringos in it, and the ship was made out of some kind of iron and glass. They was arrested as spies and taken to the capital, where they are now in the pokey."

"Who were they supposed to be spying for?" Haakon asked.

Villa shrugged. "Could be anybody; the Kaiser, the *Tejanos*, the damned Chinese, for all I know. Smugglers and spies get nabbed every day. It's just that these were found in a ship made like yours, not out of adobe or wood like sensible ships. I figured maybe these was some of them you're looking for."

"It's possible," Haakon said. "It's worth looking into, in any case. Nothing about a bigger ship, though?"

Villa shook his head. "Not reported through regular channels in Aztlan. Who can say about across the border? If they showed up here, my spies would get the word to me."

"How would we go about getting an interview with the men in prison? If they're the ones we're looking for, I can probably demonstrate that they weren't spying."

"Well, gringo, that's a little problem." Villa took a bottle of root beer from a 'bot and swigged at it. "See, it's the Federales holding these people. If they was my prisoners, I'd be glad to let you talk to them, if I hadn't shot them already. Carranza's people, though, they ain't so reasonable. Right now they're on bad terms with just about every country in the world except the Germans. Strangers show up, they ain't very friendly."

"What's to stop us from shooting our way in?" Jemal asked.

Villa grinned. "That's the kind of talk I like. Won't work, though. See, the capital is also where Montezuma's got his palace, and he don't let nobody get within a hundred kilometers of the palace in no ship, especially not in a warship."

"How would he stop us?" Haakon asked. "French seventy-fives wouldn't do the job."

"Are you serious?" Villa said. "He's got *brujos* that can call up demons big enough to eat your ship."

"Wouldn't even burp," Fierro added.

"No," Villa went on, "you want to go see them, you're going to have to walk, or ride, or maybe take the railroad, and you're going to have to cross Federal lines somewhere between here and the capital."

"Hm, we're going to have to discuss this," Haakon said. "Gentlemen, make yourselves comfortable. We'll be back shortly." He called Mirabelle and told her to keep Villa company. "Alex," he told the monkey-boy, "try to keep Fierro occupied. See if you can get any information out of him. We don't have anyone for him to shoot and I don't think he has any other amusements. Try poker or craps, if nothing else, only don't cheat except to let him win."

He summoned Rand to the bridge and they went to join Soong, who was already there. "Villa tells us that Montezuma's wizards can destroy the ship," Haakon said. "I'm not buying that even here, but I'm not so sure about the gravity in this ridiculous place. Do we dare to take *Eurynome* over that—planet, for lack of a better word?"

"It would be inadvisable," Soong said. "She is not happy with ordinary gravity. In there, it is not possible to establish even a stabilizing orbit. The one-way pull within that cylindrical field would impose a terrible strain. The result might well be irreparable structural damage."

"Don't worry about structural damage," Rand said. "The Teslas would blow long before the ship started to come apart. All our troubles would be over then."

"Can't you keep the Teslas damped?" Haakon asked. "We're not going to be making any interstellar jumps in there."

"Tesla damping is a force-field effect," Rand said. "The power torus is still going full blast. If our systems are too strained and start to fail, the force field weakens and the whole thing goes bang. Take her in there, and that's what will happen."

"I might've known that we weren't going to do this the easy way," Haakon lamented. "Now we're going to have to go down there and walk. I hate walking."

Back in the salon, they found Villa and Fierro happily passing the time with dalliance and poker. "General Villa," Haakon said, "since it looks as if I'm going to have to make my way to the capital at ground level, how close can you get me to Federal lines?"

"Let's see." Villa took off his wide hat and scratched his head. "You could go down in my ship to my headquarters at Chihuahua. There you could take the railroad to Torreon. Federal lines start just south of there. Some of my people could get you over the mountains by a smuggler's trail to Leon. There you might catch a train all the way into the capital. Hard to say, though. The tracks get cut and blown up all the time. And once you get there, you might need some fancy talking to get you into the *calabozo*."

"Actually," Jemal said, "getting *into* prison has never been a great problem with us."

"I admire your courage, gentlemen," Villa said. "Any time you want to join the Northern Division, I'll give you commissions."

"You take on gringos?" Haakon asked.

"Sure, I got lots of them: machine-gun specialists, railroaders, engineers, things like that. I ain't prejudiced."

"We'll consider your offer, but first things first. I'll have to put my expedition together. What's our best bet for getting to the capital without trouble?"

"You better not go looking like foreigners," Villa advised. "You'll be stopped and questioned everywhere you go if you do. You talk pretty good Spanish, even if your lips don't move quite right when you do it. I'll give you *charro* outfits. A *charro* is respected everywhere he goes in Aztlan. Can you ride a horse?"

"After a fashion," Haakon said dubiously.

"Probably better stick to the railroad as much as possible then. Any *charro* can ride like a centaur. Those funny guns got to go, and the knives with the switches on them. I'll give you six-shooters and real knives. I know you can't help it about the bald head, but you think you can manage a mustache? It's kind of expected of a *charro*—looks more macho."

"I'll see what I can manage," Haakon said.

"While you're gone," Villa assured him, "I shall make it my personal responsibility to see that your ship and your ladies receive no molestation or discourtesy of any kind. I shall visit every day to assure this."

"I greatly appreciate your gallant offer, General Villa," Haakon said, not informing him that Rama and Mirabelle were the most unmolestable women of his wide acquaintance.

"If you'll excuse us again," Haakon went on, "we'll get ready. No sense wasting time. Alex, take these gentlemen to the billiard room and shoot some pool."

He put his expedition together while Mirabelle was making him up. She gave him short, coarse black hair and a drooping mustache like Villa's and darkened his skin. "Should I give you brown eyes?" she asked. "It seems to be the dominant color."

"No, I hate lenses. Villa's got green eyes, so blue eyes are probably respectable. I take it you're not going along?"

"Not unless you order it," she said. "I dislike primitive worlds and animal transport. Now, if we were going to Montezuma's palace to dazzle the nobility, that would be more my style. No, with your permission I'll stay with the ship and keep General Villa romanced."

"Looks like it's just Jem and me then," he said. "Rama's out, obviously, and Numa won't go anywhere without her now. They'd both attract too much attention anyway. Same with Alex. Apparently, people with tails are a rarity down there. Rand stays with the engines, of course, and I want you or Soong on the bridge at all times. Villa's being friendly now, but he likes this ship, and he looks like he's made a practice of appropriating other people's property. If he makes any funny moves, blow that mud-brick ship of his to powder."

185

"What about our wandering Bahaduran princess?" Mirabelle asked.

"Hm, forgot about her. She'd better stay here, too. She's too much of an unknown to take along on this type of mission."

"Please take her," Mirabelle urged. "I dislike her, and she reciprocates."

"Hell, I don't like her, either. Since when should I inconvenience myself for you?"

"Don't try to snow me," she said, forcefully implanting the last few hairs in his mustache. "You do so like her. You've always been a sucker for attractive women, and the more arrogantly they treat you, the more you're intrigued by them. It's a basic character flaw I deplore."

He admired his new hirsuteness in a screen. "Not bad. I look mean enough."

"By the way," she added, "if you're gone more than a few days, you'll have a new crewmate when you get back."

"What? Oh, my God!"

"I finally managed to crack the code she uses with her medbot. Partially, anyway. We can expect labor to commence in four or five days."

"Boy or girl?"

"That I couldn't find out."

"Either is going to be a pain. Well, I better go find out if Sarai insists on going along."

She did.

# Ten

THEIR NEW OUTFITS FELT A LITTLE STRANGE, BUT NOT nearly as odd as the Chamukan armor had been. The tight pants and boots were not unlike what Haakon was used to, although the trouser legs were split from just below the knees to accommodate the boots, and everything had that indefinable, handmade feel. His gray jacket was only waist-length, with long sleeves, and he wore a colorful kerchief around his neck. It took a little practice to walk naturally with the big spurs. The wide hat felt a little silly, but everybody else was wearing one.

The holstered handgun at his waist was identical to the one Alexander had won, except for a wooden handle. Its belt was studded with cartridges, as were the two belts that crisscrossed his chest. These held ammunition for the rifles Fierro had supplied them, lever-action Winchesters that seemed, to one used to beamers, to be atrociously complicated mechanical contraptions. Fierro had demonstrated that they were deadly and accurate to two hundred meters, though. The crude iron sights and missile trajectory took some getting used to. Jemal was unhappy at having to exchange his powerblade for a steel knife, but he satisfied himself that it was sharp enough to cut anything human quite efficiently.

Jemal was dressed identically to Haakon, except for color variation. So, to their surprise, was Sarai. Apparently, soldier women, referred to collectively as *adelitas*, were quite common in both revolutionary and Federal armies. Her only concession to femininity was a long skirt in place of the tight *charro* trousers. Villa had assured her that a woman in pants would be considered scandalous and get arrested, whereas it was quite all right for her to bristle with weapons and ammunition.

They had not had time to alter her features, but her Bahaduran physiognomy did not make her stand out here. Many of the people they saw had similar features. She had replaced her brown lenses.

The town was an odd collection of low adobe structures alongside imposing stone buildings. The baroque opera house was flanked by an adobe cantina and an equally humble livery stable. There was a broad central plaza where Villa's elite cavalry regiment, the *Dorados*, went through the evolutions of a drill. The drill was nowhere near as precise as that of some ceremonial units Haakon had seen, but Villa had been right: The men looked as if they had been born in the saddle.

"If we have to get on horses," Haakon said, "our *charro* masquerade's not going to fool anyone."

"Speak for yourself," Sarai said. "The Royal House of Bahadur were fanatic horsemen. I was raised on horseback, shooting a bow."

"I used to be on my father's polo team," Haakon said, "but last time I climbed on a horse I fell off and damn near broke my arm. You'd be surprised how much you can forget in a few years." Unless, he thought, she had been living on Bahadur a lot more recently than she admitted to.

"How many hooves did the horses have on Bahadur?" Jemal asked.

"One per foot," she said. "Why?"

"These have two, and little scales around the mouth, like reptiles."

"Gene manipulated?" she asked.

"You've got to stop thinking like that," Haakon told her. "There isn't a horse gene in those beasts. They're chimeras brewed up out of whatever the Cingulans use for protoplasm. When they don't have original specimens to work with, they sometimes get details wrong. That's why the people can look perfect, because they've had plenty to use as patterns."

"Well, if they're not people, what are they?" she asked.

Jemal shrugged. "People. Just because they were concocted in Cingulan vats or something doesn't make them less so than those of us who originally evolved on Earth."

"Only some may be Cingulans masquerading as people," Haakon added.

"Maybe all of them," Jemal agreed.

189

"This place will drive me insane," she said.

"It's happened," Jemal said.

"Come on," Haakon ordered. "Let's find that railroad station Villa told us about."

They stepped off the veranda of Villa's headquarters. Haakon stumbled as his spur caught a step, but they made it to the plaza without further humiliation. The calvary was raising a good deal of dust, but dust and flies seemed to be endemic to this region. Haakon rather liked the sound his spurs made as he crossed the hot expanse. He was forced to admit, without much urging, that he cut a dashing figure in this getup.

The train station was a long, one-story building of gray stone sitting on the edge of a complex of structures through which wound a number of parallel steel rails. Jemal, fascinated, went to study them while Haakon bought them tickets for Torreon. He had brought along a sack of the gold fifty-peso pieces, made up by their synthesizer from their precious-metal stock. He rejoined the other two in the cavernous waiting room.

"I'm told the train for Torreon is due in one hour, but it's usually at least two hours late and may not show up at all, the times being what they are."

"This could get tedious," Sarai complained.

"You asked for it," Haakon said. "You could be lolling in a perfumed bath aboard *Eurynome* right now."

At a news stand featuring foreign newspapers, Jemal found one he could read: a publication called the *Houston Lone Star*. There was a cantina attached to the station, and they sipped beer while they waited for their train. Haakon studied the posters on the walls, most of which were like the one in Villa's ship, displaying a man in a tight, garish suit getting dangerously close to a horned beast and waving a cape.

"I wonder what that's all about," Haakon said, gesturing to the posters with his glass.

"A sport called bullfighting," Jemal said. "I read about it once. I think it was invented by a man named Hemingway." He squinted at the posters. "I think the bulls back on Earth only had two horns, though, and no claws."

Eventually, their train arrived. They went out on the platform and Haakon stared aghast at the approaching locomotive. "Is that sheet-metal cylinder in front really full of hot steam under high pressure?" he asked Jemal.

"That's right. See all the steam escaping from around the pistons. It's one of the earliest forms of mechanical transport. I never thought I'd see one in working order."

"I wish I hadn't," Haakon said nervously. "That thing looks more likely to blow up than a Tesla in an energy storm. Let's take a car near the rear."

"I don't think there's much danger from blown boilers," Jemal assured him. "You're a lot more likely to get killed if the train jumps the tracks. Actually, though, collision with other trains was the main cause of fatalities."

Thus reassured, they climbed aboard, well back from the engine. All the compartments were stuffed with people and their livestock. Even the tops of the cars were crowded with travelers, mostly soldiers. Many of the cars held horses and one held a fighting bull. At the very end was a hospital car for wounded soldiers. With a hiss

191

and a rattle and a screeching steam horn, the train lurched away from the train station.

Haakon had been expecting, from the look of the contraption, a truly bone-shaking ride. He was amazed at the smoothness with which the train accelerated and the soothing clickety-click sound of the wheels passing over the rail joints. "This isn't half bad," he told his companions.

"The company leaves something to be desired," Sarai said. In the middle of the floor, two passengers had organized an impromptu cockfight. Feathers and blood flew along with excited bets. Haakon studied the combatants. Both were sturdy-looking birds, one with brilliant, metallic green plumage, the other black with red wings.

"Twenty on the green," Haakon said.

"I'll take that," said a neighbor. "Twenty on the black." After a gallant and prolonged fight, the green succumbed and its owner retrieved it to fight another day. Haakon paid the man who had accepted his bet. "You people getting off at Torreon?" the man asked.

"That's right," Haakon said. "We're going to visit a sick aunt." It had seemed a fairly original and believable reason for traveling.

"I hope we make it without trouble," said the man. He wore a business suit, dirty from long travel on the train. Besides the all-pervasive dust, cinders from the coal-burning engine kept blowing in through the windows. "I hear the Redflaggers have been raiding along the Chihuahua-Torreon line."

Haakon had learned that the Redflaggers were followers of yet another revolutionary chieftain named Orozco, whose revolutionary or Federal sympathies were elastic. There was black hatred between Villa and Orozco, no matter what the political or military situation of the country.

Haakon sat back in the rump-sprung upholstery of his bench and idly spun the oversized rowel of one spur. The landscape going by outside was sere and dotted with bizarre cactuses. It must be politics they're fighting about, he thought. The land certainly doesn't look worth fighting over.

Jemal was immersed in his newspaper. "It says here," he said, "that the Republic of Texas has launched what they call a 'skyship' made entirely of mesquite."

"Isn't that some kind of insect?" Haakon asked.

"Apparently it's wood. There's also some stuff about 'bandit Villa' and 'Head Greaser Carranza.'"

"Have you seen anything about the Empire of Nippon?" Sarai asked.

"Not yet. It looks as if the Kaiser and the Republic of France are about to go to war, with the Grand Sultan of Turkey and the Tsar of Russia on the sidelines, waiting to choose up sides."

"Wasn't there a British Empire back then?" Haakon asked.

"I think that was mainly a naval power," Jemal said. "Maybe, with no oceans for them, the Cingulans decided to leave them out. I'll keep looking."

"Have you ever seen country as awful as this?" Sarai fretted. "Or a world as backward?"

"A few," Haakon said. "Chamuka was one."

"It was a demanding world," she said. "But beautiful."

"And I'll take horses over turkles any day," Haakon said, "even if they have too many hooves."

"You two are going to attract attention if you don't keep your voices down," Jemal said. "Wait a minute, here's something about Nippon."

"What is it?" Sarai blurted.

"It looks like they're going to war, too—against Russia. Not for the first time, either."

"This seems to be a contentious place," Haakon said.

"If the Cingulans didn't want it that way," Jemal commented, "they sure picked the wrong species to populate it with."

"Nothing about Tametomo?" Sarai fretted.

"I'm looking. Take it easy, it's a long ride to Torreon."

The train stopped at tiny rural stations to take on or drop off passengers, at isolated tanks to take on water or coal, and at lonely spots for no apparent reason at all. Once they pulled off the main track onto a siding while a line of troop trains went past, flags waving.

"If the revolution's in a quiet phase," Jemal said, "this place must really hop when it's in full swing."

They were dozing in their seats, hours after sunset, when the shooting started. First they heard bullets coming through the thin walls of the car and zipping by overhead. Haakon jerked awake to see most of the passengers hugging the floor. He and his two companions, unused to this particular type of disorder, took a couple of seconds to do the same.

"You three must be sound sleepers," said someone

next to Haakon. It was the man who had bet on the black cock. "I hit the floor before I was awake."

Now he could hear riders clumping alongside the train, yipping and firing shots into the cars. From the look of it, they were deliberately aiming high. The train was screeching and shuddering to a halt. "What's this all about?" Haakon demanded.

"Might be bandits wanting to rob us. If it was Federales they probably would've hit us with artillery."

"Dammit," Haakon muttered to his companions, "we can't afford to lose that gold. It's got to get us to the capital and bribe some jailers. Get ready to shoot if they try to rob us."

After a few minutes, the hollering and shooting stopped and they could hear hoofbeats fading into the distance. People began to get up and brush themselves off. Livestock owners left the car to see to their animals in the stock cars. Haakon and Jemal climbed out of the car and went forward to the engine. They found the engineer and his crew dressed in overalls, standing around disgustedly and lighting up cigars.

"What did they do?" Haakon asked.

The engineer waved to his locomotive. Steam and water were leaking from dozens of holes. "Shot the hell out of my engine. It was Redflaggers, just wanting to cripple Villa's rolling stock. Could've been worse. Good thing for us they're short of dynamite."

Haakon scratched his head through the unfamiliar hair. "What do we do now?"

"Send a rider along to the next station," the engineer said. "They'll have to send an engine out from Torreon to pull us in. Get some flares out behind us so the next train don't pile into us. You might as well make yourselves comfortable. We're not going anywhere until dawn.''

People already were spreading blankets on the ground beside the train, kindling brushwood fires. They preferred the open air to the stifling interior of the passenger cars. All sorts of ferocious noises were coming from the car which held the fighting bull. Haakon concluded that anybody who tanlged with such a beast armed only with a cape and a sword had to be crazy.

The three decided to follow suit. Might as well get used to the exigencies of life in Aztlan. They spread their ponchos and stacked their rifles and ammunition belts. Haakon took off his gunbelt and arranged it beside him with the pistol butt handy, then he lay back and tilted his hat over his eyes. "Might as well get some sleep, people," he said. "It looks like we have a long, long trip ahead."

It was well after sunup when the engine came out from Torreon to tow them in. By that time, there were two other trains stopped behind them. The mishap had been turned into somewhat of a social occasion, as people visited back and forth between the trains, and the soldiers on top told lies about the Redflaggers they had shot. As far as Haakon could determine, nobody had even been injured in the little shooting incident, either a sign of the inefficiency of the weapons or the halfheartedness of the combatants. Haakon had a suspicion that many of Villa's men doubled as Redflaggers or Federales and vice versa. It was often that way in a confused, drawn-out civil war.

Torreon turned out to be a town much like Chihuahua, but the surrounding countryside was far more lush and green. It was good farm land, and Haakon thought he saw vineyards on some of the hillsides. There was a range of low mountains to the south, which was the direction toward the center of this disc-shaped planet. In the far distance, he could see something that looked like a pyramid.

They tramped through muddy streets from the train station to the house where they were to meet Villa's agent. The adobe walls all over the town were pocked with bullet holes. This town had been fought over many times and taken repeatedly by a number of armies. The house they sought was in a poor section of town near the fragrant stockyards. It was surrounded by a wall topped with broken glass. Haakon knocked at a wooden gate with an eye-level portal closed by a shutter. The shutter opened and a villainous face glared out through the close-set iron bars.

"What do you want?" asked the face.

"Pancho sent me," Haakon said.

"They all say that. Most of them, I shoot."

"Well, this particular Pancho says you should help us or he'll find somebody else to smuggle his gold from Torreon to Leon."

"Oh, well, that's different. Come on in." He opened the gate and lowered the huge pistol he had been holding just below the portal. Two vicious-looking dogs stood

197

behind him, and there was a man on the roof of the house with a rifle and a pair of binoculars.

"You can't be too careful. I'm Cuervo, a long-time and enthusiastic supporter of General Villa. And who might you be?" He led them through a low door into the house. The outside looked like a slum, but inside it was richly furnished. Cuervo had done well out of the revolution.

"I'm Chacon, and this is my friend Jaime. The lady is named Sara." These were the closest equivalents of their names they could find.

"My house is your house. I will have dinner prepared for you and get the bathhouse warmed up. What service is it that the esteemed General Villa wishes me to perform for you?"

"Just to get us over the mountains to Leon, through Federal lines. We'll take it from there." Haakon sat in a chair upholstered in rich velvet. He wondered if it was from the mayor's palace that Villa's men had talked about looting.

"Nothing simpler," Cuervo said. "I have a pack train leaving this very night. You understand, my mules are very sensitive to bright sunlight, so we always travel after dark."

"I understand perfectly," Haakon assured him. "My own business affairs frequently take place outside regular working hours."

The bathhouse was a small hut filled with steam. A curtain divided the single room into two parts. Haakon and Jemal scrubbed down on one side of the curtain, Sarai on the other.

"I don't like his looks," Sarai said through the curtain. "I don't think we should trust him."

"You don't like anybody's looks," Haakon said. "And we've got no choice but to trust him, within limits. Maybe he's a double-dealing rat, but I can't see that he has anything to gain by selling us out. Hell, who'd be buying? Nobody's looking for us here. You saw the inside of his house. He's made a good thing out of running contraband for Villa. Why should he endanger a sweet arrangement like that?"

"You seem to have an intimate understanding of the mind of a smuggler," she said.

"Of course I do!" Haakon bellowed. "I'm a smuggler myself!"

"Now, now, Hack," Jemal soothed. "You promised me you wouldn't let her make you mad."

"That was before I got to really know her. I'm going to go over there and flog her butt with my gunbelt."

"You stay on your side of the curtain!" she yelled.

"If you're nice," he said, "and promise to quit riding me, I'll take the cartridges out of it before I spank you."

"Keep away from me!" she warned. "If you stick your face around this curtain, I'll put a bullet through it." They heard the clicks of a pistol being cocked. She meant it.

"You're not supposed to take your guns into the steam bath," Jemal said. "I don't think these people have rust-proof alloys."

They called the feud to a halt for a few minutes while two old women came in with red-hot stones from the oven. They poured water onto the stones and dense

199

steam billowed through the room. One left a basket containing bottles of chilled beer.

Jemal passed a bottle around the curtain, and Sarai took it. "You two remind me of me and my little sister when we were around ten years old," he said. "We fought all the time, too. We outgrew it by the time I was twelve."

"She always starts it," Haakon grumbled.

"He's impossible," Sarai said.

"And I thought things might go easy without Rama along with us," Jemal lamented. "I should've known better."

After they were washed up and in relatively clean clothes, they were in a much better frame of mind when dinner was served. It consisted of crushed beans, cheese, ground meat, and chopped vegetables with stacks of flat maize cakes on the side. Although the ingredients were extremely simple, everything had been highly seasoned and they found all of it delicious.

"We set out three hours after sundown," Cuervo said. "Dress warm; it gets cold in the hills at night. We're carrying nothing across the mountains. I pick up my load on the other side."

"That's good to know," Haakon said. After the authorities, hijackers were the bane of smuggling. Nobody would be interested in hitting Cuervo's train until after they had left it. "Where do we run into Federal lines?"

"There's no real line," Cuervo explained. "This side of the mountains is Villa and Orozco territory; the other side is Carranza territory. There're no checkpoints except along the main roads and the railroad. What we have to watch out for is roving patrols in the hills.''

"What do we do if we encounter one?" Jemal asked.

"If we see them first, we get real quiet and close to the ground. My mules are well trained—they won't give us away."

"And if they see us first?" Haakon asked.

"Then we got to talk to them. How good are you at looking innocent?"

"Out of practice," Haakon said. "But, if we're not carrying contraband going in, they'll have no grounds for stopping us."

"They'll know that we ain't going through the mountains because we find the road boring. I'll be lucky if they just confiscate my mules."

"Sometimes official people get reasonable when they see money," Haakon suggested.

"If you got it," Cuervo said solemnly, "keep it out of sight, because they'll kill you for it."

"Rough games you play in these parts, friend," Jemal said.

"It's rough times," Cuervo said, exposing gold teeth in a wide grin, "but it has its good points." He waved around at the expensive furnishings of his house.

There were insects buzzing and chirping as they went out of the house. In the distance, dogs were barking at nothing in particular. The chickens were roosting, and honest people were in bed. It was times like these, Haakon reflected, that people like him and his friends went to work. They had napped after dinner, facing a long, nighttime trek.

The train of long-eared beasties was waiting for them in a pen near the stockyards. Cuervo's workers had already put the empty packs on some of the animals, and saddled those that were to be ridden. Haakon went up to one and studied it. The light was dim, but he could see that its rear hooves were cloven. The front feet looked like they had claws. The animal cocked its long ears toward him and studied him with equal suspicion. Apparently, he didn't scare it much, because it lost interest before he did.

"We leave Torreon by a dry wash that'll keep us out of sight all the way to the foothills," Cuervo explained. "Once we're in the hills, the brush is pretty thick, so we don't have much chance of being spotted except by mounted patrols. Before first light, we camp in a hideout I got. Tomorrow night we go on and by morning we'll be in Leon. There you're inside Federal lines and you can go about your business."

"That sounds good to me," Haakon said. A man whose face was invisible beneath his wide hat brought a saddled mule to Haakon, and he mounted. He hadn't been on any kind of horse in years, not even an artificial one like this. He was not comfortable but he figured he could get used to it. It might be good practice to ride an easygoing mule for a while, in case he should be called on to ride one of the fiery beasts such as he had seen Villa's men riding. The mule twisted its head back and tried to bite his leg, so he rapped it between the ears with his knuckles. Maybe it wasn't so easygoing after all.

They set out with Cuervo in the head, the other mules following silently. The gait of the animals was subtly different from anything Haakon had ever ridden, and the front feet and back feet made differing sounds. It was odd but the rhythm was hypnotic, and he found himself nodding off before they had been on the trail for an hour. He shook his head to clear his senses. It wouldn't do to let his guard drop so easily. They would be up to the hills soon, where there might be danger. He made sure his rifle was loose in its scabbard beneath his right leg, then did the same for his pistol. He didn't have much faith in the weapons and wished he had his beamer and power-blade back, but if his adversaries had only crude weapons, he had little to complain about.

The long climb began around midnight. The gait of the mules changed as they began to lurch uphill, their odd but sure feet finding easy purchase along the dark, rocky trail. Soon they were hemmed in by heavy growth, indistinct in the gloom but seeming to run heavily to spiky, knife-edged shrubs that looked as if they would be unpleasant to fall into. There was a spicy scent on the warm breeze, an amalgam of the scents of local vegetation over the smell of the mules. They might have split hooves and claws, Haakon thought, but they sure smelled like ordinary mules.

The breeze grew cooler, and Haakon took his hat off and put on his poncho, a garment that was no more than a blanket with a slit in its center to go over the head. With his hat back on, he scanned the skyline for sign of patrols. Nothing. He found himself nodding off again. Abruptly, he jerked as there was a hideous squalling sound and the mules began to bray in panic. He reached for his rifle, then had to use both hands to hold himself in the saddle as his mount began to buck and twist. There was a clattering of brush and rocks off to their left as something large squalled once again, then loped away.

It took at least ten minutes for Cuervo to get all the mules under control again. "Damned puma!" he said. "If there're patrols out tonight, they could hear us a mile away. We got to move cautious now. If we spot anything, we turn around and head back for Torreon."

"You can go back," Haakon told him, "but we're going on, seen or unseen. We have a mission to accomplish and our time is running short."

"Fight your way through, just the three of you, huh?" Cuervo cackled with glee. "No wonder Pancho likes you crazy gringos—you three are just like him!" His chuckling subsided and he listened attentively for a while. "All right, looks like no Federales got wind of us just yet. Let's go on while our luck holds." They set out again, higher and later into the night.

# Eleven

MIRABELLE JERKED AWAKE SO SUDDENLY THAT, FOR A moment, she couldn't remember where she was. For the first time in years, her technothief's equilibrium was upset, mainly by the sheer volume of noise coming from everywhere. Buzzers buzzed, bells donged, sirens emitted banshee wails, and her bed was giving her a series of sharp thumps in the behind. She had never dreamed the ship had so many alarm systems.

Tumbling out of her now-hostile bed, she hit the deck on all fours and began frantically pulling on clothes, muttering dire curses of the revenge she would take if this were just Rama's way of announcing the arrival of her firstborn. The alarms were still going when she lurched out into the corridor, headed for the bridge. Alexander came barreling out of another door in front of her, and they collided.

"Alex, what the hell is going on?" she demanded as they untangled their various appendages.

"Beats me. I'm headed to the bridge to find out, just like you."

Soong was on duty on the bridge. When they arrived, he was trying to find some kind of control to shut off the awful noise. There was no sense trying to carry on a conversation until that was accomplished. Eventually, Mirabelle solved the problem with a simple voice command to the ship's computer. Their ears continued to ring in the sudden silence.

Rama's snarling face appeared in the holo tank. "Give me a good reason for this disturbance before I kill you all!" she yowled. Her face was drawn and covered with sweat. This had not been a good moment to disturb her.

"A ship is approaching," Soong said, "and it isn't that mud-brick atrocity of General Villa's. It may be we are under attack."

Rama's face sobered instantly. "Attack is rarely an equivocal concept, at least between ships. What do you mean?" It was clear that she was speaking through a veil of great pain.

"No shots have been fired," Soong said, simultaneously reading current symbols as they rose from the console, "and there have been no beams or missiles. However, our offensive and defensive systems are being probed by some force which so far defies analysis."

"That explains all the alarms going off at once," Mirabelle said. "What about this ship?"

"We're getting visual now," Soong said. "Rama, I'll relay this to your holo tank."

"Damn!" Alexander swore as the image took shape. "Ain't that pretty?"

"I must devote more time to your education, Alex," Mirabelle said. "That thing is baroque to the extent of vulgarity."

"Barbarous," Soong concurred, "but impressive."

"I like it," Rama pronounced. "Why did it have to show up when I'm in this condition? These should be guests worth receiving." Her face spasmed with unendurable pain and she let out a frightening squall. "You'll have to handle it," she said when she had breath again. "I have to sign off for a while." Her pain-wracked face winked out.

In appearance, the "ship" was a sort of flying pyramid. Its tiers blazed with marble and precious metals. Colored smoke rose here and there from what appeared to be altars set amid gardens growing on broad terraces. Crowning the pyramid was a complex of buildings covered with gold.

"Just what you would expect to come flying off a flat planet," Soong said. "In this place, ships are designed by insane architects."

"Villa's men were wrong," Mirabelle said. "It's not solid gold, just gilded on top."

"Better stop admiring their ship and figure out what it's doing to ours," Alexander advised.

"Excellent idea," Soong said. He ran his fingers over a control panel and studied his results. "Something is retarding all instructions to our weapons systems."

Mirabelle tried motion controls and frowned at the results.

"Rand," she called, "what's happening down there?"

"I wish you'd come down and look," said the engineer's metallic voice. "A description really doesn't do it justice, and a holo image wouldn't convey the true impact."

"Uh-oh," said Alex.

"We might as well," Soong said. "We're doing no good here."

Silently, they trooped from the bridge, down the companionway to the main salon, past the crew quarters and recreation rooms, past the hatches to the small cargo holds, the hydroponics, the machine shops and robot laundry, and finally to the holy precincts of the engine rooms. Rand met them at the barrier hatch.

"There I was," he explained, "minding my own business, keeping the Teslas damped like the captain ordered, with half an eye screen on the holo of that ship out there, when what should show up unannounced?" He jerked a metal-sheathed thumb at the area where, on ordinary days, the humped forms of his Tesla engines were the largest objects to be seen. Today was different.

Coiled completely around the whole engine complex, nearly filling the engine room from bulkhead to bulkhead, was an immense serpent. It was not of the usual, scaly variety but was instead covered with feathers of eye-searing brightness and riotous colors. An especially spectacular feather ruff surrounded its head, which was as large as a human body and rested on one of the lower coils. The huge, saucer-shaped eyes were set directly in front, above its snout, watching them with amusement.

The surprisingly mobile face grinned, exposing a whole mouthful of half-meter-long teeth.

Soong cleared his throat with some difficulty. "Are you someone we should communicate with?" he asked. The serpent said nothing, and Soong turned to the others. "It is always a good idea to be polite to dragons."

"That's what I always say," Alexander said, looking a little sickly. He took a few tentative steps toward it. "You know, you gotta be careful with the Teslas. They're—" It flicked out a long, forked tongue at him, and he jumped back. "Don't talk a whole hell of a lot, does he?"

"I don't think he's a messenger," Mirabelle said. "Soong, you'd better get back to the bridge. I'll join you there in a few minutes."

"What'll you be doing in the meantime?" Alexander asked.

"Getting properly dressed, of course."


"They are taking their time in opening communcations," Soong said. It had been more than an hour since the ship arrived in their tank. It was now floating within a few hundred meters and was more than a bit intimidating so close. Its base was nearly a kilometer on a side. Now they could make out some of the mosaics covering the vertical walls of the rising terraces. They could see people walking about or standing, some in military-style formation, but they could make out no details at such a distance.

"Maybe we should try first?" Alexander hazarded.

"Never," Mirabelle said. "In polite society, it is

incumbent upon the attacking party to establish a dialogue. That goes even here. Besides, it would be embarrassing to try to call only to find out that they control the communications as well."

She hid her anxiety well, but it set her nerves on edge to know that an unknown party had control of any of *Eurynome*'s systems. The ship had become their world, and it was very nearly impregnable. She had always been proof against human tampering, but things didn't always work out that way within the Cingulum.

"I suspect," said Soong, "that they are busily analyzing us. Remember, our ship is as bizarre to them as theirs is to us. I would love to have an analysis of whatever it is that holds that thing up. No anti-grav we've ever developed will support more than a few tons."

"Wouldn't do you no good when we got back to real space," Alexander said. "It's got to be something as crazy as that flat planet or Villa's gunpowder-driven ship."

"I suppose so, but—" he stopped abruptly as a low note of uncertain origin sounded through the bridge.

"That sounded like a conch shell being blown," Mirabelle said.

"I shall take your word for it," Soong said. "But where is it coming from? Not over the ship-to-ship."

"Visitors," said a pleasantly modulated voice, "the Emperor Montezuma welcomes you to his domain, and hopes you have suffered no undue inconvenience because of our security precautions."

"We desire an explanation for this behavior," Soong said. "Our ship's systems have been assaulted in a most unprovoked fashion. We have done no harm, nor did we seek to flee at the approach of your ship. Why have you treated us as enemies?" He felt that a little bluster would do no harm just now.

"It is our policy to establish the origin of any vessel that enters our space before allowing it any kind of contact with Aztlan. We have been unable to do so with your ship. What is the origin of your vessel?"

"Just a moment," Soong said. "Upon arrival, we were met by a General Villa. We cooperated with him and assumed that he had some authority in dealing with us. Were we incorrect?"

There was a pause. "The status of General Villa must be discussed at some other time. We accept that you dealt in good faith. Now please inform us as to the origin of your ship."

Soong took a deep breath. "We come on a mission from the Republic of the Cingulum."

There was another pause. "Are we to believe that your vessel and yourselves did not originate on this planet?"

"You may assume that with perfect confidence."

Another voice came on, this one deeper and more melodious. "I'll take over now. This has become a diplomatic matter." Apparently, the second speaker was addressing the first. "Unknown ship, I am Emperor Montezuma the Ninth, Great Speaker of the Tenocha and Supreme Ruler of Aztlan. It is necessary that we speak as soon as possible. I propose to bring your ship to rest in a dock aboard my own. Is that agreeable?"

"Impossible," Soong said. "We would very much like to have a meeting with Your Majesty, but our ship is not designed for docking in a gravity environment. She would suffer irreparable structural damage, not to mention the disastrous consequences to the engines. I fear it is impossible."

"You need not worry," Montezuma said. "My wizards have performed a thorough analysis of your ship, and they have prepared a cradle in which it will be perfectly secure and happy. As for the engines, we have taken the liberty of sending a guardian deity to prevent them from becoming angry."

"Ah, yes, the great serpent. A magnificent creature but not, I fear, a damping mechanism of which we have experience."

"Have no fear," said Montezuma airily. "We are taking you aboard now. I shall meet you personally at the dock."

"So much for our fears of mortal danger," Soong said. "Are you ready, my dear?"

"As ready as I can be on insufficient data," she said.

Taking the fantastic craft confronting them as her cue, Mirabelle had constructed the most garishly stunning outfit she could dream up from the resources of her extensive wardrobe. As her main garment she wore a "Danae-Cloud," which consisted simply of a generator that surrounded her from neck to ankles in a veil of shimmering golden light. She was not quite visible beneath it and, as the light was equipped with artificial inertia, she always seemed about to step out of it, but it always caught up just in time. It had been extremely popular with herm courtesans a few years back. Her hair had been gilded, each hair individually plated with a molecule-thick layer of the metal. She wore metallic golden lenses over her irises and put on a good deal of barbaric jewelry and other ornamentation. Without Rama to outshine her, she had pulled out all the stops to impress their reception party.

"I wasn't expecting to have to vamp the emperor himself so soon," she complained.

"All the better," Soong said. "Possibly, we can get this matter settled while our esteemed shipmates are floundering about in General Villa's backward bailiwick."

"What about me?" Alexander asked. "You want I should go along with you? I get along with kings real good."

"Sure, come along," she said. "You're baroque enough to delight the most jaded monarch."

Soong was resplendent in a dress uniform for which he possessed no qualifications. Its decorations were made of spectacular gems and coruscating ribbons of brain-searing brilliance. His cape was lined with the nacreous fur of Pirian ice lizards, and his dress sword's handle and sheath were carved from solid jade. He had won the outfit from the doorman of a luxury hotel on Balder and saved it for just such an occasion. He pulled on his white gloves as they made their way to the airlock.

*Eurynome* was now under guidance of whatever power Montezuma's "wizards" disposed of and was drifting in toward a broad notch sunk into a side of the pyramid. On the screens in the airlock chamber, they could see a cradle made of a netting of gigantic ropes, which looked newly made.

"Surely that won't support *Eurynome*!" Mirabelle said.

"I would suggest," Soong said, "that if these people can make a pyramid fly, they can most probably dock a light cruiser in a net. There is nothing we can do about it, in any case."

Slowly, almost imperceptibly, the ship settled into its improvised cradle with no groans or squeaks of protest. Mirabelle glanced at Soong and shrugged. In its slowest and stateliest fashion, *Eurynome* opened its side hatch and lowered a long ramp until it touched ground. Rods rose along the sides of the ramp and extruded slender poles of bronze which met to form an elegant, latticework railing.

Facing them was a long stone stairway. A huge red cylinder appeared at the top of the stair, hesitated there, then toppled toward them and rolled precipitously down the steps. In moments, the steps were red-carpeted.

"Damn!" Mirabelle said. "We didn't think of getting a red carpet. And this was a royal ship, too."

Now a lone figure appeared at the top of the opposite stair. They timed themselves as precisely as possible and stepped off onto the ramp just as he stepped onto the first step. A few steps behind the descending figure came two files of strange-looking, uniformed persons, presumably bodyguards. Mirabelle had no attention to spare for bodyguards. She was busy storing and analyzing information about Emperor Montezuma IX.

He was tall and appeared to be about thirty years old. His hair was thick and black and his features were narrow, with medium-dark skin. An upper cape of white ermine spotted with black tails covered his shoulders, and from below it spread an undercape of brilliant green feathers. He wore a suit of shiny gray silk, its jacket bearing lapels of black velvet and its trousers terminating above shiny black shoes. His white, high-collared shirt had a narrow-patterned necktie, and across his waistcoat was looped a narrow, golden watch chain with a tiny fob. *Edwardian*, Mirabelle thought, *but we found no Great Britain here. Can you have Edwardian with no Edward?*

She read his bearing with the clarity of a trained observer. This was no usurper or puffed-up, fake monarch like so many. He walked with the confidence of a god. He made even the absurd juxtaposition of clothing look perfectly natural, as if he would be equally at home in a cigar-smoke-filled gentlemen's club or presiding over a human sacrifice. Now she noticed the bodyguards behind him. For a dizzy moment, she thought they were Felids, but then she noticed the tails. They were cat-people of some sort, but far more feline in appearance than Felids. They were covered with short fur, splotched tan and black, and they wore comic-opera uniforms with lots of brass buttons and tall shakos sporting towering feathers. Their weapons were businesslike revolvers and bolt-action carbines.

"Welcome to *Floating Mountain*, honored guests," Montezuma intoned. "I trust you have not been excessively inconvenienced by our invitation? The fact is, we couldn't let you just drift there in defiance of natural law and at the possible mercy of our esteemed General Villa."

"We are, of course, quite charmed to accept your invitation," said Soong, for lack of any viable response. "To tell you the truth, we weren't quite sure what to make of General Villa, or his rivals, in relation to yourself, so we thought it best to retain a diplomatic reserve."

"That was wise," Montezuma said, speaking to Soong but with his attention on Mirabelle. He took her hand and kissed it gallantly. She responded with a curtsey that threatened to drop her out of her golden cloud; it dipped in time to preserve modesty, but only barely. "Now that we have made contact, you need not concern yourself further with our squabbling generals. You shall be my guests and we shall learn of your place of origin and arrange for diplomatic relations. I may assume that you are diplomats?"

"We have no credentials to present, Your Majesty," Mirabelle said. "Actually, we are on a rescue mission. However, we are empowered by our government to make pre-diplomatic arrangements with newly discovered sovereign powers."

This was made up on the spur of the moment, but it was not a complete falsehood. In fact, the Cingulum was so anarchic that it was not unusual for its minions to invent official capacities for themselves. If everything worked out, these powers could be ratified ex post facto.

"Then we shall proceed on the assumption that you constitute a genuine embassy. That means I can throw a banquet for you. I could anyway, of course, but it's always good to have an official occasion the first time. Are you three our only visitors?"

"No," Mirabelle said, "the captain of our ship and two others went in search of our rescuees a few days ago. At that time, we thought General Villa was going to be our only contact. One of our number is about to have— well—I suppose you might say she's about to have a baby, for lack of a better term. Her mate is on guard over her. They're not quite human. Our engineer likes to stay with his engines, even if you have wrapped them in a snake. He's human, but just barely. That leaves us. I am Mirabelle and this is Soong."

"Charmed. And your official status?"

"At present," Soong said, "diplomats. The one rudely poking your bodyguard is Alexander. You may consider him minister without portfolio and nearly without conscience."

"What an amusing group you are. Most of the diplomatic corps here are a dour and humorless lot, but you'll learn all about them. They used to be more fun, but now they're getting ready to go to war with each other, so diplomatic functions have become rather chilly. You'll liven things up considerably and earn my eternal gratitude for doing it."

"We shall be honored to brighten Your Majesty's

days," said Mirabelle, remembering the ancient injunction concerning the gratitude of princes. He turned with the kind of gracious gesture that is possible only with centuries of royal breeding and led his guests up the long stair.

"Your ship shall be quite safe, under the authority of the captain of my personal guard. None shall be allowed to enter. And your—person of delicate condition, will she require the services of my personal wizards? They are expert at these things, having delivered more than a hundred of my own offspring. No losses yet."

"Ah, thank you," Mirabelle said, "but our medical, ah, machines are tending to her. She is in a condition which makes her more hostile than usual to strangers." More than a *hundred*? she thought.

"Medical machines? How droll. My wizards would never hear of it, I fear."

"Mind if I ask a queston, Chief?" Alexander chimed in.

"Please do," Montezuma said.

"What's holding this pile of rock up?"

"Why, spells, of course. My priests chant in relays to keep *Floating Mountain* aloft and on course. Direction control, needless to say, is performed by appeal to the appropriate stars."

"Needless to say," echoed Mirabelle, green about the gills beneath her makeup.

"I, in turn, was wondering what kept your own ship from disintegrating," Montezuma said. "We could detect no conventional wizardry at work, not even the faith factor that European ships utilize. And your engines! I confess, my wizards were appalled. Even the obsolete gunpowder drive isn't so dangerous. That is why we took the precaution of sending the guardian deity to keep the demon from breaking loose. You must come from an odd place if that is your customary means of travel."

"The universes," Soong said, "are full of odd places."

They entered the flying palace, an amazing warren of tapestried hallways, sinister shrines, drawing rooms full of overstuffed furniture, menageries where some of the caged inhabitants looked rather human, ball courts, billiard rooms, swimming pools, sacrificial altars, an observatory, gardens both indoor and outdoor, a trophy room full of skins, stuffed beasts, and human skulls, and an amusement room with a carousel and bowling alley.

They came to a portrait gallery, which Montezuma insisted they tour. At one end were sculptures and mosaics. Midway were oil paintings, which gave way to monochrome photographs. There were no holographs of any kind. Mirabelle stopped before a marble sculpture of a man whose face greatly resembled Montezuma's, but whose hair was longer. He wore a feather headdress and an elaborate loincloth with much jewelry.

"I rather expected you to look like this," she said.

"These days I only wear the loincloth on ceremonial occasions," he said. "This is an ancestor of mine. They were more uninhibited in those days. He boasted that he personally cut out the hearts of five hundred prisoners between sunrise and sunset one day."

"I do hope your religion is no longer so sanguinary," Soong said apprehensively.

"Human sacrifice? Haven't done it in generations, although rumors persist that some of the more backward peasants do away with an infant or two in bad years. Strictly forbidden, of course. No, our priests quit trying to bribe the gods and buckled down to the proper study of science back in my great-grandfather's day. However, since you come from some other planet, it strikes me as odd that you should have any preconceived notion of how I should look at all. How is that?"

"That," Mirabelle said, "is a long, long story, and should wait for the banquet. You are about to find out what a very odd place the universe is."

"I always suspected it was rather peculiar." Montezuma led them to a towering pair of doors and two of the jaguar-guards hauled them open. "This is the grand ballroom, and most of the diplomatic corps should be here to meet you and propose improper alliances. Pray do not commit yourselves."

The immense room was crowded, and all its inhabitants turned to face Montezuma to bow deeply as he entered, but their eyes were on the three who came in with him. The men looked calculatingly at Soong, then admiringly at Mirabelle. The women stared at her Danae-Cloud, looking at first scandalized, then fascinated, then envious.

"Jesus, look at all the uniforms!" Alexander said. "It looks like a doormen's convention in here."

Military uniforms did seem to predominate, along

with luxuriant mustaches. The uniforms were bright with colors and gold braid, ceremonial swords, and garish decorations. In accordance with some tacit understanding, people began to line up to be introduced, although nothing as vulgar as a common queue actually formed. It was a stately minuet of the pecking order. Position of birth seemed to come before diplomatic rank or importance of nation represented, although they had no way of judging this last factor.

"This," said Montezuma, "is General Helmuth Johannes Ludwig von Moltke, ambassador of His Majesty Kaiser Wilhelm the Second."

Moltke was an old and sick man, but his back was ramrod-straight even in a bow, and his heels were noisy. The ambassador from the Republic of France was suave and wore a row of military decorations on his tuxedo. Well down the line, they reached a man who was younger than most, in a blue uniform gold-braided across the chest, graced with white gloves and high black boots. His sword hung on slings and was far heavier than the court swords worn by the others. It had a long handle and rather resembled those Soong had encountered on Chamuka.

"From the court of Emperor Yoshihito of Nippon, we are honored by the presence of the Shogun Minamoto Tametomo."

Mirabelle managed to keep her jaw from dropping, and Soong made heroic efforts at inscrutability. Alexander hadn't even noticed, and was occupied in making salacious overtures to the wife of the ambassador from Austria-Hungary.

Tametomo was somewhere in his early thirties, as advertised, if this was the same man. He was tall and had hard, handsome features. His bearing was military, but it was more that of a highly trained commando than the military-school rigidity of many of the other uniformed men. He regarded them coolly. "I greet you in His Majesty's name," he said noncommittally.

They were introduced to a host of others, but one thought now predominated: how to get Tametomo alone for a few minutes? In this welter of soon-to-be-at-each-other's-throats diplomats, spending more than a few minutes in conversation with any of them would trigger suspicion in all, and accomplishing anything without being overheard would be impossible. Ah, well, doing the impossible was what they were noted for. So they told themselves.

There were a very large number of apparently minor states represented, some of which had names that sounded vaguely familiar, others completely mysterious and bizarre. Everywhere, though, were evidences of militarism, and a general air of chest-thumping and saber-rattling was the order of the day. There were snarls in the smiles that some ambassadors gave others, and a few did not bother to hide them. Everyone was effusively polite to Montezuma, and by extension to his guests, Soong and Mirabelle. Nobody knew what to make of Alexander.

"There is going to be a general bloodletting on this world soon," Soong muttered when they had a moment of privacy.

"It's what the twentieth century was noted for, is it not?" Mirabelle asked.

"True. Pity the sorry business has to be repeated here. One would think once was enough, even in a multiplicity of universes."

"Worse has happened since," Mirabelle said. "And we aren't here to influence internal affairs. Let them work out their own destiny. Our problem is to get Tametomo aside and ask a few pertinent questions."

"Where is Sarai now that we need her?" Soong lamented. "She might be able to recognize him. And she has the damned Three Treasures."

"I'm more concerned with the man in his putative capacity as leader of the second expedition into this place. I want whatever information he has, and I want to pick up the others if they're still alive and I want to get out of here. Even the real universe, complete with Bahadur and Timur Khan, is better than this make-believe fantasy."

"It isn't make-believe," he reminded her.

"I know," she said wearily. "Uh-oh, what's that kid up to?"

Alexander had cornered several of the female sevants and was regaling them with tales of his importance. Alexander loved attention, and female attention was best of all. Unfortunately, he was seldom content with mere female adulation. He was proceeding in his forthright fashion to more personal attentions when Soong hauled him away by one oversized ear.

"This is no way for a diplomat to behave," Soong chided gently.

"I was just being friendly," Alexander complained. "Ain't that what you wanted me to do?"

"I did not intend that you take my instructions quite so literally," Soong answered. "However, I now have another assignment for you. Go back to *Eurynome* and find out what Rama's situation is. You may be a godfather by this time."

"Well, I hate to leave the party, but if you say so."

Actually, he was already bored stiff with the diplomatic affair and was curious about Rama, but it never paid to seem anxious to run errands, because then people got in the habit of assigning them. He dropped to all fours and took off. He made better time that way.

He attracted some curious looks as he scampered through the hallways, but since all the really important people were still in the ballroom, nobody stopped him. The cat-guards eyed him for a few moments but, whatever else he looked like, Alexander didn't look threatening to even the most paranoid. Without Montezuma giving the guided tour, it took only a few minutes to get to the outside. At the top of the stair leading down to *Eurynome*'s landing ramp, he found somebody waiting for him.

What he saw at first was a bulky, looming form in a blue uniform, which he took to be one of Montezuma's guards. Never anxious to trade pleasantries with officialdom, Alexander darted to one side to pass around the man, but the shiny black boots sidestepped in front of him and he had to stop. He noticed the big sword dangling in its harness by the man's leg, and he looked up to see a serious face that he vaguely recognized from the greeting line at the diplomatic bash. It wasn't one of Montezuma's people, but he couldn't remember which country the man was from.

"I would like to speak with you," the man said. The words came across through Alexander's translator almost without accent or inflection, but he could see that this guy was agitated, although trying manfully to hide it.

"Sure, why not," Alexander said. "Come along. I got to check up on a shipmate. She's gonna have a baby or something."

They descended the steps to the bottom of the ramp where one of the cat-people was on guard. "The Emperor has ordered that nobody is to be allowed aboard the foreign ship." The words were hissed and gargled. The long fangs and narrow tongue were not well adapted for human speech.

"It's okay," Alexander assured the guard. "He's my guest. Nobody told me nothing about not bringing guests aboard."

The guard looked hesitant, then said, "I suppose it's all right. I was ordered to let no unauthorized persons board while the foreigners were away." He displayed the immemorial discomfort of soldiers whose orders had not been specific enough. At least, Alexander thought, this breed of cat-person didn't broadcast its discomfort with a disagreeable smell.

As they climbed the ramp, Alexander noticed that his companion was greedily devouring *Eurynome*'s lines with his eyes. He slid his hand along the bronze railing like a drowning man clutching at a rope. It was decidedly odd. They went through the lock and into the main salon. A 'bot came floating up and Alexander took the beer it held out.

"Order up. That was a pretty wet party back there, but here you can sop it up, and we don't expect you to be polite or anything. We believe in being comfortable here."

"No, thank you. I must ask some questions and it is unlikely I shall be able to get a private interview with your officers. This may be my only chance."

"Shoot. Oh, I'm Alexander. I'm sorry, but I didn't quite catch your name."

"I am Shogun Minamoto Tametomo of Nippon." He looked a little crestfallen.

"No kidding! You mean it was this easy? You're the guy we've been looking for!"

He looked stunned and confused. "Looking for me? After all this time?"

"Sure," Alexander said, puzzled. "According to the word we got back at Meridian, you and your expedition disappeared about three months back, standard."

"Three months!" Tametomo's face flushed. Yes, no doubt about it, this guy was agitated. "I left the Cingulum *fifteen years* ago!"

"Oh," Alexander said. "Well, in that case, I can see you'd be kind of pissed off. They tell me time works different here, but I never quite understood it. Anyway, it looks like you did pretty well for yourself, making shotgun and all."

"Shogun," Tametomo corrected.

"Yeah. I mean, the captain and Jemal and that lady from Chamuka went looking for the expedition that went in just before yours, and those guys ended up in the slammer."

"Chamuka," Tametomo said. "Did you say from Chamuka?"

"Yeah, that's where we were before we got suckered into this mission. Chamuka, I mean. Anyway, while we was there, we picked up this lady named Sarai."

"I never heard of her."

"Probably not. Anyway, she's not really Chamukan— she's Bahaduran."

"Bahaduran?"

"Right. A princess of the royal house, if you believe her. Anyway, she was sent out to find you on account of you're gonna be Emperor of Chamuka. If they find you, that is, which it looks like we have."

"I think I will take that drink now," Tametomo said. His hand shook slightly as he lifted the glass.

"Oh, hell! I just remembered I gotta check up on Rama. Hold it here just a minute, Chief. I'll be back." He left Tametomo looking dazed and staring into a half-empty glass of wine.

First he tried Rand in the engine room. "Hey, Rand, you heard anything about Rama?"

The engineer turned his visual receptors toward Alexander. "Not a thing. I've been keeping an eye on the snake, and the damned thing just keeps staring back at me."

"Could get tedious."

The feathered serpent flicked its forked tongue lazily. Alexander stuck out his own, then he darted back up the passage and stopped in front of Rama's door. He took a deep breath and rapped, ready to take flight the instant he was faced with hostility. To his surprise, the door opened, and Numa stood there, not smelling too bad.

"Who is it?" came Rama's voice from inside.

"The apeling," Numa rumbled.

"Ah, everything okay?" Alexander asked brightly.

"You may as well come in," Rama said.

Gingerly, Alexander edged past Numa and tiptoed into Rama's bedchamber. He didn't get to see this part of the ship very often. Rama was extremely jealous of it. He saw her propped up in the center of her huge bed, looking haggard but healthy. Her striped hair hung in lank strands, but a 'bot was working on it. She also looked a lot smaller than in recent weeks. She was holding some kind of bundle of flashy silk in one arm.

"Come closer," she ordered. "I am in a good mood. Admire."

He went to the side of the bed and looked into the bundle she held out. "*Gaah!* Twins!" Two incredibly tiny faces peered blindly from the bundle. Their eyes were so squinty that it was difficult to determine their color, but the thin fuzz on top of their heads was striped yellow and white. "Orange tabbies," Alexander said wonderingly. "Kind of small, aren't they?"

"They are perfect," Rama insisted. She beamed down at them and licked the tops of their heads.

"Boys or girls?" Alexander asked.

"One of each."

"Oh. I can see already they're gonna be loads of fun. Do they have names yet?"

"Not yet. That will take time and consideration." The infants began broadcasting a faint scent that Alexander recognized. When Rama shed that one, she was hungry. She opened her robe and let the babies nurse. "Now, apeling, tell me how you and the other bunglers have brought catastrophe upon us during my incapacity."

"It's not as bad as all that," Alexander told her. "The captain and Jemal and Sarai are wandering around on the ground somewhere, lost."

"That is good to hear," Rama said. "Their absence is always welcome, and with luck perhaps they won't return."

"Soong and Mirabelle are still hobnobbing it with the local bigwigs in the palace. Looks like the last big party before this whole silly planet goes to war."

"And I would have been such a glittering addition to so distinguished an assemblage." She sniffed. "Oh, well, they shall have to get along with that unattractive person. I had more important things to concern me."

"And we located Prince Tametomo. That is, I did. He's here, in fact. Things are a little funny, though. He's been here fifteen years instead of a few months."

"As I suspected, things are in chaos. I suppose they will all expect me to sort things out now." She turned to the 'bot. "Holo," she ordered. In the tank, her own image appeared, slightly magnified. Her hair was now in order. "Give me some time to apply a few cosmetics, then bring this Tametomo person to me."

"In *here*?" Alexander gasped.

"Surely you don't expect me to get up so soon and greet him in the salon. Yes, bring him here. I wish to speak with him. Besides, it isn't every day that we get a visitor who is a prince, if he truly is such a thing. Such a distinguished guest should have the opportunity to admire my offspring. Now go."

A few minutes later, Alexander came back in with the bemused-looking Tametomo. He made appropriate noises upon being shown Rama's new pride and joy. "My congratulations on your, ah, reproduction, Lady Rama. Now am I to understand that you are in some position of authority on this expedition?"

"I am now, in the absence of anybody else. They are all idiots anyway. None of them even smell good. Recently, I have been indisposed, but I shall be back to full capacity soon. As anyone can tell you, the full capacity of a Felid is an awesome thing to behold. Now tell me, you handsome devil, how did you get to be shogun or whatever it is of Nippon?"

There was a loud throat-clearing sound at the door as Soong and Mirabelle strode in. "Perhaps we should be in on this," Soong said.

"Who invited you?" Rama demanded.

"Shall I throw them out?" Numa asked her.

"No, this way I won't have to repeat everything to them."

Mirabelle ignored Tametomo for the moment and

delivered the necessary admiration of the cubs. She poked one with a finger and its tiny hand closed over the fingertip. The little claws were soft and bent freely. It gurgled and exuded a scent that was not altogether disagreeable.

"When do their claws harden?" she asked.

"Not for a few years," Rama said.

"That's a relief. Will their eyes stay blue?"

"Possibly, but they could be almost any color. I'm hoping for green; it goes so well with orange hair."

"This is supposed to be a rescue mission?" Tametomo asked.

"Only secondarily," Soong assured him. "You recall the hole in Meridian that you were to explore?"

"I could hardly forget."

"It is still there and getting larger all the time. This ship had no difficulty passing through."

"Still there," Tametomo said, "after fifteen years?"

"Did you say fifteen years?" Mirabelle asked. She handed an infant back to Rama. "This is going to take some explaining."

"Take it from me," Alexander said. "It ain't gonna sound any better after he explains." They ignored him.

"I have been here too long already," Tametomo said. "By now that guard may have reported that I boarded this ship. Or someone else may have seen. If I am aboard too long, plotting will be suspected."

"So what?" Mirabelle asked. "That bunch is so paranoid they'd be suspicious if you retired to a monastery. We have crucial business to discuss and damned little time to get it all accomplished. We have to pick up our captain and the other two, with or without the men they went out to contact, but mainly we have to find the answer to that expanding hole in Meridian. What about the other men from your expedition? Are they still alive?"

"All but two. They are all still with me. When we made the crossing all those years ago, we landed on this impossible world in the Empire of Nippon. This whole planet is an analog of Earth in the early twentieth century, but there are radical differences. Nippon was still under the last Tokugawa shogun, and Emperor Meiji had not dismissed him. Much of the restoration had been accomplished, but the samurai class had not been abolished.

"We were immediately taken into custody and questioned for several months. Eventually, we were allowed parole, and I became a close advisor of Prince Yoshihito. He was determined to carry on the work of defeudalizing Nippon. I kept my former crew as my personal staff, independent of the political factions within the court and government. The two who died were killed by assassins who worked for reactionary feudal lords."

"Do you think you can bring yourself to leave your cushy job and go back to the real universe?" Mirabelle asked. "Assuming we can find our way back, that is."

Tametomo smiled. "His Majesty already has my resignation. I have told him for years that the time is long since past to abolish the shogunate. If it will get us back to our native universe, I would make my resignation effective immediately. The question arises: Can we get back?"

"That is a tricky one," Soong admitted. "Did you come through a glass tube full of florescent neon gas?"

"A what? We passed through the hole in Meridian and found ourselves in what passed for orbit around this flat planet. Actually, it's not such a bad planet, although technologically backward. If only it weren't flat. I could never get used to that."

"I can understand how it could get on your nerves," Mirabelle assured him. "But your mission was to find an answer to the expanding hole as well. You've had, by your own claim, fifteen years to research the matter. Any luck?"

"I believe so. Conditionally, in any case. The problem is, I require an artifact that simply does not exist in this universe. Back on Chamuka, it was simply called the Jewel."

# Twelve

HAAKON SLAPPED SOMETHING STINGING HIS NECK. "Of all the damned things to copy efficiently," he muttered, "why did they have to get mosquitoes right? Blood-thirsty little buggers."

They were coming down from the hills above Leon. This country was wilder than that on the other side of the mountains, with prominent rock ridges separating valleys full of lush, near-tropical vegetation. And bugs.

"Cheer up," Jemal said. "These aren't a tenth as fierce as the bugs on Chamuka."

"They make up for it in nuisance value," Haakon contended. "This little expedition had better turn out to be worthwhile. So far it's been nothing but toil and tedium while we could have been taking it easy on the ship."

"It was your idea," Sarai said. "You insisted that we

had to come down here and sneak into the capital to talk to these putative Cingulan explorers."

"Well," he said, scratching his scalp, "maybe I did misjudge the time and distance factors a little. This place looked a lot smaller from orbit."

"And these beasts have worn permanent sores in some of my most vulnerable areas," she complained.

"The medbots can fix you up in no time," Haakon said. "Just as soon as we get back."

Absently, he rubbed his own sore areas, which hurt far worse than he would admit. He could barely walk and wasn't sure that he would ever be able to sit again. It wasn't that he minded suffering in the pursuit of duty, it was just that suffering should be more dignified. Thank whatever gods held sway in this universe, though, they were almost out of the hills. If they could just get into Leon, they could travel the rest of the way by railroad. Uncomfortable and inconvenient as that was, it was infinitely preferable to this.

Cuervo came back along the line of mules. "We wait here," he said quietly. "After dark, we go into the city. You'll be safe once we're in town. Nobody will give you a second glance then. I'll leave you at the railroad station, and you can make the rest of your arrangements from there."

"Sounds good," Haakon said, unutterably relieved to be able to dismount and rest his poor, aching backside for a couple of hours.

Gingerly, they climbed down and picketed their animals. With many a wince, the little group of three sat on the ground and passed a bottle to pass the time. If this place had a single redeeming virtue, Haakon thought, it was that it produced excellent tequila.

"Odd," Haakon mused, "but you get used to living high all too easily. A few years ago, when I was breaking rocks in the Bahaduran pits, this would have seemed like heaven—mosquitoes, saddle sores, and all. Running free in the hills, even with patrols to dodge, was my idea of the best life had to offer."

"Were you really in the slave pits?" Sarai asked. "Everybody who does business with the resistance movements claims to have gone through that, but I've never met anyone who really was in the pits."

"You can believe it," Haakon said. He held out a hand, palm foremost. She reached out and ran a fingernail down the horny plating of callus, producing a rasping scratch fit to raise hair on a corpse. "Jem was there, too," Haakon told her. He contemplated his palm. "The sledge marks are on the bones, too, I'm told."

"I wasn't there as long as he was," Jemal said modestly. "Hack was dumb enough to get caught twice. Once was enough for me, so I took up prizefighting instead."

"From what I've heard of the pits," Sarai said, "I'm not really surprised that you don't trust me."

"Don't let it bother you," he said. "I wouldn't have trusted you anyway."

"You—" A hand signal from Jemal shushed them both. There were sounds from nearby: a scraping of rocks and a slight, metallic clinking. Cuervo came scrambling by.

"Keep down and keep quiet," he whispered. "It's a patrol."

"Forget it," Haakon said. "They're all around us, sneaking up. Might as well talk to them. Maybe they're amenable to a bribe."

"Don't count on it," Cuervo said disgustedly.

A man appeared, striding up onto a lip of rock straight toward what had been their path. He wore a khaki uniform and high, dusty leggings. He held a pistol casually in a gloved hand. "Ah, if it isn't our old friend Cuervo from Torreon! You never know who you'll run into out in these hills. How good to see you, my friend."

"Greetings, Lieutenant Polycarpio," Cuervo said with a broad, gold-toothed smile. "It gives one a secure feeling to know that our soldiers are out on patrol, ever vigilant to apprehend malefactors."

"Speaking of such persons," the lieutenant said, "how does it happen that your pack train takes the mountain paths instead of the road, which is favored by honest men?" His grin had even more gold in it than Cuervo's.

"You know how it is, Lieutenant," said Cuervo, spreading his hands in a dramatic gesture for understanding. "In these times, a merchant has to pass back and forth acros Federal and Villista lines and be searched, and every time something sticks to the hands of the searchers. It is no way for a poor man to make a living."

"Well, things are no different up here in the hills, Cuervo, except that here we're more suspicious, naturally. Let's have a look in your packs."

"By all means, Lieutenant," Cuervo said. "Search to

your heart's content. You'll see that we have nothing to hide."

Cuervo's tone was nonchalant, but Haakon could see the sheen of sweat on his brow. Polycarpio's thumb never left the hammer of his revolver. Signals like this had far more meaning than men's words. Without moving, Haakon prepared for trouble.

"Keep them covered," Polycarpio said.

His patrol rose from their position among the rocks, six hard-bitten men in dirty khakis with short, bolt-action carbines. Some carried long machetes at their waists as well. They closed in, doubtless anxious not to miss their share of whatever the trapped travelers were carrying. That suited Haakon. If there was going to be a fight, he wanted them close. That way, he and his friends would have a chance of surviving. Rifle-armed men would have it all their own way at any distance.

Polycarpio made a perfunctory search of the packs. "So, you are going to pick up your cargo in Leon? I should have waited until you returned. But who is this?" He licked his lips theatrically as he eyed Sarai. "You don't look like most of the *contrabandistas* we get around here, young lady. But we'll get to you later. First, what's in your saddlebags?" He opened one of the bags and pulled out a silk-wrapped bundle. Frowning in puzzlement, he unwrapped the Jewel. "What's this thing?"

"A keepsake," she said, with no more than a slight shakiness of voice. "It was my mother's."

"Well, it's mine now, whatever it is. What else do you have?"

Haakon decided on one forlorn try. "Lieutenant, I realize that your government insufficiently rewards its faithful soldiers. It's that way everywhere. If you'll let us go on unmolested, I would be willing to improve your financial position. That goes for your men, too, of course."

Polycarpio smiled at him. "You carrying cash? That's good to know." He turned to his men. "Leave the woman for now, but shoot these men. Don't ruin the boots."

Haakon drew and fired, drilling Polycarpio just below the chin, then he turned and fired again before the man started to fall. The soldier nearest him fell, and he dived and rolled as a rifle bullet struck a rock next to him. Jemal jerked a soldier in front of him and stabbed him with his left hand as he drew his pistol with his right. He fired before his target got his carbine lined up. Cuervo hauled a pistol from beneath his poncho and shot a confused man who hadn't quite figured out what was happening yet, and Haakon shot the next to last soldier in the side just as Jemal was shooting the same man in the chest. The last man, standing farthest away, didn't even try to shoot. He began running, but he got no more than ten paces before Cuervo snatched up a dropped carbine and drilled him between the shoulder blaes.

Cuerevo dropped the carbine and scanned the six dead soldiers and their lieutenant. "Damn!" he said. "You men act like you been in this kind of situation before."

"More often than I care to remember," Haakon told him.

"Well, if you ever decide to take up the *contrabandista* trade seriously, you can always work with me. Right now, though, we got to hide these bodies and find their horses."

"Do we have time to do that and still make Leon before it gets light?"

"Sure, but you're going to Leon, not me. Soon as we have these stiffs stashed, I'm heading back for Torreon. No sense trying to make my run now. By tomorrow night, these hills will be crawling with Carranzista cavalry. I'll come back in a couple of weeks. You got no problem, though. You can be on the train and halfway to the capital before these men don't report in and headquarters gets suspicious."

Haakon turned wearily to see Sarai standing numbly, looking at him with a different expression. "What's the matter?" he asked. "This was no worse than that dust-up back on Chamuka."

She shook her head. "It's the noise," she said unconvincingly. "These weapons are brain-rattling. Besides, back there all I noticed was the cat-man. I didn't get a chance to see you at work."

Haakon shrugged. "Most people are good at something, I suppose. This is what I'm good at. Not the kind of thing I enjoy, but over the years I've learned to cope."

"So you have," she said. "Did anybody think to bring a shovel?"

The train from Leon was not much different from the first they had been on. They were nearing the capital, so there were fewer rustic types aboard, and more business types. There was the same rhythmic rattling, the same shower of sooty smoke through the windows.

Jemal had found another newspaper, this one blazoned with a red headline in six-inch type. "It says here," he reported to his bored companions, "that President Wilson of the United States, President Long of the Confederacy, and President Maverick of Texas have sent a joint expeditionary force under a General Pershing into Aztlan after General Francisco 'Pancho' Villa."

"So this country is at war with a foreign enemy for a change?" Haakon asked.

"They don't seem sure. There's so many governments here they apparently have to get a consensus. The Kaiser is trying to whip up a war against the Tsar, but the French say they'll declare war if Germany does. I don't know what these people would do for news if they weren't fighting or getting ready to."

"Anything about Tametomo or Nippon?" Sarai asked.

"No, just—hold on, he's here."

She shot upright in her seat and snatched the paper from his hands. She scanned the columns for a few moments, then handed it back. "I can't read this," she admitted abashedly.

"I could have told you that," Jemal said. "Now where was I? Oh, yes, here it says that Emperor Montezuma has been hosting a massive international diplomatic function, in hopes of bringing about a peaceful resolution of the seemingly insoluble conflicts which are leading to war among the major powers of the world—hah, big chance—the diplomats having agreed to meet here on neutral ground."

"Get to the part about Tametomo!" she hissed.

"Be patient, we won't be off this train for several hours. It says that although the Empire of Nippon has no alliances with any of the powers about to go to war, they have sent a mission to be in on the negotiations. The mission, in keeping with the belligerent practices of everybody else, is not headed by a member of the diplomatic corps, but by the supreme military commander, the Shogun Minamoto Tametomo."

"Now we're getting someplace," Haakon said. "Where is this grand diplomatic bash being held?"

"Aboard something called the *Floating Mountain*. The nature of the craft is not described, but it's supposed to be somewhere in the capital."

"We're not dressed to crash a really high-class party," Haakon said, surveying his dust-and-blood-stained *charro* outfit. "This was fine camouflage for getting here, but maybe we'd better get ourselves some go-to-meeting clothes when we hit the big city."

"How long is this mission to be in the capital?" Sarai asked, desperation edging her voice.

"The whole thing breaks up tomorrow," Jemal said, "but no word as to when the individual delegations leave."

"We'll assume they head for home immediately," Haakon said. "That doesn't leave us much time to get those men out of jail and weasel ourselves aboard this ship or whatever."

"Forget them," Sarai insisted. "Worry about them later. I must get the Three Treasures to Tametomo."

"You're assuming a lot," Jemal said. "We still don't

know that he's the man you're looking for. We're pretty sure that these two in the slammer are from the Cingulum."

"You go meet them," she said. "I'm going to find Tametomo. You two know your way around jails better than I do anyway."

"No arguing about that point," Haakon admitted, "but I'm disappointed at your lack of team spirit. Here we are, getting ready to do something daring, demanding, even heroic, if I may be gaudy, and do you want to help? No, you want to go off on your own and find your prince."

"I fully intend to," she said. "Whatever it takes to gain access to him, I'll do."

"Hell, you can kiss frogs until he turns up for all I care!" Haakon shouted. Heads turned to find the source of this unseemly outburst.

"Quiet, children," Jemal cautioned. He glanced out the window. "I think I see our *Floating Mountain*."

They pressed their faces to the windows. "Damnation," Haakon said, "what's holding it up?"

The pyramid hung above the volcano-ringed city at an altitude of about a thousand meters. They could see its base clearly, a featureless square of cut stone. The angle was not good for viewing the towering pyramid, but what little they could see looked lavish and unlikely.

"Not gunpowder this time," Jemal said. "Not enough smoke. Hell, maybe they use happy thoughts and pixie dust."

"I don't understand the reference," Sarai said.

"You're deficient in classical literature," Jemal told her.

"Don't mind him," Haakon said. "He's always doing that. Now that you've seen it, are you still confident you can talk your way onto that thing?"

"I don't know," she admitted, "but I am going to try."

"Give it a try, then," Haakon said. "But don't expect us to come rescue you when you screw up."

The train was pulling into an immense station at the base of a wooded hill studded with ancient, monolithic sculptures. Most of the station was taken up by a cavernous shed roofed with dingy glass and spidery wrought iron. Long fingers of brick separated tracks where trains disgorged their passengers, who filed along the brick into the terminal. They filed right along into the terminal themselves. Everywhere there were soldiers in the khaki or blue Federal uniforms, but nobody paid the slightest attention to two more *charros* and an *adelita* coming in from the back country for a visit to the big city.

The terminal was papered with posters, some new and bright, others tattered. There were posters for bullfights, posters for festivals, election posters, posters advertising everything from guns to shoe polish. Outside the terminal were clustered little stalls selling flowers, second-hand clothing, toys, and a multitude of other goods along with fortunes and spells.

They were in the market for higher-class goods, though, and a stallkeeper directed them to a thoroughfare called the Avenue of the Twentieth of Thermidor, where the expensive clothing shops were to be found. They took a rattling streetcar powered by overhead cables and got off at a square centered by a small, ruinous pyramid.

"Here comes trouble," Jemal muttered. A short, fat

policeman wearing a blue uniform wadded with gold braid was striding importantly their way.

"Hey, you three," he called.

"Us?" Haakon asked innocently, his hand near his revolver butt. Please, he prayed, no trouble *here*. We're so close.

"Yes, you. You can't walk around here wearing guns like that. Where do you think you are, in Pancho Villa's army? Keep those irons out of sight when you're in the city. You *campesinos* always think the capital is just another village." He snorted disgustedly through his walrus mustache.

"Easy, Chief," Haakon said. "We're just not used to the big city."

"Just hicks, that's us," Jemal said. They unbelted their pistols and rolled them up in a poncho. The rifles, still in saddle scabbards, apparently caused no offense.

"That's better," said the cop. "Now behave yourselves while you're in my city." He waddled away, lord of all he surveyed.

"Officious little prick," Haakon said. "How come, no matter how many planets I visit, no matter how many *universes*, for God's sake, I keep running into that little bastard?"

"There's probably a great philosophical-cosmological concept there, Hack," Jemal said. "Let's give it to the loonies at the U. of the Cingulum when we get back. The Cosmological Cop Theory or something like that."

"Yeah," Haakon said sourly, "when we get back. Come on."

They found a discreetly expensive shop with a French

name and walked in, causing a little bell to tinkle. A man with a tiny, curled mustache walked out, dressed in clothing so impeccably tailored that he looked like some kind of illustration. He clasped his hands together as he came from the back of the shop, smiling for all he was worth, then he saw them and the smile was replaced by a look of horror. The horror disappeared when Haakon dropped the heavy bag of gold on the front counter and told the man what they wanted.

It transpired that there was no such thing as a fashion shop that catered to both men and women, and this was a man's shop. The flunky directed Sarai to a similar establishment for women across the broad avenue, then he set to taking measurements. He was pleased at Jemal's excellent proportions, appalled at Haakon's extravagant musculature. He had nothing to fit. Haakon paid for the quickest-possible tailoring job. He had an important party to attend that night, he explained. The shop's staff got to work.

Four hours later, the three emerged from the lobby of their luxury hotel—bathed, barbered, and dressed to the nines. Haakon's drooping mustache was now curled tightly at the ends. His feet sported not only shiny, uncomfortable shoes but something called "congress gaiters." They had tucked their smaller weapons discreetly about their persons beneath their clothes.

"This is impossible," Sarai complained. "What if I have to run or fight?" Her clothing was so voluminous that not a square centimeter of flesh was visible from the neck down. Her dress was a mauve silk and only cleared the ground sufficiently to allow a partial view of her high-button shoes.

"Standard attire for the pre-industrial upper classes," Jemal said, lighting an expensive cigar. "It's designed to display the uselessness of the upper-class woman. Read your Veblen." He coughed and made a face at the cigar. "Why do they smoke these things? They smell awful and taste worse."

"Smoke it anyway," Haakon said, lighting up one himself. "It's camouflage." He got his first snootful of the horrid smoke and fought to keep from losing the elegant lunch they had just eaten. His eyes watered despite his best efforts. He took the thing out of his mouth and glared at it. "Well, maybe not everybody smokes these things. Fierro said Villa doesn't." He threw the cigar into the nearest gutter, where it was immediately snatched up by a beggar. The man stuck the butt into his mouth and walked away with a blissful expression.

"Come on," Haakon said disgustedly. "Let's go find the jail."

"You go ahead," Sarai told them. "I'm heading for the floating pyramid."

She carried a shoulder bag which the woman at the shop had said was horridly unfashionable, but she needed some place to stash the Three Treasures and her pistol. Her broad hat had a flimsy veil that did little more than make her features somewhat obscure. It made her expression no less disapproving. She turned away from them and began to make her way toward the center of the city, where the hotel clerk had told them the palace complex lay.

"Just us now," Jermal remarked.

"I know," Haakon said, following her with his eyes. "I'd just hoped . . ." he trailed off. "Ah, hell, let's go to jail."

They caught a streetcar headed in the right direction. It was primitive, but they had to admit that it was a hell of a fun way to travel. It was better than the railroad and didn't have all the smoke. Evening was coming on and bands were beginning to play, both indoors and outdoors, all over the city. For a country in the midst of an interminable civil war and which had just been invaded by a foreign army, Aztlan seemed determined to have fun.

They got off in front of a forbidding building that presented a tiny-windowed red brick facade to the square it fronted. A pair of blue-uniformed soldiers flanked the doorway.

"How do we get past the guards?" Jemal asked.

"Let's try walking," Haakon suggested. They crossed the square from the streetcar stop and walked through the entrance. As Haakon had suspected, the guards were for show. They did not even glance at the two well-dressed men as they entered. The interior of the building had no character except generic institutional. There was no decoration and the paint was flaking. A bored-looking man sat behind a wide desk near the entrance. He glanced up, then stood when he saw the expensive clothes and the respectable bearing of the wearers. "May I help you gentlemen?"

"Possibly so," Haakon said, remembering to make his manner businesslike rather than aristocratic. Jailers didn't like aristos, but they knew that businessmen meant money. It was that way everywhere. This place was pretty innocuous, but it made Haakon nervous anyway. He just didn't like jails.

"Would it be possible for us to speak to the director of this establishment?"

"What might I tell him is the nature of your business?" the functionary asked, all cooperation.

"We are journalists for the Paris *Gazette*," he said, naming a newspaper they had seen on a stand in their hotel. "There are two prisoners here whom we would like to interview."

"I shall speak to the commandant," the man said. "Please wait here."

"Easy so far," Jemal said.

"So far," Haakon echoed.

The desk man came back out. "The commandant will see you now, gentlemen."

They went into a large office behind the desk. Inside was another smaller desk behind which sat a gray-haired man in uniform. Next to the desk was a coat rack with a hat and a gunbelt hanging from its pegs. Over a stone fireplace hung two portraits. One was General Carranza, whose picture was everyplace, usually plastered over the visages of former presidents. The other was of a man in an ermine robe. That, Haakon thought, was probably Emperor Montezuma.

The man behind the desk stood and came forward, stretching out his hand. "Sergeant Gomez tells me that

249

you are journalists for a French newspaper. Welcome to the Benito Juarez Correctional Facility." He took their hands in turn, giving each hand the customary cop's once-over. "How may I be of assistance to you?"

"We have heard," Haakon said, "from a source in the north, that you have two prisoners here, men who appeared some few months ago, in a flying craft of unknown origin. The owner of my newspaper feels that there might be a story of some interest here, and sent us to interview them. My employer would be most grateful for any cooperation and help you might be able to give."

"I see," the commandant said and pondered deeply. "I am afraid I must disappoint you. These men are still under the authority of State Security, and as such I have no authority to allow them visitors, not even representatives of a distinguished Paris journal."

"That is unfortunate," Haakon said, "however, my employer has empowered me to be extremely generous in showing my appreciation for any aid in facilitating this interview."

The man stroked his graying goatee. "I see. Perhaps something might be done. Allow me to make some small preparations." He bowed grandly and left.

"Jackpot," Haakon said.

"I hope to hell these two know something," Jemal said. "If they've seen nothing but this lockup, they're probably as much in the dark as we are."

"Don't borrow trouble," Haakon said. "Maybe we'll at least be able to buy them out of this place. That's part of our assignment."

The commandant reappeared at the door. "If you

gentlemen will come with me, I have dismissed certain of the guards for the evening. I know that you will wish privacy for this interview."

"You are most kind," Haakon said. They followed the commandant through a thick, iron door into a corridor made up of barred cells. Glancing through the bars, they saw no prisoners in any of them. Their guide stopped at the last cell and opened it.

"You two have visitors," he called. Stepping aside, he waved Haakon and Jemal into the cell. "I can give you one hour," he said.

The two walked into the dim interior of the cell. There were two humped forms on benches at the rear of the cell. "Wake—" Instantly, Haakon knew that there were no men beneath the blankets. He did not even have time to turn before the door slammed shut behind them. When he did turn, he found himself looking into the muzzles of two rifles held by guards.

"You will now surrender your arms," said the commandant.

Haakon grasped at a last bluff. "Of course, Commandant. We have just come through unsettled country and thought it best to arm ourselves." Gingerly, he handed over pistol and knife and Jemal did the same.

"When you came into my office," the commandant said, "I found myself asking certain questions, such as: What kind of journalist has hands like a silver miner, without a single ink stain on them? What kind of journalist carries dagger and revolver, but no fountain pen or note pad? What kind of journalist shares an interview with a colleague? This is an important facility, gentlemen, which from time to time houses distinguished prisoners. As a result, journalists are nothing new to me, and I know the breed."

"Excellent questions, sir," Haakon said. "I congratulate your astuteness. However, my offer of generosity stands." What the hell, it was worth a try.

The commandant's face grew grim. "Agents of State Security will be coming for you soon. Make yourselves comfortable, gentlemen." He strode away and the guards went with him. Seconds later they heard the massive iron door slam shut.

Haakon sat on a bunk. "Jem," he said, "what the hell is a fountain pen?"

Jemal shook his head. "Damned if I know. Must be something we should have checked up on before we decided to pose as reporters."

"We didn't last long once we got to the big city, did we? Oh, well, I was always better at getting into jail than getting out."

"We can take comfort in one thing," Jemal said.

"What's that?"

"Well, maybe Sarai can figure a way out of this. That woman certainly had her brains about her when she decided to have nothing to do with us."

# Thirteen

"HEY, HACK, WAKE UP." JEMAL WAS SHAKING HIS shoulder. Haakon sat up, yawning and stretching. Long experience had taught him to sleep as best he could when in jail. Sleep was always good for you, and often as not there was nothing else to do anyway. He could hear a metallic clatter in the distance.

"Somebody's coming," Jemal said. They both did their best to straighten their sadly rumpled clothing. What good was dressing like a lord when you had to look like you'd slept in the stuff?

"Who is it?" Haakon asked. He sat on his bench and refused to look anxious. Jemal was standing at the barred gate and peering down the hallway.

"It looks like Numa, only about six rungs down the evolutionary ladder."

"This should be worth seeing," Haakon said. He got

up and smoothed down his lapels. The creature that appeared at the door did, indeed, look a bit like a Felid.

"You two are to come with me." The voice sounded like a man gargling with his mouth full of marbles. Whatever pseudo-deities had been at work here, the scientists back in the real universe had done a better job with Felids. No sense in telling him, though.

"What is the meaning of this?" Haakon asked in his best bluster. "We are law-abiding citizens, journalists for a great publication, and we are treated like criminals!"

"Shut up," the cat-man said. "We have searched your rooms. No passports, no identification. We have cabled Paris. The newspaper you claim to write for has never heard of you."

"My, you're thorough," Jemal said. "What now?"

The commandant was unlocking the cell. Behind him were several guards who plainly knew their business. No sense fighting. "I am going to cuff and shackle you two," he said, "and you are going to accompany this officer to one of His Majesty's own facilities. This whole matter has been taken out of the hands of General Carranza's government. I trust you shall be able to settle matters to your satisfaction. As prisoners go, you two have been interesting and very little trouble. I do suggest, however, that you refrain from lying or attempting bribery. His Majesty's minions may not share my tolerant nature."

They were marched outside to the square where something that looked like a palanquin awaited. They climbed in and sat glumly on the overstuffed seat. "Very little trouble," Jemal echoed, shaking his head sadly.

"Kind of makes you want to take up an honest living, doesn't it?"

The jaguar-man sat in the facing seat. He looked rather elegant in his ornate uniform, but he was totally without humor. "Be silent for the remainder of the journey. We go to His Majesty's flying palace, *Floating Mountain*. There you are to be interrogated at His Majesty's pleasure. Save your breath for that."

There was no point in arguing. A man in an exotic loincloth and feather cape appeared next to the palanquin. He climbed into a small cockpit behind the passenger compartment where they sat. He settled his feathered headdress, took a sulphur match out of his loincloth and lit a fire in a tiny brazier in the cockpit. With palms turned upward, he began a long and complicated chant. The palanquin lifted from the plaza under the curious gaze of a few idlers.

"My God," Jemal gasped, "he's *praying* this thing into the air!"

"Should that surprise you?" Haakon asked. "In this place—" A teeth-baring snarl from their guard silenced him.

Idly, he fidgeted with his chains. They weren't heavy, but breaking them would be quite beyond even his strength.

The city below them provided a spectacular view in the early light. There appeared to be two cities occupying the same area. One was a "modern" city, a bustling early industrial metropolis held together by a network of streets, most of them striped with streetcar tracks. The other was an ancient city represented by temple complexes dominated by towering pyramids. Some of the temples had smoke coming from them, but most were semi-ruinous. It was an interesting mixture, and speculating on its history helped take their minds off their predicament.

The pyramid was nearing. It was a mind-boggling sight, with its layers of sculpture and gardens, its temples and endless walls decorated with mosaic and fresco. They ascended almost even with the highest level and began to circle the flying edifice. Then they were over a deep notch let into the side of the pyramid and saw what was cradled there.

"That's *Eurynome*!" Jemal said.

"What the hell is holding her together?" Haakon said. "She's not designed for stresses like that!"

"Silence!" snarled the guard.

Haakon snarled right back. "That's my ship, you fur-faced bastard! Now leave us alone or I'll bite your goddamn face off."

"Easy, Hack," Jemal cautioned.

Their guard grumbled but gave them no further trouble. It was a good sign. They might be more important than they had thought.

The palanquin came within a few meters of the impossible net cradle that held *Eurynome*. Haakon scanned the ship for damage, but she showed none of the signs of stress he would have expected. It had to be more of the magic that kept the pyramid floating and the palanquin flying. The priest's chant slowed and Haakon stood to exit the palanquin. The guard's hiss stopped him.

"Never exit a craft while the priest is still chanting!" the cat-man said. "Do you know nothing of safety procedures?"

"Sorry," Haakon said, settling back down.

A minute later, the chanting halted and the guard stood, signaling them to do the same. They climbed awkwardly from the craft, careful not to let their leg irons trip them. They eyed the tall stairway ahead of them gloomily.

"Can't you take these irons off?" Haakon asked. "It's not like we'd try to run. Where could we go?"

"I have no such orders," the guard said, and that was that.

"Bastard would make a good BT," Jemal said. "Old Hulagu'd welcome him to the Tuman, except for certain racial disqualifications."

"Move," said the cat-man.

They began to climb, the chains making their progress miserable and humiliating. Ordinarily, they would have sprung up the steps with effortless, athletic grace. This chain-induced shuffle deeply offended their fine sense of style.

Once atop the steps, they entered the manmade mountain. There were corridors, chambers, stairways, all of a surpassing magnificence, but their condition left them in no mood to admire the appointments. The guard ushered them into a wood-paneled room furnished with oppressively heavy, overstuffed furniture and bizarre tapestries. A sideboard held decanters of fluids and a humidor full of the digusting cigars.

"You wait here," the guard said. "I go to report."

257

"Wait here, huh?" Jemal said when he was gone. "What the hell did he expect us to do?"

"Pretty posh lockup," Haakon said, eyeing their surroundings. "I've been in worse." He crossed to the sideboard and pulled a crystal stopper from a decanter. "Nobody said we couldn't sample the drinkables," he said, "and screw 'em if they did." He sniffed one, made a face, and put it down. "Peach brandy. Can't stand the stuff." He sniffed another and smiled. "Claret. That's more like it." They each poured a glass.

"Now," Jemal said, "just what the hell is our ship doing here?"

"I imagine we're about to find out. I wonder how Rama is?"

"We're here as prisoners," Jemal said. "Our ship's in the control of strangers, we have no idea of what shape the rest of the crew is in, we don't know where Sarai is, we haven't found a single one of the people we were looking for, we're no closer to finding an answer to Meridian's problem than when we came through the neon tube, and you're wondering whether that insufferable enemy of humanity's had her kittens yet? Hack, we've been friends a long time, but sometimes for the life of me I can't figure out why we agreed to let you be captain!"

"Because that's the way Timur Khan wanted it," Haakon said, "and besides, I'm a superior human being. In worrying about one of my crew, I'm fulfilling one of the prime duties of a captain."

"There are others who require worrying about more," Jemal said darkly. "Rama is never in danger from anyone except herself."

Haakon sat in an easy chair. "Hell, maybe we should have let that punk back at the Bloody Bucket plant his damned luck detector or whatever it was on the ship. The readings he'd get would probably fry his brains." He had brought the decanter to his chair and poured himself another generous glass. He started to wave his arms in an expansive gesture, but his shackles frustrated that. "What the hell," he declared, the excellent wine on his empty stomach loosening him up fast, "look on the bright side."

"If there is one, I wish you'd point it out to me," Jemal said through slightly gritted teeth.

"We took a roundabout route, but we got here to the palace," Haakon said triumphantly. "I bet Sarai never even made it here."

"Don't count on it; she's pretty resourceful. And from the look of things, we'd have got here quicker by staying with the ship."

Haakon ignored that. "Plus, it looks like this is where those two from the Meridian expedition are as well, so we're closer than we were. All we have to do is push our luck. We've always been good at that."

"Our luck?" Jemal's face was growing red. "What the hell luck are you talking—"

He was interrupted by the door opening. The man who came through the door was tall, with black hair and dark, handsome features, slightly inbred in lineament. He wore an ordinary suit in a simply patterned weave instead of ceremonial vestments, but they recognized him from his portrait.

"I am Emperor Montezuma," he said. He waited a

few moments. "It is customary to rise in the presence of royalty."

"Screw that," Haakon said. He sat back in his chair and his feet remained propped up on the low table before him. "So you're an emperor. I used to be a viscount. Hell, I have a woman in my crew this trip who's the daughter of an emperor. Not just any old pissant emperor, mind you, but the Khakhan of Bahadur. That son of a bitch owns enough firepower to squash all your squabbling little countries like so many bugs. Wouldn't bother sending a major fleet to do it, either."

Montezuma smiled. "You're exactly what your friends told me to expect." He turned to the cat-guard who now stood behind him in the corridor. "Take the shackles off these men." He turned back to Haakon and Jemal while the guard plied his key. "As I understand it, your Khakhan occupies a universe other than my own, so I need hardly worry about him. We have a great deal to discuss, gentlemen, but first I think you should have some breakfast. You've made quite an inroad into my excellent claret, and it would be a shame not to provide some complementary food. I shall be back when you have eaten."

Haakon sat back from the litter of plates, replete. "They just waltzed in here and found him," he said disgustedly. "Hell, he stood in line to get *introduced* to them! While we were down in the hills getting our butts mule-blistered! Is there no justice?"

"Oh, there certainly is, Captain," Soong assured him.

"It is my belief that these follies of yours are punishment for the sins of a former life."

"You could have been more patient," Mirabelle said. "Nobody in his right mind would have committed himself to such a hare-brained expedition on nothing better than General Villa's talk."

"He was honest with us," Haakon muttered. "He has other good points. He shoots rebellious subordinates, for instance." This was doing his mental state no good. He was still shattered by the news about Rama. Twins! What kind of madhouse would his ship become now?

The door opened and Sarari came in. She had been to the ship, because she had gotten rid of her ridiculous disguise and was wearing a one-piece gold coverall. Haakon glared at her. "Well, at least we beat you here."

"No you didn't," she said. "I've been here since yesterday evening."

"How?" he asked, crestfallen.

"Simple. According to the newspapers, half the high-level diplomats on the planet were in this palace. That meant there would be some serious entertaining going on. I got directions to the most exclusive brothel in the city and volunteered my services. I told the madam that I was doing it just to make connections, and she could keep all my fees. I was here within an hour, attending a ball."

Haakon turned to Jemal. "This woman has not led as sheltered a life as she lets on."

Things might have been worse. Mirabelle had brought his customary clothes and had removed the fake hair and mustache while he ate. This made him feel more like himself and, therefore, a bit more in control of his situation. His ego had taken some bruises, though.

Servants cleared away the plates in time for Montezuma's arrival. He was accompanied by Tametomo and made the requisite introductions. Montezuma took a cigar from the humidor and lit it up; the others managed not to gag. He took a chair and crossed his long legs casually.

"I must admit," he began, "that if I had nothing but your unsubstantiated word for your origin and activities, I would recommend that you all be committed to a madhouse." He waved his cigar in a graceful gesture. "However we have two of your ships, and there can be no question that they are genuine and that you arrived in them. My priests and sorcerers are at a loss to explain how you harness the forces that drive your craft between the stars, but we can be sure that you do so.

"As to the nature of your universe, I am lost to hear you try to explain it. Your cosmology and mine are too different. I have some understanding of the gods of this world, as much as any human being can truly understand gods. You believe that my gods were once beings that inhabited your own universe, am I correct?"

"That is our firm belief," Soong said. "In their long era in our universe, they attained truly godlike powers, and within the worldlet we call Meridian, they created one or more, probably several, universes in which they could give their creative powers free reign."

"But is it not as possible," Montezuma said, "that your own universe was created by a god or gods from mine?"

"Ridiculous," Haakon said. "Our universe was there first."

"Are you sure of that?" Montezuma asked. "This world has a natural order that we understand. It has a geological and fossil record extending back many millions of years, as I understand yours has. The history of man on this planet is documented, somewhat incompletely, for about six thousand years, with an archaeological record extending back many thousands more. So which of our universes is older?"

"It is possible," Soong said, nodding. "Time is different here, and we only vaguely understand the periphery of inter-Cingulum space. It could be that our reasoning is backward."

"I don't believe it," Haakon said stubbornly. He had no particular reason not to believe it, but the prospect opened a void so huge and so black that it did not bear thinking about.

"These are deep cosmological questions," said Montezuma after a silence, "but we have a more immediate problem. You need to close the gate between our worlds, lest it destroy this place you call Meridian. That gate makes me uneasy as well. So far, three of your craft have landed on this world. I do not believe that we are ready to deal with you. We are by comparison technologically backward, and just now we are poised on the brink of a vast and insane bloodletting. Your presence could be ruinous at a time like this. I hope you will not think me callous if I tell you that, were it not for the chance that you might be able to close that gate, I would almost certainly execute you all, and destroy your ships."

263

They said nothing.

"However," he went on, "it need not come to that. The ex-Shogun Minamoto, whom you know as Prince Tametomo, may have the solution to all our problems. Please tell these people of your plan, Your Excellency."

Tametomo, now dressed in civilian clothing, clasped his hands behind his back and paced nervously as he spoke. "I led the third expedition from Meridian. By some incomprehensible warpage in the status of time, I arrived here first, as far as I know. I have heard nothing of the first expedition, which explored the gate in pressure suits. In fifteen years, neither I nor my surviving crew have aged."

"I was wondering about that," Haakon said. "You look about the age we expected when we traced you to the Cingulum."

"None of this was unplanned," Tametomo said. "We all arrived here in a fashion which appeared to us to be as random as the fall of cherry blossoms." Haakon wondered from which cultural grab bag he had pulled that simile. "But there was nothing random about it. We were *brought* here."

"That assertion," Haakon said, "is going to take a little explanation."

"Bear with me," Tametomo said. "I began life as a minor prince and became a mere runaway youth, swept wherever the waves of war took me. I ended up in the Cingulum, the last bastion of defiance to Bahadur. One day I happened to be in Meridian and attended an officers' meeting where a mission to explore the alarming gate was proposed and volunteers were asked for. I

264

volunteered for a simple reason: I was bored. Years of danger had left me unsuited to a life of peacetime routine, and it would be many years before the war could resume, perhaps not in my lifetime." He took a sip from a glass of claret.

"I came through the gate, and I made landfall on this planet. Unerringly, I landed in Nippon, the analog of the land of my ancestors. Just as unerringly, you landed in the empire of Montezuma, not only the sole ruler who would give you a sympathetic hearing, but one who was hosting the greatest diplomatic conference in this planet's history, in hopes of averting a worldwide war. None of this is coincidence."

"That isn't hard to believe," Haakon said. "We've seen how coincidence works inside the Cingulum before this. Go on."

"You must understand, Captain," he said, searching for the most tactful words, "you yourself were not of primary importance in the plans of the gods here."

"My friends," Haakon said, "have been letting me know how insignificant my actions have been. Don't be bashful."

"I regret," Tametomo said, "that I do not express myself well. I was always a better soldier than diplomat."

"Don't worry," Jemal said. "He can take it. Go on."

"What I mean is that the important intermediary in all this is Lady Sarai. By the logic of our universe, she is the most unlikely factor of all. She is a renegade princess of the royal house of our enemy, stranded under unlikely circumstances on the world of my birth, eventually to be entrusted with a fool's mission: to find amid all the flotsam of a lost war the sole surviving heir of the royal line of Chamuka and deliver the Three Treasures to me."

"I said it was silly right from the start," Haakon agreed.

"But it was necessary," Tametomo persisted. "Two of the Three Treasures, the Sword and the Mirror, are irrelevant. They are venerable heirlooms of the royal family, no more. But the Jewel is different. It is not original."

"Come again," Haakon said.

"We spoke somewhat of this earlier, Captain," Soong said. "I said that one or more of these treasures, perhaps all three, were reproductions, the originals having been lost centuries ago."

"That is so," Tametomo confirmed. "The other two need not concern us. The Jewel is a replacement, but it is also the original."

"I just love paradox," Haakon said. "Let's hear about it."

"According to legend, the Three Treasures were given to the Imperial House long ago, in the age of myth. By historical times, they had already been in the possession of the family for centuries. In the twelfth century, by the old calendar, a long feud was fought between the clans of Taira and Minamoto. The Taira managed to gain possession of the child-emperor Antoku and the Imperial Regalia. The climax of the feud was the sea battle of Dan-No-Ura. The Minamoto prevailed, and the last surviving Taira jumped into the sea rather than admit defeat. They carried with them the young emperor and the regalia. The sea was dredged and two of the Three Treasures were recovered. Some believe that the Sword was lost, but that is not true. It was the Jewel.

"At some time in succeeding years, the lost treasure was replaced, but who crafted it has never been established. Indeed, the knowledge of which treasure had been lost had faded. In my time here, I discovered where it originated. It came from here."

"Hold it," Haakon said. "You're saying that many centuries ago on Earth an artifact arrived from this planet, in a totally different universe?"

"Exactly that. In the analog Nippon of this world, there were two Jewels. One of them disappeared in the ancient past, in a similar battle on one of the great rivers. In the legends of both this Nippon and the Japan of Earth, there were once many Jewels, belonging to the gods. Here more of the lore of the Jewels has been preserved. They were concretions of the power wielded by the gods, dating from the days when they still needed artifacts to concentrate their will. You might compare them to Tesla nodes or catalytic crystals, although these are infinitely more sophisticated. I do not think they consist of matter at all. They are the means by which this universe is regulated, and the loss of one in our world caused another one to disappear from here. This universe gradually, over the centuries, grew out of balance. The result was the unstable gate which appeared in the Cingulum. It had to be repaired."

"You mean," Jemal said, "that we're just repairmen for these gods, by whom I suppose you mean the original Cingulans?"

"I mean more than that," Tametomo said fervently. "We have believed for years that the Old Cingulans fled into their created universes before the beginning of human history. I believe that they are still manipulating events in our universe now!"

Haakon took yet another long drink, then reflected that he was really putting it away. What the hell, he could always take a sober-up pill if he needed it. "This is stuff for the happy people at the U. of the Cingulum. Tell me—have you figured out how to fix our dilemma?"

"Yes," Tametomo said, "but we must go to Nippon."

Haakon looked at Montezuma. "Does that meet with your approval?"

"Decidedly. Most of this is gibberish to me, but if it will get all of you safely home and close the gate that let you in, I'll chance it. Go with my blessing. As fascinating as you all are, I shall breathe a sigh of relief at your departure. My diplomatic conference did not succeed. My poor world is about to plunge headlong into the greatest war of its history."

"Get used to it," Haakon said. "There'll be lots more of them."

"Isn't it funny," Jemal said, "how happy people are to see the last of us?" They were back in orbit, circling the periphery of the flat world. Nippon was on the side opposite Aztlan.

"Can't imagine why," Haakon said, studying the bridge consoles. "We always put ourselves out to be agreeable."

268

Off Nippon, Tametomo's ship came up for them. It was a small scout, and there was some crowding to get everyone aboard. Only Haakon, Jemal, and Soong elected to go along on the ground mission. They wanted to see it through to the end, if that was what it was. Tametomo's crew wanted to hear all about it. They were amazed to find that they had experienced fifteen years while only months had passed in Meridian.

"But if we go back," one said, "we'll start to age again."

"That's all right," said another, "if it gets us out of this crazy place and back to where the worlds are round and there's more than one of them."

"I have a feeling we would begin to age here, too," Tametomo said, "as soon as we accomplish our mission."

They were coming down over a mountaintop. The mountain was dotted with buildings and topped with an immense temple complex. The largest of the structures had a golden pagoda roof. It was before this building that the scout ship settled. A group of priests and monks, looking flustered, came out to greet them. When they caught sight of Tametomo, they went into a seizure of furious bowing.

"Your Excellency," said the senior priest, "we had no idea you were going to visit us. We have had no time to prepare a proper welcome."

"Do not concern yourself," Tametomo said. "I have resigned the shogunate. The office is abolished. His Majesty reigns now without rival. I have come to return a thing to this shrine which has been missing for many centuries."

"Your Ex—ah, Minamoto-sama," the priest said perplexedly, "I do not understand."

"Just take us to the great image of Jizo-Bosatsu," Tametomo requested.

"Of course," said the rattled priest. "Come this way." He led them to an entrance near a corner of the gigantic temple.

"The main chapel," Tametomo explained to the others, "is a very ancient shrine of Buddha. His statue is ten meters high and made of wood so old that it has turned completely black. We go to the shrine of a lesser deity, one much revered by Buddhist and Shintoist and Daoist alike."

They entered the shrine, which was of impressive proportions, even if it was not so grand as that devoted to Buddha. In the dim light, they saw the standing figure of a serene-looking deity. The statue was made of wood, with touches of gold leaf here and there. In its belly, at about eye level to a standing person, was set a teardrop-shaped stone, glossy black in color.

"Lady Sarai," Tametomo said.

A look of wonder on her face, she handed him the silk-wrapped parcel she had carried so far. He unwrapped the Jewel, and the priests drew in their breath in a unanimous gasp of awe. Tametomo placed the Jewel in its setting, interlocking with the other to form a perfect circle.

"That's what it reminded me of!" Haakon said triumphantly. "Yang and yin! I've seen the symbol in hundreds of places."

"Exactly," Tametomo said. "It is male and female, light and darkness, everything and its opposite, and neither is complete without the other. Now they are together again and this universe will begin to heal. I think it is time to get through that gate while it is still there."

"But," Sarai protested, "we'll be going back to Chamuka. Can we return with only two of the Three Treasures?"

Tametomo turned to her. "I believe that another Jewel will turn up before long. That's how these gods work."

"The neon circle is still there," Soong reported. "It has begun to flash off and on."

Haakon made a scan of the area. "We'd better get through and see what happens. Just a minute, I'm getting another reading. Something just appeared."

"It is two pressure suits," Soong reported.

Haakon's face was grim. "It must be the first two to come through the gate. God knows how long the poor bastards have been floating out here. We might as well pick their bodies up and take them back. If we get back ourselves, that is."

He signaled Tametomo's ship, close behind them, that he was making the pickup. A robot probe went out to catch the two floating forms and bring them in. Haakon went to the airlock to see what shape the corpses would be in. It was not two corpses that came in through the lock, however, it was two men, alive and squawking. One undogged his helmet and yanked it off. A wild ruff of hair and beard opened around his face.

271

"What the hell took so long about getting us a pickup?" the man shouted. "We've been floating around out here calling for help for at least six hours!" He composed himself and looked about at his surroundings. The other did the same.

"Christ, Ike," said the other, a bald man with a paisley pattern tattooed on his scalp, "what a whorehouse! This has got to be *Eurynome*." He looked at Haakon. "You must be Captain Haakon. Thanks for the pickup, but we didn't know you were in the Cingulum."

"Let me get this straight," Haakon said. "You two were the first mission to investigate the hole, and you came through six hours ago?"

"More or less," said the bearded man. "What the hell do you mean, 'first mission'? We're the only one as far as I know."

Haakon shook his head in surrender. "This is going to take a lot more explaining than we have time for. Just make yourselves at home. Get a drink from the 'bots or something. If our luck holds, we should be back in Meridian in a few minutes."

He dashed back to the bridge. "This just keeps getting weirder," he announced to everybody. "What has me worried is, what if we get back to Meridian and fifty years have gone by, or a hundred?"

"Then maybe Timur Khan will be dead," Jemal said.

"Hm, hadn't thought of that," Haakon admitted. "Well, I won't worry then. Set course for the center of that circle, dead slow." He looked at Mirabelle, who wore an abstracted expression. "Why are you looking so moony-eyed?" he demanded.

"Oh, I've just been playing with Rama's babies. They're so beautiful."

He gave her a horrified look. "Now don't you go getting ideas! Our situation is crazy enough already."

"What is crazy about it?" Rama asked, barging onto the bridge with an infant in each arm. "She was complimenting the beauty of my offspring, the first sensible thing she has ever said."

They were getting close to the ring now. Haakon looked closely at one of the babies and poked it in kitchy-koo fashion with a blunt finger. It squalled and swatted feebly at his finger, the soft but unsheathed claws scraping lightly over the skin. "Got your mother's temper, I see."

"We are going through," Soong announced.

Once more the shimmering veil slid through the bridge, then they were in the clear and looking into the Meridian atrium. The ledges were packed with people, but there were no transports of joy. Haakon hit the loud hailer and his voice went blasting through the atrium. "Hey! Why aren't you cheering? We've been out doing heroic stuff! We're back, we've picked up the other parties except for two that got killed, and we've fixed the problem with the hole. What kind of welcome is this?"

Tredegar's image appeared in holograph. "What do you mean, Haakon? The nose of your ship came through the hole almost before your tail disappeared. You didn't even have time to turn around. How did you do it?"

Haakon looked at him solemnly. "Tredegar, by this time don't you realize we can do anything?"

\* \* \*

Haakon was sweating, but Timur Khan wouldn't think that was suspicious. He was used to people trembling and sweating from terror at his mere presence. It was always a chancy business, putting one over on Timur Khan Bey. If he caught on, the punishment would be slow death under conditions of unbelievable pain. He had faced it before.

Timur Khan was studying the holograph Haakon had brought him. It was a portrait of Sarai, dressed in Chamukan garb, but actually taken in the Cingulum. She had not worn brown contacts, just to make identification positive. She had agreed to this to save Haakon's skin, along with the others. She was safe in the Cingulum, and the ruse might serve to distract Timur Khan from the true nature of the rebellion on Chamuka.

"So it is true," Timur Khan said quietly. "She is still alive. No wonder the rebellion has been so successful." If he had been capable of smiling, Timur Khan would have been beaming. He turned his fierce gaze upon Haakon. "Do you know who this woman is, or the significance of the silver eyes?"

"No, Noyon," Haakon said. "She is the ring leader in the rebellion, and they call her Sarai, but all we could get was this holo of her." He added maliciously, "Our investigations were much hindered by the Subadar Hulagu, who persisted in acting as if some vendetta lay between us. We were lucky to stay on the planet at all."

"He was doing his duty," Timur Khan said. "He was right to be suspicious." He studied the holograph for a few more moments. "Your report pleases me. Forget all of this and speak of it to no one. You are free to go. Be ready to receive your next assignment."

"Yes, Noyon." Haakon bowed his head to the floor, then backed out of the room.

"What was it all about?" Jemal asked. He had met Haakon at the port and now the shuttle was taking them back to *Eurynome*.

"I don't know," Haakon admitted. "I don't really think he's interested in the rebellion on Chamuka, though. I think he's just scored some points on the royal family. I think it's some kind of power play between him and the Khakhan, or maybe between him and the Second Lady, the one who tried to kill Sarai."

"Bourtai," Jemal said.

"That's the one. Anyway, we survived another one. That's all I can say for certain. And maybe not for long." He thought for a while. "Jem, do you think he could be right? Tametomo, I mean. Could the old Cingulans still be manipulating things here, us in particular? That punk from the U. of the Cingulum showed up again just before we left, with another gadget that's supposed to measure coincidence quotient, whatever the hell that is. He says our whole crew goes completely off its chart."

"That kid is insane, and what could we do about it if the gods or whatever they are really are messing with us? Don't worry about it, Timur Khan is enough to keep us occupied." Jemal was worried about Haakon. Usually he was in a state of manic ebullience after surviving another interview with Timur Khan. Now he was strangely subdued. "What is it? Sarai?"

"I can't figure her out," Haakon said. "I thought—well, hell, I didn't expect her to drop me cold like that."

Jemal knew better than to give him the needle. "Hell, Hack, I told you before: that woman is intelligent. What kind of woman with half a brain would have anything to do with us? She might have been crazy about you, for all I know. But your life expectancy is not the kind that puts women in mind of a blissful future."

"I guess you're right," he said. "All the good ones know enough to clear out."

Mirabelle met them at the airlock. She handed Haakon a drink. "Do we get to live a while longer?" she asked.

"Looks like it," Haakon said. "Where is everybody?"

"In the salon," she answered. "Come on, you look like you need to tie one on."

He went into the salon. Even Rand was there. Rama sat with her infants clasped to her newly bounteous bosom, where they were feeding noisily.

"Temporary reprieve," Haakon announced. "He's not going to kill us yet. We were headed for Balder before we got interrupted, and we're rolling in credit. What say we go blow it all in a few weeks of riotous living?"

"Yay," Alexander said.

"Suits me," said Rand with a metallic shrug.

"Let's do it," Mirabelle said. "I've been bored to death since we got the summons."

"Eminently satisfactory," Soong proclaimed.

"Balder?" Rama said. "That sink of iniquity is no place for children!"

"Then stay with the ship while we live it up," Jemal told her. "Let's go."

Haakon strode up to the bridge and dropped into his captain's chair. For a split second, a vision of silver eyes floated before him, then he punched the console viciously. "Take us to Balder, damn it. Be quick about it." He leaned back in his chair. Eventually, he relaxed. There were worse things than being captain. Especially with a ship like *Eurynome*.

## THE BEST IN SCIENCE FICTION

## THE BEST IN FANTASY

# POUL ANDERSON
## Winner of 7 Hugos and 3 Nebulas